"YOU KNOW WHAT YOU ARE,"
THE WOMAN SCREAMED,
"A WITCH!"

"You'll put a curse on the town just as your mother did. Your aunt had to take you away. Now she's bringing you back. Why? To perpetrate more mischief by predictions which will bring grief and heartache on families who ask only that they be allowed to live in peace."

This woman was rude and what she said was shocking, but was it the truth? If so, I had the right to know. The very thought was repugnant, yet I couldn't disregard everything this woman said. I'd seen both this woman and her daughter in my hallucination. I'd also seen myself lying dead at the foot of the Apollo statue. Was it a forewarning that this woman meant me harm and I must be on guard?

Warner Books

By Dorothy Daniels

The Marble Hills
The Caldwell Shadow
The Apollo Fountain
Hills of Fire
The Silent Halls of Ashenden
The Duncan Dynasty
The Larrabee Heiress
Dark Island
The Lanier Riddle
Shadows From the Past
The House of Broken Dolls
The Summer House
A Mirror of Shadows
Jade Green
Diablo Manor
The Tormented
The Beaumont Tradition
The House of Many Doors

Dorothy Daniels

The Apollo Fountain

A Warner Communications Company

WARNER BOOKS EDITION

ISBN 0-446-84800-X

Cover art by Vic Prezio

Warner Books, Inc., 75 Rockefeller Plaza, New York, N.Y. 10019

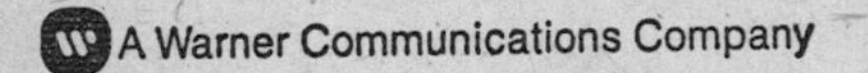

Printed in the United States of America

Not associated with Warner Press, Inc., of Anderson, Indiana

First Printing: January, 1974

10 9 8 7 6 5 4

THE APOLLO FOUNTAIN

PROLOGUE

The strains of the string orchestra playing a stirring gavotte drifted up the grand staircase. Mingled with it was the sound of voices raised in gaiety and high spirits. It was a magnificent affair, as well it should be, for a fortune had been spent to make it so.

I was wearing a shepherdess costume, with a high headdress of curls intertwined with velvet ribbon and real roses, heavy with scent. In my hand I held a shepherd's staff, covered with ribbon and topped with a bow.

I wanted to close the door of the room upstairs to shut out the overpowering perfume of the flowers that had been placed about the house. Yet it would have been rude to do so, for this room had been set aside for the ladies to rest and check to see whether their outrageously fascinating hairdresses had come askew. Even here, the delicious bouquet of gardenias filled the room. Their lovely blossoms drifted in wide, shallow dishes, their heavy bouquet all but intoxicating.

I'd slipped away from the party to keep a rendezvous outside. The place designated was the Apollo fountain that stood in majestic splendor at the foot of the waterfall stairway. I was eager for the meeting, which apparently had to be clandestine. That was why I'd excused myself and come up here. Truth to tell, I'd deliberately undone the huge bow at my waistline so I might have an excuse to get away. I was dallying with my coiffure, awaiting an opportunity to step out on the gallery and move along it to where a stairway, cleverly concealed by a heavy growth of vines, led to the grounds proper.

The room was almost deserted except for a maid who hovered in the background waiting to attend me if I had need of her. She'd already served me a *café noir* in a narrow, delicate china cup almost thimble-like in size. I thanked her and was trying to think of an excuse to send her from the room when a portly matron and her daughter came in, the former puffing from the exertion of climbing the stairs. She immediately kicked off her satin slippers and requested a room in which she could lie down.

The maid asked that she follow her. The woman did, calling for the young girl to come. The latter scooped up the discarded slippers and with a hurried, "Yes, Mama" did so. I felt a touch of compassion for the girl. It was obvious she was completely dominated by her mother. Though plain in appearance, with proper clothes and a change of hairstyle—she was not in costume—she could have been made most attractive.

I fussed with the sash I'd already tied, regarding myself in the enormous gold-framed mirror that graced the wall. However, once they left the room, I picked up my shepherd's staff, moved quickly to the french doors, opened one, and slipped through, closing it silently behind me. It was an unnecessary gesture, for the mere snick of a latch could never be heard. Though my rendezvous was secret and I was already impatient to reach it, I was also cautious. There was a need for that, and I felt I'd been extremely clever in outwitting my escort, who had sensed I was up to something.

I laughed inwardly at the thought, for I could visualize his troubled features, concerned at my continued absence, and imagine him sending a servant upstairs to summon me. I wondered why I hadn't just stated my reason for wishing to leave the house. I supposed it was because I was, and always had been, spirited and mischievous, and reveled in intrigue. I'd enjoyed outwitting my elders and would laugh derisively when they'd caution me that one day I'd learn a lesson that would cause either me or them grief. I'd always scoffed at their admonitions and rejected any idea of prudence.

I skirted the front of the house by moving cautiously through the formal garden and its well-manicured shrubbery. Twice I had to change my course when soft laughter and voices gentled with love almost blocked my path. But eventually I reached the stairs and started down them.

It was a double stairway with fountains in between. In the center of each was a statue of a Greek god or goddess. At the top was Daphne and at the bottom Apollo, where I was to rendezvous.

I touched the bodice of my costume and felt the crackle of the letter that had been delivered—by an unknown hand—to me that day. It stated that one who greatly admired me had news which, it was hoped, would send my heart soaring. Who could have written such daring words? I wondered. The handwriting was strong and masculine. The very boldness of the words served to heighten my curiosity.

My steps quickened in anticipation, then gradually slowed, for a mist had suddenly slipped over the area. Whereas before, the night had been beautiful, with a moon lighting the grounds in magical rays, now there was an eerie grayness all about me. I paused and turned back to look up at the house. It too was slowly being enveloped in a ghostly shroud, and the music was barely discernible.

I thought of turning back, then shrugged away the feeling of uneasiness the change in the night had brought. However, my descent was slowed, for the mist drifted around me so thickly I couldn't see the steps. I bent slightly and reached for the low stone wall edging the fountain.

Now the music was no longer evident, but the sound of the water cascading down to each successive level was quite audible. I told myself I had nothing to fear and if I wished, I could always return to the house, where I knew the festivities were at their height. However, the adventuress in me took precedence and I continued my descent, though moving cautiously over each long step, letting my staff find the way.

I don't know how long it took me to reach the bottom, where smooth stone covered a large circular area enclosed with a wall of statues of Greek gods. Directly in the center was a magnificent bronze of Apollo, poised above a fountain. He faced the stairways leading up to the house, and it seemed as if the various gods and goddesses gracing each fountain were paying homage to his manly beauty.

I paused, waiting hopefully for the sound of footsteps or a voice, hesitant but with a touch of triumph that I'd come. But all was silence, a sepulchral one, made so by the mist that swirled about me. I strained my eyes hopefully for a sign of a human. From time to time, the mist would thin and I'd see a figure I thought was that of a human, yet its size told me it was just another statue, each of which was more than life-size.

Then I did hear a cautious step, followed by a few more that seemed to skirt me, rather than approach . . . as if whoever it was wanted to make certain of my identity. If I was correct in my reasoning, I could end the suspense by speaking out. Or was the person playing a game? If so, it was time to end it. I was tiring of the sport, if such it was.

And so I spoke out, identifying myself and asking who it was. I even reached out a hand in a gesture of camaraderie. But no one grasped it. I was annoyed now, and my voice sharpened as I demanded to know if the person inches away from me, yet completely invisible, was the one who had sent the missive. If so, I went on, he was to identify himself and announce his reason for having written the note, or I'd return to the house.

I was already chilled by the mist, and when my hand lowered to my side and rested against the softness of my frock, I felt it moist with dampness. I had no desire to catch cold and knew I would if I remained here. Yet I wondered how I could best manage getting back. I couldn't even see the statue of Apollo. My face was wet with dew, and I shivered, though not from the cold. Then I felt a warmth against the back of my neck. Someone's breath! I exhaled in relief and was about to laugh at my growing uneasiness when I was practically jerked off my feet as something soft but strong enclosed my throat.

My hands raised to free myself of this constriction, but the bond tightened and my breath was being cut off. I tried to cry out, but the effort was hopeless. My knees sagged and my head swam. I was being murdered by strangulation! I don't know how long the silken cord held my throat, but I felt consciousness leave me as the life poured out of my body. Not even when I lay prone on the ground was the bond loosened.

Instead, it was tied tightly about my throat. I couldn't untie it, nor could I call out for someone to do so. And for a very simple reason. I was dead. I clearly saw myself lying there. I suppose it was my spirit which had left my body that observed my mortal remains.

Yet what had I done to deserve such an end? Who could have wished me dead? Had I been evil in life? Was I murdered in cold blood because of revenge? Or jealousy? It mattered not. It was too late for questions. My death was an accomplished fact.

My spirit seemed to soar off into space until the body lying on the cold, wet stone far beneath disappeared in the mist that now acted as a protective shield. A protective shield? How amusing. And stupid. It was the mist that had been my undoing.

No, my spirit corrected; my foolish, reckless, adventurous way had, at last, caught up with me. Just as everyone had predicted. I was a fool not to have listened.

Now the mist which had enveloped was dissipated. There was blackness all around me and I seemed to be a part of it. This was Death. And death was nothingness. A formless eternity of which I was now a part.

ONE

I was struggling, attempting to free myself, but I was being held down. I tried to cry out, but no sounds came from my throat. I said, "I'm dead. I'll never speak again."

Then I heard sounds that seemed to come from a great distance. They were voices—human voices—and I tried to make out what they were saying, but the words were a jumble of sound. I had to know what they were saying. I fought to open my lids, which seemed leaden.

"She's past the crisis." It was a male voice, but I couldn't place it. "She'll recover."

"Thank God. Oh, thank God." That was a woman, and the voice was familiar, but my brain couldn't stir itself sufficiently to place the owner.

I tried to speak again. "Dead. Dead. I . . . am . . . dead."

The man spoke again. "You've been very ill, but you've passed the crisis." The hand of the speaker rested lightly on my brow. "The fever has dropped. She'll sleep now, and when she wakens, she'll no longer be confused."

"I . . . died." Couldn't they understand? What kind of game were they playing?

"My dear," the male voice was trying to reassure me, "you were stricken with yellow fever and have been gravely ill, but you're going to get well."

"I . . . am . . . dead . . . !" They had to know. They were fooling themselves that I was alive. I knew I was dead. I'd seen myself lying on the cold stone below the statue of the Apollo fountain—wherever that was. But if they looked, they'd find my body.

"What is she saying, Doctor?" The low, cultured tones of a woman asked the question.

"Her words are unintelligible. I believe that while in coma, she hallucinated," came the reply. "It happens often to those near death, and her dream is still very real to her. But she'll come through now."

"I'm going to the chapel and pray she will get well and live a full life. I have no one else. I devoted my life to raising her, and to lose her now . . . well . . . the thought is unendurable."

"Have faith, Yvonne," came the reassuring reply. "If not in me, then in God. Go to your chapel and say prayers of thanks that He has seen fit to spare her. And don't further upset yourself with tears."

"They're tears of gratitude." Her voice wavered as she spoke. "Thank you, William, for the care you've given my niece."

"She'll sleep now and gain strength through it. I suggest you not return until tomorrow. Send Sister in."

Perhaps she nodded, for I heard no reply. Only the sound of soft footsteps departing, followed by those of another approaching.

"You did well with this girl, Sister Amelita. Now all she needs is rest."

"I will see that she gets it, Doctor," came the reply.

Her hand also rested briefly on my brow. "Yes, the fever is broken. God is good."

"It was you who sat by her side, not even taking time to sleep," came the gruff reply.

"My prayers were answered, Doctor," she chided mildly. "When was the last time you prayed?"

He chuckled softly. "I trust you to do it for me, Sister."

"Be assured I do," came the brisk reply. "Now go get some rest."

"If Julie is lucid when she wakens, give her a little light broth. Only nourishment will return her to good health."

"That and a change of climate. I've already spoken to her aunt about it."

"You're right, as always. Is she amenable?"

"I'm not sure. Perhaps you could convince her."

"I will. As soon as the girl has recovered her strength sufficiently to travel, she must get away from here. A recurrence would be fatal."

"My thoughts exactly."

I felt consciousness slipping away and I tried desperately to fight it, for I dreaded another sight of my lifeless body, with the silken cord tight about my neck. But my efforts were useless, and the soft voices which drifted over me became unintelligible and finally drifted into the void I found myself slipping back into.

A week passed before I recovered sufficiently to take cognizance of my surroundings. I was in the Queen of Mercy Hospital, operated by the good nuns whose tender and competent care did much to hasten my recovery. My room was sparsely furnished, but it was neat and immaculate.

The good doctor in my case was William Tanney, a lifelong friend of my aunt, whose voice it was I'd heard the day I came out of the coma.

Today I was seated in a chair by the window, awaiting her arrival. Sister Amelita and I had wanted my progress to be a surprise. My aunt had not been able to visit me since the day I'd heard her and Dr. Tanney speak across my bed. She'd come down with a cold brought on by exhaustion and worry, and the doctor had ordered her to stay in bed and away from me.

I was eager to see her, for she was my only living relative. And it was true—she had raised me and been a devoted guardian. I didn't remember either of my parents. I was three when Mama died. Papa had preceded her in death by a year. I'd been raised abroad in private schools, very exclusive in nature. My aunt was an inveterate traveler and during vacations and holidays always arrived at the school to take me on a journey to a nearby country. I'd had a cosmopolitan education. Yet, while I had thoroughly enjoyed my life, I now had a desire to remain in the country of my birth. The thought of traveling again held little interest for me, and I would so inform my aunt when she came today. I was eighteen years of age, and I felt that I should be entitled to think and do for myself, though certainly I was dependent on her, for my education had taught me only the gracious and grateful attributes considered necessary to live a ladylike life of leisure.

Despite the illness I'd contracted in this city, I loved its cosmopolitan atmosphere. New Orleans reminded me of the sophistication and gaiety of Paris. The fact that I was thinking in such a way was the best proof I was well on the road to recovery. I was eighteen, adult and modern in my thinking, and I felt I had bridged the chasm from girlhood to womanhood competently, though when I informed my aunt of that fact, laughter trilled from her.

I heard her brisk footsteps click-clack along the corridor and stole a quick glance in the bureau mirror on the opposite side of the room.

I was still pale, attesting to my recent illness, and perhaps seeming more so because of my flaxen hair, which I'd managed to brush myself this morning. It fell to my waist and center-parted, served to frame my oval features. I was no beauty, for my mouth was too large for my face.

But my eyes were interesting, being green and slightly uptilted at the corners, giving me a flirtatious air. However, I was really quite shy in the company of the opposite sex. Having been raised in the sheltered atmosphere of the convent, I'd had little association with gentlemen.

My aunt paused a moment in the doorway. She did that before entering a room and, as always, I was enthralled by her radiant beauty. Her hair was jet black, with a deep wave. She wore it piled high on her head, with ringlets on either side of her brow and behind her ears; the effect seemed casual, as if they'd slipped from her coiffure, but I knew, from having watched her dress her hair, it was done with meticulous care. Nothing about Yvonne Moniere was careless. Wherever we went, heads turned. She'd had endless proposals and turned them all down. To me, it seemed a waste, but her answer had always been the same. They would have to accept me, be a father to me as she had been a mother, and while some had consented, she'd doubted their sincerity.

Her mauve silk afternoon dress followed the trim lines of her figure. She was tall for a woman, but not the least self-conscious about it, and carried herself beautifully, the tilt of her uplifted head almost regal. She must have been forty-five or more, yet looked no more than thirty. I was not only proud of her; I idolized her.

"Ah, my dear." She dropped the pose and entered the room, her arms extended to embrace me, and pausing before me to study my face. "Very pale. Too much so. But the sparkle is returning to your beautiful green eyes. Just like your mama's. Your papa's were brown, like mine. But his had the softness of a babe. He was a gentle man. Your mama was spirited—like me, I'm afraid. You have more of your papa in you."

She embraced me, and I was submerged in the fragrance of gardenias. It brought back the dream—or hallucination—I'd had and I shuddered involuntarily.

"Julie, *ma petite*, you're not catching a chill, are you?"

"No, Auntie." I smiled reassurance. "You're wearing the fragrance of gardenia."

She looked puzzled. "It's my favorite scent. And you've always liked it. If it offends you, I'll change to another."

"Oh, please don't," I exclaimed. "I'm sorry I shivered. It's just that the scent reminded me of the hallucination I had when I was in coma."

She eased herself into the chair facing mine, her features still registering concern. "What was that? I do know you were mumbling something that night when William and I were bent over you, but your words were unintelligible—at least to me."

"I died," I said. "I died in that hallucination."

She leaned forward and patted my hand resting on the arm of the chair. "Of course, my dear. I've heard of instances where people near death saw themselves dead."

"I was murdered. I was at a costume ball. I remember a letter had been sent to me that day. A letter telling me to meet the sender at the Apollo fountain—that I would hear news that would send my spirits soaring. I remember I was wearing a shepherdess costume complete with staff and I undid my sash so I might excuse myself and go upstairs. I knew the room set aside for the ladies had french doors that led onto the gallery. There, a staircase hidden from view by wisteria vines led to the grounds proper. I used that exit to go to the rendezvous. How strange that even now I see it as clearly as if I were once again hallucinating."

"Tell me the rest of it, Julie." My aunt sobered at the grimness of what I'd related.

"Now that I think of it, I'd never been to that place. Yet in my dream, I knew my way about easily. Twin staircases, rather, and in between them was a fountain. Several—one cascading into the other. There were small landings between the stairways and at each descending fountain was a likeness of a Greek god or goddess. I knew at the very bottom was the Apollo fountain, which was my destination."

I paused as she exclaimed audibly. "What is it, Auntie?"

It was my turn to evidence concern, for her lovely skin had paled and I thought she was about to faint.

She gave her head a brief shake and inhaled deeply, as if to get a grip on herself. She even managed a smile. "Nothing, my dear. Do go on. Let me hear the rest of the hallucination."

"I think it would be better if we forgot it. I didn't mean to frighten you."

"I was frightened for you," she said. "What a dreadful dream! But I do want to hear the rest of it. Perhaps if you relate it, it will leave you. It has affected you as deeply as it has me."

"That's why I think I shouldn't continue it."

"I insist you do," she said, softening her tone with a smile. "It will be better that you talk about it. All of it."

I sat back and resumed my story. I told about the descent to the Apollo fountain and how I was enveloped in mist.

My aunt leaned forward. "One moment, dear. Who wrote that note to you?"

"I have no idea. That's why I was so excited about going there. I knew I would enjoy the intrigue."

She settled back in the chair. "Please go on."

My aunt's eyes revealed the anguish she felt when I told how the silken cord had pressed against my neck, as if to stifle an outcry. Yet I knew she wanted to hear the rest and I continued, feeling as she did, that if I told it, it might leave me. I'd thought of it a great deal in the loneliness of this room, and I wanted mightily to be rid of the vividness of the dream. And so I continued, raising my hand to touch my neck as if I could still feel the tight, choking death.

"I collapsed and lay on the stone floor, helpless, as the cord was tied tightly so there'd be no chance air would reach my already suffocated lungs. I died there. Then my spirit was released from my body, and I saw myself lying limply. And as I watched, the mist was dispelled and there was only blackness. Blackness of which I was a part. And I told myself that that blackness was Death and I was now a part of it."

I covered my face with my hands. "It was dreadful. But that hallucination must have been the crisis of my illness. I remember now hearing the voices of you and Dr. Tanney speaking as if from a great distance."

My aunt regarded me with compassion. "Is that what you were trying to tell us?"

I nodded. "I didn't know who you were, but I thought you wouldn't accept the fact that I was dead, and I felt you had to know."

"Thank God, you were wrong—that it was merely a hallucination. But what a strange one!"

I managed a smile. "I hope never to have another."

My aunt rose from the chair and walked over to a window behind me. I could see her reflection in the mirror opposite. Her hands were clasped before her, and though she appeared to be looking out the window, I sensed her eyes saw nothing. My story had affected her deeply, and I almost wished I hadn't told it. Yet I did feel better now that I'd related it. Whereas before, it had seemed so real, now it seemed foolish—a product of a mind trapped in a body ridden by illness.

My aunt broke into my thoughts. "Dr. Tanney wishes me to take you away from here. Mostly because he's fearful of a recurrence of your illness. New Orleans is no place to be in summer, even when well."

"Sister spoke of it also. But I want to stay in America. I've lived most of my life in Europe."

"So have I, my dear," she said. "And I wasn't thinking of Europe."

"Where, then?" Excitement coursed through me.

"A place one hundred miles from here. I'm thinking I'll have our trunks sent there immediately and we will follow whenever Dr. Tanney feels you are capable of the journey."

"That sounds exciting." I stood up so abruptly I'd have

fallen had not the brass foot of the bed been handy for me to grip.

My aunt came to me quickly. "Please get back in bed. I shouldn't have excited you with such news."

"I'm glad you did. Have you ever thought of how little time I've spent in this country?"

"Yes," she replied. She'd drawn aside the mosquito netting and was now urging me into the bed. "But I wanted you to complete your education abroad. I'm glad, for if you'd contracted yellow fever while a little girl, you might have succumbed to it."

"How soon do you suppose Dr. Tanney will let me go?"

"If you promise me you'll nap, I'll leave here and go to his office immediately and talk with him about it."

"Please do, Auntie. I have a feeling my progress will be much faster once I get beyond the walls of this room. It seems as if I've been in it forever."

"Almost a month," she said. She stood at the foot of the bed and regarded me. "I'm going to lower the curtains, but I'll not leave this room until you're deep in sleep."

I blew her a kiss.

"Don't wait for that. I'll be good. I want very much to go."

My eyes were closed and I heard the soft rattle of the window shade as it was lowered, followed by the light, departing steps of my aunt. I opened my eyes to make certain she was gone. She was, but Sister Amelita entered the room and placed her cool hand on my brow.

She smiled down at me and whispered, "Sleep, my dear. It is the greatest cure of all."

It was exactly ten days later when we set out for our destination, which was still a mystery to me. My aunt told me it was to be a complete surprise, and with that I was content. I wanted only to remain in the country of my birth.

My aunt brought traveling clothes to the hospital and we left from there. Dawn had scarcely broken when we set out, for she wanted the greater part of the day's journey completed by midday, when the heat would become overbearing.

Dr. Tanney had given permission for me to travel and had given my aunt the name of a doctor in the town where we were headed. Sister Amelita saw us off and bade us godspeed. My aunt pressed a sealed envelope into her hand which I was certain contained a generous contribution to the hospital. Sister Amelita embraced my aunt and exclaimed at her goodness.

"My entire fortune would not be sufficient reward for nursing my niece back to good health," my aunt replied. "God bless you, Sister, and my everlasting gratitude."

"Ours also, Mademoiselle Yvonne. *Adieu, ma petite.* God go with you."

"*Adieu,* Sister," I replied and embraced her.

As if the departure wasn't exciting enough, my aunt had gifted me with a new coupe, drawn by two beautiful black horses. The exterior was dark blue and the interior upholstered in blue goatskin with satin of a matching hue. The floor of the vehicle was thickly carpeted, and tasseled silk shades could be drawn as protection against the sun.

I settled back in the seat alongside my aunt as the driver urged the horses into motion.

"How can I ever thank you, Auntie, for your goodness?" As I embraced her, she blushed, looking even more beautiful than usual.

"My dear, as you must have guessed, I am an extremely wealthy woman. One day you will inherit that wealth. I have done all in my power to prepare you for when the time comes to assume that responsibility."

"Auntie, don't talk that way," I exclaimed.

"It has to be talked about, my dear. I shan't live forever."

"I can't picture life without you," I said.

"You mustn't sound so petulant. Only children can afford to live in a world of make-believe."

"You're right," I admitted, though reluctantly. "It's just that I've had such a wonderful life with you. All the traveling we have done together . . . "

"So much, I suppose you've forgotten you're an American."

"I'll never forget that," I said. "I feel I'm privileged to be one. This country has gone through many agonies to achieve real freedom. I did a tremendous amount of reading about it in school, and I have only one regret."

"What is that?"

"That I know nothing about this part of the country where I was born."

"I hope you don't resent me because of that."

"Oh, no. After all, I know New York City and Boston and Philadelphia—even Chicago. We did explore the northern and central parts of America, so I'm not completely ignorant, but somehow once I started to recover from my illness, I felt I wanted to remain here. Not necessarily in New Orleans, but in Louisiana, the state in which I was born."

Her features relaxed in a smile. "I'm glad, because this time I felt I'd brought you home. I'm tired of traveling."

"You know you still present a youthful appearance."

She gave me a knowing look. "Thank you, my dear. And you know I shall take excellent care of myself to retain it as long as possible. I'm a vain creature. I suppose in part because I have the means to indulge myself."

"You're not selfish, Auntie. Sister Amelita spoke at length of your many generosities to the hospital and of how you refused to allow any publicity regarding your charitable contributions.

"Tush, tush, my dear. I was blessed with wealth. There is much poverty in the world. I will do whatever I can to alleviate it. But enough of that. I haven't told you that we will stop at an inn tonight. It will be the half way point to our destination. They're expecting us—I wrote as soon as Dr. Tanney gave me permission to take you. Also,

I sent our trunks ahead to our destination, plus hired servants who will also be there on our arrival, so all will be in readiness for us."

"Won't you give me even a hint of where we're going?"

She looked pensive. "I would rather not. Somehow, I feel it would be wiser for it to be a complete surprise. I want to see your reaction. I hope it will be favorable."

"I give you my word it will be," I said

A smile touched her lips. "You've been a great solace to me. Now settle back and enjoy the scenery. Despite the comfort of the carriage, we're getting jounced and we'll become fatigued. My concern is for you, so I suggest you conserve your energy by not talking."

I didn't mind, because the countryside was new to me. Now and then I caught glimpses of the Mississippi, but it seemed that we were veering away from it. There were lovely homes along the way with verdant lawns leading up to them. Now and then we passed another carriage and leaned forward to exchange waves with the occupants.

My aunt had kicked off her slippers, and her feet were resting on a silken pillow. Her eyes were closed and for the first time, I noticed fine lines about her mouth. Probably fatigue. She'd had to pack for both of us and had seen to closing up her townhouse, which she had opened for the first time in years when we returned from Europe.

After I'd completed my education, I pleaded with her to bring me to New Orleans. Even girls I'd attended school with had been there. I never had—at least, not that I could remember. And so she had acquiesced. Her townhouse was luxurious. I reveled in the busy activity of the city and was impatient to take part in it.

But alas, I'd ignored the fatigue brought on by my travels and had taken leave of the house early one morning to explore the city. I didn't return until nightfall, at which time I was promptly scolded by my aunt—one of the rare occasions when she'd lost her temper because of something I'd done. I deserved it, though, because the next day I was delirious with fever and was brought to the hospital.

I gave myself a mental reminder not to overdo again. Dr. Tanney had made me promise, as had Sister Amelita. Otherwise, he'd not have given his permission for me to leave the city.

We reached the inn around midday and I was as grateful as my aunt that half of our journey was ended. The road was badly rutted, and the driver had to maintain a goodly pace for us to cover the distance necessary to reach the halfway mark of our journey. The inn was wisteria-covered and on the wide porch were white rockers, their backs and seats padded with green cushions. Flower boxes decorated the railing, giving the place a colorful air. The grounds behind had been carefully cultivated and were a mass of color with rose-covered arbors in full bloom. The very air was heavy with their perfume.

"How beautiful, Auntie!" I exclaimed. "I want to explore the gardens at once."

"No, my dear," she contradicted me. "We will bathe, have a light repast, and then nap. In the cool of evening, you may explore and get your exercise which, Dr. Tanney told me, is most necessary for you. You were inactive for so long, your muscles became weak from disuse."

"It will be a pleasure strengthening them among such beauty." I could scarcely tear my eyes away from the enchanting setting visible behind the inn.

Our driver presented a striking appearance in his green livery. He was about thirty, dark-skinned, quiet of manner, and extremely competent in the way he handled the animals and the carriage. His name was Henry, and after assisting us to the ground, he proceeded to take our luggage from a storage area beneath his seat.

The foyer of the inn was empty except for a clerk at the desk. However, sounds of muted conversation drifted from the dining room, which was visible through the open doors. My aunt identified herself and we were brought upstairs, though not before she received assurance that there was a suitable stable for the horses and that Henry had clean quarters.

She used her dainty, lace-edged handkerchief to fan herself as we mounted the stairs. She looked relieved that we'd arrived, and I knew the ride had fatigued her more than it had me.

Our rooms were large and high-ceilinged and looked out on the rear gardens. A small sitting room separated the bedrooms, which were clean and pleasantly furnished, with a view of the gardens. A maid came in to help us unpack, but my aunt asked that she go downstairs and have food sent up to us in a half-hour. She did so and we went to our separate rooms and removed our travel clothes. The light in the rooms was muted, for the jalousies were closed against the heat of day, and the dusky interior helped create the illusion of coolness.

I bathed and slipped into a negligee and returned to the sitting room to await my aunt. She came presently, as did our trays of food. The food was delicious, but we ate in silence, both of us overcome with fatigue. Then the maid removed our trays and we retired to our rooms for a much-needed rest.

I stirred restlessly and came awake suddenly, as if someone had called my name. Recollection returned quickly, and I glanced at the open door leading to the sitting room that connected our bedrooms. I wondered if my aunt might have called. I reached for my negligee and donned it quickly as I moved noiselessly across the darkened room in my stockinged feet.

I glanced at the clock on the sitting room mantel and was startled to see it wasn't even three o'clock. I'd been asleep no more than a half-hour. Noting that, I moved more cautiously to my aunt's door, which was partially open. I stepped into the room, but had to pause until my eyes had further adjusted, for she'd drawn the shades on the closed jalousies, turning the shadowy room into pitch blackness.

But I had only to listen to hear her measured breathing, and I retreated as cautiously as I'd entered, not wishing to stir her from her slumbers. I knew she placed great store in her afternoon naps and had spoken to me at length of the importance of them, especially when a woman wished to retain her looks. I didn't have the kind of beauty my aunt possessed, and so such cautions were lost on me.

I returned to my bedroom, still puzzled by what had wakened me. I was certain my name had been called. Yet it couldn't have been. No one here knew me except my aunt, and she was deep in slumber. Then the answer came to me. She might have called out my name in her sleep. She'd been a devoted guardian and the concern she showed for me during my convalescence revealed the deep worry she must have felt when my life wavered in the balance. Not until the day before I left the hospital did Sister Amelita tell me Dr. Tanney at one point had given up hope and had told my aunt to be prepared for the worst.

I bathed my face and selected an afternoon dress of a gauzy material. I'd already decided what I would do—take a stroll in the garden. The heat wouldn't bother me, and I had no desire to lie down again. I felt quite refreshed.

I went to the window and tilted the jalousies just enough to let me peer down into the garden. I was thrilled by the riot of color and beauty.

I noticed cushioned benches beneath shade trees. How wonderful to go down there and sit. I would bring a book and luxuriate in the quiet and enchantment of the garden. I was about to turn away when I caught sight of two feminine figures. One, an older woman with buxom figure and gray hair, was seated on a bench. At her feet was a young girl. There was nothing unusual about that, except that they seemed to have a familiar look to them. I couldn't place them, yet I was certain I'd seen them before.

The girl seemed to be occupied with some sort of chore, yet from time to time I noticed she raised a hand to her eyes, as if something was impairing her vision. Then the older woman bent forward and, in raised voice, seemed to be scolding the girl. The girl nodded, but didn't raise her head. Then I could see that she was massaging the older woman's feet. Yes, the shoes were placed side by side beneath the bench. Yet why should these two look familiar?

Then the woman, still scolding, looked up as if to see if there was anyone about to overhear. I exclaimed aloud, and my cry must have been overheard by both, for the girl looked over her shoulder and directly at the window whose jalousy concealed me. Despite the warmth of the room, a chill of apprehension encompassed me, for I suddenly recognized these two. They were the mother and daughter who'd entered the room I'd dreamed about while in coma—the mother who had kicked off her shoes and asked the maid for a room in which she might rest, then imperiously called for the daughter to follow. It couldn't be. I was imagining it. The hallucination had seemed so real I was carrying it about in my mind.

I looked again. The girl was plain, dressed in a fashion of twenty years ago and in a frock that was much too old for her. *Dressed exactly as she'd been in the dream!*

Impelled by curiosity, I left my room and moved silently along the carpeted corridor to the stairway. The lobby of the inn was deserted, the guests still enjoying their rest. The clerk behind the desk had his straight-back chair tilted against the wall and he was sound asleep, gentle snores emanating from his throat. I opened the screen door cautiously, hoping it was oiled. It was, and I shut it carefully. I listened a moment to see if the snores continued. They did, and smiling, I moved off the porch to the grassy lawn, where I could walk silently, neither calling attention to myself nor disturbing anyone.

Once in back, I paused. Not to admire the beauty of the grounds, but to get my bearings. I would walk past the two women and take a closer look. Perhaps I'd had a recurrence of my dream and that was what had awakened me, rather than the thought that I'd heard my name called. I hoped so.

The tall arbors cut off my view of the area visible from my window, so I moved along a path, heading for the shade trees beneath which benches had been placed. This was where the two women were. As I proceeded, I felt more and more certain my imagination had played tricks with me, that they would in no way resemble the two in my dream.

I followed the curving path and came to another, which should lead to the area I sought. But I was doomed to disappointment, for none of the benches was occupied. Nor was there a sign of the two ladies. In my haste, I'd forgotten to bring a book, so I decided to stroll among the paths and admire the carefully laid-out gardens. They were extensive and beauteous to behold.

I dismissed the two women from my mind and meandered about, pausing now and then to admire a perennial of unusual size. Then I noticed an arch of oaks and I was enticed not only by their beauty, but by the thought that it would be cool beneath them. Because of the heat, fine beads of perspiration were already covering my brow.

I entered the oak arch and paused, delighted not only by the coolness, but because it was almost like stepping into the make-believe world of Lewis Carroll's *Alice in Wonderland*. With the oaks towering above me and their branches so intertwined as almost to turn daytime into nighttime, I felt almost tiny and wanted to laugh aloud. But my mood was quickly changed by the sound of someone sobbing softly. It sounded like a woman whose hands covered her mouth, muting the sound in order not to draw attention to herself.

My first instinct was to withdraw and return to the inn, but as quickly, I remembered the young girl and the gesture she'd made of raising her hands as if to brush away tears, and I wondered if it might be she. As I advanced farther beneath the arch of oaks, the sobs became more apparent, then stopped. I did, too, wondering if I'd been seen. I'd made no attempt at stealth, but now that the sobs had ceased, I felt like an interloper. Yet how could I be, when I'd not even seen the person who was crying?

Though I'd have enjoyed continuing my stroll beneath the trees, I felt I should turn back. Certainly, whoever had been crying had come here so that her tears would not be heard. But as I turned, a young girl came from around an oak. She stopped, startled, as she saw me and would have retreated except that I smiled a greeting. Her eyes were swollen from weeping, and though she didn't return the smile, she did nod.

I said, "I was lonely and decided to come out and explore the grounds. I think the arch of oaks is spectacular, don't you?"

She looked up at them as if seeing them for the first time and again nodded. She was the girl in the dream I had had, and she was dressed in a frock of a bygone era, just as the girl of my dream had been. The realization might have unsettled me, except that my concern was for her. I wondered what could have made her so unhappy.

I wanted to learn more about her, yet knew I must be cautious. She seemed uncertain of me and was regarding me with suspicion—or was it distrust? I had the feeling it would take little to make her flee.

I said, "I hope you won't think me rude to speak to you, but I was so pleased to see someone my age. My name is Julie."

"Mine is Adrienne." Her tone was lusterless.

"It's a beautiful name," I said.

"It's the only thing about me that *is* beautiful," she replied tonelessly. She turned and started to walk away. I moved up and fell in step beside her.

"Why are you unhappy?" I couldn't keep from asking the question.

"Please go away," she exclaimed, and I thought for a moment she would burst into tears again.

"I'd like to be your friend," I said quietly. "Even if it's just for an afternoon."

"I'm not allowed to have friends." She averted her head as she spoke.

"Why not?" I was careful not to evidence surprise or shock.

"Because I'm not. I don't wish to talk about it."

"That's understandable. But you'd feel better if you did talk about it. I know. When I was away at school, I had a girl friend whom I trusted dearly. She trusted me also, and when we were unhappy or troubled, we would talk things over with one another. And somehow, things we thought so terrible didn't seem so bad once we talked about them."

She slowed her walk and turned her head to eye me. The cold glance was anything but reassuring, though I pretended not to notice.

"Where did you go to school?"

"Switzerland."

"Then you're not an American."

"Oh, yes."

"You mean you were born here?"

I knew what she meant. "In this very state. However, my parents died when I was small, and my aunt raised me. She preferred living abroad, and that's why I was educated there."

"Then that explains why you don't sound like an American."

I smiled. "I suppose it does, though Americans in New York don't sound like those in Boston. You have the soft drawl characteristic of the South. My aunt, despite her travels, still has it."

"Is she with you?"

"Oh, yes. But she's resting. I caught a glimpse of the gardens when we arrived, and I couldn't bear to leave without exploring them."

"Then you didn't follow me into this glen of sorts."

"Good gracious, no! Though I heard you crying. Why are you unhappy?"

"Because I'm young and not allowed to be."

"Is your mother jealous of your youth?"

She looked startled at the idea. "I'm sure she isn't."

"I think she is," I said boldly. "That's why she won't allow you to dress in the present era. And your hair. It's a lovely chestnut color and would look beautiful piled high on your head, rather than pulled back tightly in a bun."

Her face flamed in embarrassment. "You're very rude."

"I don't mean to be. I want to help you. Come to my room. I'll dress your hair in a style becoming to you."

Her face colored pleasurably, but her voice was doubtful. "Would you really?"

"I'd love to." I caught her hand in mine and pulled her along with me. "I'm sure my aunt is still sleeping and we'll have my room to ourselves."

Her sallow skin seemed to take on color at the thought. "If only you could make me attractive."

"You can do it better than anyone." I spoke in the manner of one inspiring a confidence. "First of all, an inner happiness is essential."

"Easier said than done," she replied, though not so dismally.

"You must convince your mother that you're old enough now to make decisions, select clothes, and choose friends—and you must insist on having friends."

Her manner cooled. "How do you know it's my mother who's responsible?"

I shrugged lightly. "A mother has the most influence on a daughter, does she not?"

She nodded, convinced. I could scarcely tell her I'd seen them both in a dream I'd had while in a coma.

"It's my mother. I don't know why she dominates me so. Or won't allow me to have a life of my own. I've even tried to fathom a reason for it, but I've never come up with an answer."

We'd reached the end of the grove, and she stopped abruptly. "I hope Mama is sleeping. Our room looks out on the garden, and if she sees me with you, she'll make me come upstairs directly and rest."

"I suggest we separate. I'll go first, and you follow me to my room."

She nodded, even managing a smile. Once I stepped from the arch of oaks, I dared not look back or even glance up at the shuttered windows. I hoped Adrienne wouldn't change her mind. It made me angry to see one so young, hesitant and fearful to face the challenge of womanhood.

I'd closed the door of the sitting room that separated my room from my aunt's so that we had complete privacy. I'd seated Adrienne before the dresser and had brushed her hair until it glistened, then slowly put it up, showing her how to arrange it herself and place the pins so that it would stay. Her hair was thick and of good texture. The styling acted as a tonic on her, for her eyes had taken on a soft glow and the corners of her mouth were widened in a smile of disbelief. She was actually pretty, and I noticed the tip of her nose tilted upward, giving her a saucy look.

She stood up, turned and embraced me, then stepped back and turned once again to the mirror. "I can't believe it's me," she exclaimed. "But Mama will be furious."

"Be firm," I said.

"I will be," she exclaimed. "After all, I'm nineteen."

"So am I," I said.

She held out her skirts, turned sideways to regard the bustle, and shook her head in dismay. "No one wears a bustle any more."

"Then don't wear it," I said.

"But my dresses will all be too long in back," she said.

"Would you like to wear one of mine down to dinner?" I asked.

"Yes, but Mama would be furious, and she'd have a right to be." She was still regarding her reflection. "I know what I'll do. I'll go to our room and shorten the dress I've been wearing to dinner. I packed it because we're leaving tomorrow, but I can unpack it."

"Do that," I exclaimed. "I'll look forward to seeing you make an entrance in the dining room."

"How can I ever thank you, Julie?" she said. "I feel reborn."

"You look it," I said. "I have a feeling you're going to meet a young man who'll fall in love with you instantly, and you with him."

"What makes you say that?"

"Just looking at you, I see it."

"You sound like a gypsy," she giggled, but suppressed it by covering her mouth. "Are you secretly one?"

I walked her to the door. "Secretly," I whispered, "I'm your fairy godmother."

She laughed softly. "You're too young."

I made a somber face. "In wisdom, I'm as old as Methuselah."

I closed the door on her soft laughter and turned to see my aunt regarding me with a quizzical expression.

"Who was that?" she asked.

"A girl I met in the garden."

I was about to tell her the girl in my hallucination was real, then decided it would be a betrayal of Adrienne. I'd managed to bring her out of the doldrums. I didn't want anything to force her back to the way she was.

"She's a girl I met in the garden," I repeated. "We were discussing hair fashions and I suggested a new way of wearing hers. I even brought her up here and did it for her."

My aunt came forward and embraced me. "How like your mother you are! She was always performing kind, generous acts for others. I'm proud of you."

"Thank you, Auntie," I said.

"What is her name?"

"Adrienne."

"Adrienne what?"

I looked my chagrin. "I haven't the faintest idea. We just exchanged first names."

My aunt's smile was one of tolerance. "The impetuosity of youth. Ah, well. No matter. You'll probably never see her again."

"I shall."

My aunt's brows raised questioningly.

"In the dining room tonight. With her mother."

"Then I suggest you start to dress. We must endeavor to look charming—like true Continentals."

"You miss Europe already, don't you?"

She smiled wistfully. "Perhaps." As I sobered, she added quickly, "Relax, my dear. I know, though you've spent more years abroad than in this country, you feel that you've come home."

"I do, Auntie. And I want very much to stay."

She gave my cheek a light pat. "We shall see."

I recalled telling Adrienne how she must assert herself, and I wondered if I would be forced to do the same thing with my aunt. I was determined not to make another voyage to Europe for at least a year.

The dining room was two-thirds full, and the soft murmur of conversation drifted about the room. It was a charming room, with carpeted floor and walls covered with damask. The tables were placed far enough apart to ensure privacy. Each was covered with a white linen cloth, and a low pewter bowl filled with flowers decorated the center of each, along with a twin candelabrum. Soft light drifted down from oil lamps that hung from the ceiling.

My aunt and I were enjoying a sherry when Adrienne and her mother entered. Without meaning to, I exclaimed aloud, for on a closer look, I knew for a certainty the mother was the same woman who had appeared in my dream. They were being led to a table just beyond ours, and from the flushed look on the older woman's face, I knew Adrienne had had a confrontation and that the young girl had triumphed, for she was still wearing the hairstyle. In addition to that, she had removed the bustle from her frock and had shortened the hem, managing to drape the extra material so skillfully it served to emphasize her shapely form. She was shorter than I, but trim of figure, and carried herself beautifully. Perhaps defiantly would be a better word. As they reached our table, our eyes met. She smiled and nodded graciously to my aunt, who nodded in return.

But not so her mother. A cry escaped the older woman as her eyes met mine. All I could think of was that she looked as if she'd seen a ghost. Then her glance flicked to my aunt. I was certain her lips formed the word Yvonne.

When my aunt greeted her with, "Good evening, Louisa," I knew I'd been correct.

The woman did not return the greeting, but quickly gathered her wits together and moved beyond my range of vision.

"You know them!" I exclaimed.

"The woman," my aunt replied. "Mrs. Zaffery Leloude. I presume the young lady is her daughter."

"Adrienne," I said. "She's the girl . . ."

My aunt nodded. "I caught a glimpse of her when she was leaving your room. I fear you've made an enemy of her mother."

"I hope not," I said.

"So do I," she replied. "Since their plantation adjoins our estate."

"Then Adrienne and I will be friends," I exclaimed happily, already forgetful of my aunt's prophecy.

"Only time will tell," my aunt said wisely.

"Auntie, since you know them—or at least Mrs. Leloude—I have a little news for you."

"Regarding them?"

I nodded. "When I was in coma and hallucinating, Adrienne and her mother were part of that dream."

My aunt was so startled at my statement she almost spilled her sherry. "Are you certain?"

"Very," I replied. "I saw them both in the garden this afternoon. I was in my room and was awakened by hearing my name called. At least, I thought I had. I got up and went to your room, thinking you might have called to me. You were sleeping, and when I returned to my room, I glanced out into the gardens. I was admiring their beauty when I observed the two women. The older woman was seated on a bench, and her daughter was massaging her feet. In my dream the woman came into the room reserved for the ladies at the masqued ball. She kicked off her shoes, asked the maid if there was a place where she might lie down, and called to her daughter to follow. The girl scooped up her mother's shoes and obeyed."

My aunt seemed startled. "Are you positive?"

"Yes," I insisted. "You look as if you doubt me."

"I don't, my dear. But I must be sure."

"Why?"

"I find it a little frightening." She observed me carefully, then asked, "Don't you?"

"At first, I guess I did. But I don't see why it should be."

My aunt smiled. "It shouldn't. Here comes our dinner. Let's forget about it."

But it was not so easy to do. The incident had left me restless and unable to sleep. I was disturbed, and didn't know why. I'd done nothing wrong. Certainly, a girl is entitled to happiness and the thrill of being young.

Nonetheless, I was still disturbed by the look of unconcealed hatred the woman had bestowed on me. Mrs. Louisa Leloude. A pretty name—French. Almost without realizing it, I'd been pacing back and forth the length of my room. The maid had drawn down the bedcovers, but

I knew I'd toss restlessly. I also knew I was feeling the fatigue brought on by my prolonged illness. The sitting room was in darkness, and when my aunt had bade me good night, I'd heard the door to her room, adjoining it, close softly.

I lowered the bedlamp and moved across the room. I opened the door softly and listened. The inn had quieted for the night. I wanted to go downstairs and walk in the gardens. I wondered if my appearance downstairs would be unseemly. If so, I'd not allow myself to dwell on it. I had to rid myself of this feeling. It was almost one of foreboding. As if that dream had been meant to warn me to beware of her. I knew I was being foolish to let my imagination run away with me.

I was trembling when I reached the stairs and used the bannister for support. I looked neither to right nor to left as I crossed the lobby, so I had no idea if other guests were still about. I heard no footsteps or voices. I opened the screen door quietly, stepped off the porch into the wet grass, and moved around the building to the rear. My satin slippers would be ruined, but it didn't seem important.

I slowed my pace once I reached a path, for I was breathing rapidly. Whether from exertion or nervousness, I didn't know, and it didn't seem important. Something was driving me, yet I didn't know what. I tried to forget my nervousness and slowed my pace so I might observe the flowers, glistening with dew. Crickets and katydids made their song evident, augmented by an occasional croak of a frog. I paused to observe and listen. The moonlight gave the grounds the brightness of day, yet there was a softness to it that I found soothing. I resumed my stroll, slowly now, caught up in the magic of the evening. I'd have thought the grounds would have been well frequented on such a night, but most of the guests had traveled great distances and were only too glad to retire, knowing they would have to be up again for an early start on their journey.

The path made an abrupt right turn that was completely concealed by a rose-covered arbor of considerable length and a goodly height, shutting out the moonlight and placing the entire area in shadow. I shivered, though I felt no chill, but I sensed I was no longer alone. I didn't wish to continue along this path and turned back to retrace my steps. But my path was blocked.

It was Mrs. Leloude, and even in the dimness I could see the look of hatred with which she was regarding me. I was about to ask her to allow me to pass when she spoke.

"I saw you leave your room. Is this a night favored for your witchery?"

"What are you talking about?"

"As if you don't know." She kept her voice low, but her tone was contemptuous.

"I don't," I said. "And if you can't speak courteously, I don't wish to speak with you."

She reached out and grasped my wrist, as if fearful I might flee. I struggled to free myself, but to no avail.

"I don't wish to speak with you," she said. "I know the chance I'm taking. But you are to stay away from my daughter."

"Mrs. Leloude, I believe I've done more for your daughter in the brief time I was with her today than you have in all the years you've had her under your domination."

"She's a dutiful girl. She never defied me until today when you dressed her hair so that she resembled a . . . a huzzy."

"That isn't true," I exclaimed with rising anger. "She's a dutiful girl and a lady. If you really loved her, you'd let her enjoy her youth."

"I love her and will not see her destroyed by you. You know what you are. How could you escape it when your mother was one?"

"One what?" I demanded. I'd given up trying to free myself, for the effort had left me weak and shaken.

"A witch," she exclaimed. "You are a witch. You'll put a curse on the town just as your mother did. Your aunt had to take you away. Now she's bringing you back. Why? I'll tell you why. To perpetrate more mischief by predictions that will bring grief and heartache to families who ask only that they be allowed to live in peace—peace that was lost once your papa brought your mama there as a bride."

I wanted to ask the name of the town, but would not give her the satisfaction. When I returned to my room, I'd ask my aunt. The time for secrets and surprises was over. This woman was rude, and what she said was shocking, but was it the truth? If so, I had the right to know. The very thought was repugnant, yet I couldn't disregard everything this woman said. I'd seen both this woman and her daughter in my hallucination. I'd also seen myself lying dead at the foot of the Apollo statue. Was it a forewarning that this woman meant me harm and I must be on guard? If so, I would be as discreet as possible so as not to further enrage her.

"I can't believe what you say is true. I will question my aunt, who has never given me even a slight hint of my being other than a normal young woman. Frankly, I don't believe in witches."

"Your mother was one," she hissed. "Everything she predicted came true. We don't want you back."

"To my recollection, I've never been there."

"You were born there and lived there until you were three. That was when your mother died. And good riddance, I say."

Was there no limit to this woman's malevolence? I would endure no more.

"Stop speaking ill of my mother. And release my wrist. Should we meet again, I will be pleased if you do not in any way acknowledge my presence."

Her smile was a sneer. "No one in that town will acknowledge your presence. You would be much smarter not to go back, because you'll be driven from it. If you're lucky enough to live."

"Are you threatening my life?" I began to struggle anew, but not only were my efforts fruitless, she grasped my free wrist as I raised my arm in an attempt to push her from me. I reeled as a wave of weakness overcame me.

"I'm telling you to stay away from my daughter. She's not to be influenced by you again. You're evil, just as your mother was. You'll put a curse on my daughter. I know you will. At least you'll try, but I warn you. I'll see you dead before I'll let you do to her what your mama did to others."

"Let me go!" I raised my voice, hopeful that I'd attract the attention of someone still awake. I couldn't believe this woman intended to murder me now, but I was thoroughly frightened of her.

She threw me from her with such force I struck the wooden edge of the arbor. I doubt that ordinarily I'd have been more than shaken up by her rough gesture, but I was already overcome with weakness by my exertions. All I remember before blackness enveloped me was an overpowering wave of dizziness.

I stirred and tried to open my eyes, but the effort seemed too great. My head was throbbing, and I raised an arm, letting my fingers touch the side of my brow. I moaned softly, and a hand closed around my wrist, gripped it lightly, and drew it down to my side. The gesture startled me, and I remembered my last conscious moments in the garden with Mrs. Leloude when I'd struggled futilely to free myself of her grip on my wrists.

I again tried to free myself, but a masculine voice spoke close to my face. "It's all right. I'm taking your pulse. I'm a doctor."

"Thank God she's alive, Doctor. Where did you find her?" It was my aunt, and I felt reassured.

"I was strolling in the gardens and I heard a lady's

voice cry out, asking to be let alone. From her tone, I feared she was being molested and ran in the direction of the voice. I found your niece on the ground. She was in a faint."

"She's been very ill," my aunt said, "and should not have been out tonight."

"She's exhausted," came the quiet reply. "What was the nature of her illness?"

"She had yellow fever, and I was bringing her back to my home in Flagton to convalesce."

"My practice is there," he said.

My aunt said, "You wouldn't, perchance, be Dr. Bruce Manning?"

"I am he." The hand released my wrist and drew the bedcovers to my chin. "She's not to get out of bed. It won't hurt her to sleep in her clothes. I fear the slightest exertion might cause her to have a relapse."

"I won't leave her bedside," my aunt said.

He said, "I want you to get your sleep. Are you intending to travel tomorrow?"

"We were, but we can stay over. I'll not submit Julie to the rigors of the journey in her weakened condition."

"She might be all right tomorrow. If so, you must get your rest so you'll be alert should she suffer a weak spell. I'll remain by her bedside tonight. She's perspiring profusely, though it might be from weakness brought on by fatigue."

There was a few moments' silence; then my aunt spoke. "You said you heard a lady's voice cry out in alarm. Did you see anyone accost her?"

"No. Nor did I see anyone flee. But I was under the arch of oaks, and that was a fair distance from where I found your niece. I located her only by the general direction I assumed the voice came from."

"I see. Very well. I'll have to check it to make certain, but I believe yours was the name Dr. Tanney gave me. He wanted to be assured Julie would continue to have care until she had completed her convalescence."

"I know him well, and if I'm the doctor he recommended, I'll be privileged to assume the care of your niece. She's very pale now, but with proper food and rest, I believe she'll be as good as new in a few days."

"Thank you, Doctor. I'll leave the adjoining doors open, so should you need me, I'll be available."

"I shan't disturb you," he replied. "The door leading to the corridor will be ajar, and I've asked one of the maids to sit out there. She'll be available should I need her."

"Then I shall rest, knowing Julie is in good hands."

I wanted to thank my aunt and the doctor, but the effort to open my eyes was more than I could manage. I felt myself slipping off into slumber, and I awoke only to the sounds of birds chirping and trilling their morning song.

It was no problem opening my eyes, and when I did, I looked up into a pair of gray eyes that were observing me in a professional manner.

"Good morning, Julie. I'm Dr. Bruce Manning."

"Good morning, Doctor."

"Feeling better?"

"Quite a lot better," I replied. "It was good of you to stay the night with me."

"So you heard your aunt and me talking."

"Yes. But I couldn't open my eyes or even say a word to reassure you."

"You were completely exhausted. What happened out there?"

I opened my mouth to reply, then paused. Certainly I couldn't tell him I'd been accosted by a woman who accused me of being a witch. Since he came from the town of Flagton—at least I knew where I was headed—he might be a good friend of Mrs. Leloude. Or he might think me delirious. Far from fearing Flagton or its inhabitants, I was impatient to get there. I didn't for one moment believe a word that woman had said. Either she was mad, or she bore an intense hatred for my parents, and now my aunt and me.

I said, "Fatigue overcame me. I became frightened I'd not make it back to the inn and called out for help."

He made no reply, but I saw his brows raise slightly. In disbelief, or amusement that I'd lied? I felt my face flame, but if he noticed, he gave no visible evidence of it. Instead, he moved aside the mosquito netting, took out a watch from his vest pocket, and grasped my wrist lightly as his fingers sought out my pulse. While he studied his watch, I observed him, noting the unruliness of his auburn hair, his fair skin, his strong chin, and the nose that had a slight bump on it, giving him a rather fascinating air, I thought.

He was about six feet in height, and though I knew he'd had no sleep—for he'd drawn a straight-back chair to my bedside and had spent the night there—his suit was not in the least rumpled. He replaced his watch in his pocket, let his hand rest lightly on my brow, and nodded in satisfaction.

"I think you'll do nicely, Julie. I'll leave you now, but I'm sending in a maid who'll help you from bed."

"I feel quite capable of managing, myself."

He smiled at that. "I'm sure you do. I think you're a rather spirited young lady, and I admire it—to a point. Just now, you're under my care. You may check with your aunt about that. I'll expect to see you in my office tomorrow. You're not to get out of this bed until the maid comes in and sees if you're capable. And she's to remain in here while you bathe and dress. Afterward, she'll report to me on how you did. If I get a good report, you may start out on your journey. I think I already hear your aunt moving about."

"Thank you, Doctor, for your excellent care."

He laughed a little at that. "I did nothing. You slept the night through. A pleasant journey."

"To you also, Doctor. Apparently you're leaving today."

"At once."

"But you had no sleep!" I exclaimed.

"A doctor learns to get along on little." He waved a farewell, but did not close the door. I knew better than to get out of bed. I sensed that though his manner was compassionate, he could, when the occasion warranted, become stern. I had no wish to antagonize him, for he had been most kind, and I knew that for a while I would have need of him.

Then the maid entered. She was young and her smile pleasant. She insisted on helping me from bed, but once she saw I was able to manage for myself, she busied herself replacing the garments I'd unpacked, in my bag. I felt quite fit, except for a slight headache. There was discoloration on one side of my brow where it had hit the arbor, but other than that, I was none the worse for what had happened last night, though I knew I had a dangerous enemy in Mrs. Leloude and I was impatient to discuss the woman with my aunt and learn how much if anything of what she said was true.

Much to my surprise, my aunt had ordered breakfast served in our sitting room. Naturally, the idea pleased me, since I was eager to discuss my meeting with Mrs. Leloude. However, I waited until we had breakfasted and were lingering over coffee before I told her of my encounter with the woman. She listened quietly and kept her eyes lowered, so I could not tell what she was thinking. But the fact that she did not dispute a word of what I said made me fear the worst. Not until I'd told my tale in its entirety did she speak.

"Well, my dear, I'd not wanted you to know anything about that."

"Surely you can't believe I'd have been unaware of it once I returned to Flagton."

"How did you know the name of the town?"

"I was too exhausted to speak or open my eyes last night, but I heard every word you and Dr. Manning said."

"I was hoping the town would have forgotten," she

said. "I've wanted to go home for many years, but I felt if I remained completely away from the place all wounds would heal."

"Do you mean Mama was a witch, and I am also one?"

"I mean no such thing," she scoffed, though she looked uncomfortable. "I will say this. Your mama could foretell the future. It's a gift only a few have. To me, that does not constitute a woman being a witch, or a man a warlock if he should have that gift."

"Did Papa have it?"

"No. Your papa was killed in a duel which your mama predicted no one would win. Neither man did."

"What do you mean?"

"Both your papa and his adversary, Lester Bergeron, died of their wounds. It made your mama bitter. She made other predictions of what would happen to the townspeople. Her auguries always came true."

"Why did you leave?"

"Had your mama lived, she'd have taken you away. She had become so hated she feared for her life, and even more for yours. Little as you were, you were already being called the daughter of a witch."

"Poor Mama. Did you take me away from there before she died?"

"No, my dear. The day following her burial."

"What happened to her?"

"She was found unconscious in the garden. I'm sure she was afflicted with a heart condition brought on by the strain of what she'd had to endure in that town. She suffered an attack, fell, and struck her head on a marble bench. She lingered for a day, but never regained consciousness."

"Where are Mama and Papa buried?"

"In the family cemetery that's situated on the grounds." My aunt pursed her lips thoughtfully. It was a gesture she used when she was pondering a step she would take. "We'll return to New Orleans. I'll not subject you to the hatred of Flagton."

"Then let me subject myself to it," I said firmly. "I want to go there."

"But what if you have the gift of prophecy?"

"If I have, I pray to use it well."

She looked pleased at my reply. "You're a woman, Julie. Inside as well as outside. I admire your courage, but I'm not sure I shall permit you to go."

"If you won't accompany me, I shall go alone."

"I'm fearful of Mrs. Leloude."

"She's formidable, I'll admit. But I'll not be intimidated by her."

"Did you tell Dr. Manning about her?"

"No."

"Why not? He heard you cry out."

"I know. And I sensed he did not believe me. I told him I cried out because I became frightened when weakness overcame me."

"Why did you go out there in the first place?"

"I was restless. I couldn't get Mrs. Leloude out of my mind. Or her daughter, though I like Adrienne. We got along well. But to learn that two women who I believed existed only in my dream world are actually living human beings quite unnerved me. I thought a walk in the garden would soothe me. It did, until I encountered Mrs. Leloude."

"I can't believe she means you harm," my aunt said.

It was my turn to smile. "If you'd seen and heard her, you'd believe it, but I'm not afraid. She made the threat I've repeated to you. She'll do nothing so long as I remain away from her daughter. She apparently doesn't want Adrienne to have friends in her age group."

"A possessive mother. There are none worse. They destroy what they helped to create. Sometimes because they're jealous of their daughter's youth. Sometimes because they want to govern every thought their daughter has. In either case, it's sickening."

"Very," I agreed.

"Well, my dear, it's time to get started. It will be afternoon before we arrive at Flagton. I'm sorry about last night."

"Perhaps it's as well it happened. At least, I'm prepared."

"True. Are you certain you wish to proceed?"

"I insist we do. I will even plead with you."

"No need for that." She stood up. "I'm proud of you. You have your mother's courage. She fought the entire town."

"And lost."

My aunt answered with a brief nod of her head. Her lips were compressed tightly, as if she didn't trust herself to speak.

TWO

We didn't reach Flagton until late afternoon. My aunt was fatigued to the point of irritability. I too felt the discomforts of the journey, but my curiosity exceeded my fatigue. I moved aside the drawn shade enough to get a view of the town as we drove along its main street. The raised sidewalks were of wood, and though there was a goodly sprinkling of stores, I saw no one about.

The heat was overwhelming, and even the lowered shades did nothing to alleviate it. My aunt had turned down my suggestion that we open the windows, and perhaps it was as well. The horses did kick up the dirt of the road, and though the carriage was becoming unbearably stuffy, at least we weren't covered with dirt from the journey.

"Sit back, Julie. I don't like you moving aside the shades to peek out. It's unseemly."

I knew she'd not speak to me in such a peevish fashion

were it not that she'd missed her nap and was weary from our travels.

"I'm sorry, Auntie." I released my hold on the shade and sat back.

She patted my hands folded in my lap. Hers were still gloved, but I'd dispensed with mine shortly after our departure.

"I'm the one to apologize," she said contritely. "I shouldn't have subjected either of us to this. Another day at the inn wouldn't have hurt. It was pleasant there, except for that terrible Louisa Leloude."

"Does she dislike you, or is it fear?"

"She has nothing to fear from me."

I frowned. "I'll admit her manner was antagonistic, yet somehow, I got that idea. When she saw you in the dining room last night, she seemed afraid. At least, for a moment."

"It's dislike, more likely. People envy money. They respect it, but in Flagton, they've always assumed a scornful attitude toward our family."

"Why?"

My aunt shrugged listlessly. "Because our wealth was ill-begotten."

"What do you mean?"

"Don't look so shocked, my dear. I'm really too weary to tell you in detail, but for now you must be content when I say one of our ancestors was a right-hand lieutenant of Jean Lafitte. As such, he profited enormously."

"The pirate!" My voice registered my distaste.

"The same. However, your great-grandfather was also a scholar, and his favorite tales were those of the gods and goddesses. He called his estate, where we are headed, Olympus."

"After Mount Olympus, the abode of the gods and goddesses?" The idea seemed preposterous.

"Exactly. And we'll be there shortly. Thank goodness, I had the foresight to send servants on ahead to get the place in readiness. The grounds have been kept up. Mr.

Louis Taylor, a famous New Orleans attorney who also has a residence in this town, has looked after the place for me. He's an old friend and would not accept compensation, even though he assumed full responsibility for hiring the help—outside help, that is. But even inside, everything had dust covers and should be in good condition. I'm sure all the house needs is a thorough airing and cleaning. When we arrive, which should be in minutes, since I already gave Henry directions on how to reach the place, I will excuse myself after showing you to your suite. I doubt I'll come down for dinner. But you must have nourishment. It's most important."

"After a rest. Just now, I'm much too excited to eat."

"That's understandable." Much to my surprise she raised the shade on her side. "In minutes now, you'll catch a glimpse of Olympus."

I smiled. "I have visions of a castle perched on the top of a mountain."

"Not a mountain," she replied. "But it cost a king's ransom to bring earth and rock so as to erect a palazzo."

"Are you serious?" My voice was no more than a whisper.

"Completely. Appreciate it, but don't be in awe of it, Julie, *ma petite*. One day it will be yours."

"Nonetheless, it is frightening," I reasoned. "A palace, when all I've known is one spartan room in a girls' school run by nuns who taught us modesty, humility, compassion, and love of our fellow man, regardless of his station in life."

"Isn't a good ruler loved by his people?"

"I'm not a ruler, Auntie."

"No," she agreed. "You're a modest girl, but one of spirit, and I feel you will fit in nicely. One day all of it will be yours. You must be ready for it. That's why I've brought you home."

"I'm grateful," I said. "But I had no idea I was returning to such luxury."

She looked amused. "Why should you be over-awed,

when we stayed at the best hotels wherever we traveled?"

"I always thought because it was a holiday, you made it more gala for me by stopping at those fashionable establishments. I had no idea you were possessed of such wealth you lived like an empress."

She laughed softly. "I did, sometimes, for I missed Olympus. That was the family residence. My brother brought his bride there to live. You were born there."

"I don't remember it."

"I suppose not," she said. "Though perhaps, when you see it anew, something will jog your memory."

"I hope so," I said enthusiastically. "I just wish we'd get there."

We rounded a corner and my aunt said, "Your wish is granted."

She instructed me to raise the curtains on the front and side glass panels and knock on the windows in a signal for Henry to stop. He obeyed just as we reached the drive leading up to the awesome structure at the top of the hill. I could think of no other word for it. It wasn't a mountain, certainly, but it was a steep rise. Then I caught a glimpse of water sparkling in the sun's rays. It was really a waterfall, and flanking each side of it was a stairway. I cried out in dismay as I saw the statues on each landing and realized I was observing what I'd seen when I hallucinated.

I looked at my aunt, who was, in turn, observing me carefully. She nodded and said, "It's what you saw in your dream."

"Why didn't you tell me when I described it to you?" I demanded.

"I was too astounded. Then I thought it would be wiser if you saw it. Particularly after you saw Louisa Leloude and her daughter, Adrienne."

"What did that have to do with it?" I was more angry than frightened, and my anger was directed at my aunt.

"I'm thinking of your mama."

"What about her?"

"She was a seeress. She, too, dreamed things that afterwards came true. Apparently you do also."

"I never did before my illness," I protested. "And it wasn't really a dream. I was hallucinating. I had fever and was out of my mind. Dr. Tanney said so."

"My dear," my aunt's tone was placating, as if addressing a recalcitrant child, "you were born here and lived here the first three years of your life. Some part of that has been stored in your memory all these years. During your illness, your mind, sick as it was, recalled Olympus and gave you a clear-cut picture of it, which you described perfectly to me."

"If that is so, then you've sealed my doom by bringing me back here."

My aunt's voice raised in dismay. "That was not my intent. You're speaking in riddles."

"Have you forgotten I saw myself dead beneath the Apollo fountain?"

She pressed a hand over her lips and her head moved slowly from side to side, in negative fashion. "You were gravely ill and near death. You thought yourself dead. That's all it was."

"If Mama had dreams that foretold the future, that's what I had. A dream in which I saw myself dead. There will be a masked ball, I'll dress as a shepherdess and be murdered—by strangulation. A silk cord—one used to hold back a drapery."

Her arms enclosed me. "No, my dear. Don't talk that way. If I suspected you would come to harm here, I'd not have brought you back."

"Mrs. Leloude threatened my life. What did Mama ever do to her that she should threaten me?"

"Oh, my dear, forgive me for bringing you here. We must stay overnight, for I am too fatigued to travel further, but we will leave tomorrow and head back to New Orleans."

She tapped on the window for Henry to proceed, then fell back against the cushioned back as if the effort had exhausted her. It probably had. The corners of her mouth drooped and her eyes held a drawn look, though that could have been caused by my emotional outburst. I was on the verge of tears, not of fright so much as resentment that she had not told me the truth—that the place in my dream was my own birthplace.

Henry urged the horses into motion and we skirted the palazzo, moving completely around it during the ascent. The vehicle finally came to a stop at the front after traversing the entire structure. The driveway had been deliberately planned that way so as to give the visitor a complete view of the place. It was magnificent and breathtakingly beautiful, as were the surroundings. Olympus was a fitting name for it, for no expense had been spared in creating it.

The gardens were formal in treatment, Italian in design and interspersed with marble statuary. But what held me the most was the fountain stairway. When we alighted from the coupe, we had to pause to steady ourselves. The long ride, plus the jouncing, made us unsteady on our feet, as if we'd been on a sea voyage and had to regain our sense of balance. I regarded the twin stairways with landings at various levels. All was exactly as I had dreamed it.

However, I told myself sternly, that did not mean I was a seeress. It did mean my memory had stored away a picture of the setting. I'd do my best not to dwell on the figure I'd seen lying prone on the stone floor surrounding Apollo's fountain.

"Come, my dear." My aunt, despite her fatigue, was once again in command of the situation. I turned dutifully and walked with her to the marble stairs that led to the entrance. The building was of gray stone, the entranceway pink marble.

The door opened and an elderly man in butler's livery bowed as we entered. My aunt acknowledged his greeting and told me his name was Martin. There was a buxom housekeeper named Tammy, and Melisse, a personal maid for my aunt. At least, those were the ones who stood in line to greet us. My aunt informed me there were others who would attend to keeping the house sparkling. Looking around, I judged it would take a corps of them to do it, for except in museums I'd visited, I'd never seen such luxury.

My aunt brought me upstairs, an expedition that seemed endless. The staircase circled round and round, and I bent my head back to look above. The light was almost blinding, for the circled dome at the top was of colored glass and caught the bright rays of the sun. It seemed as if red and green flame glowed from the roof. It was spectacular and awesome, as it was no doubt meant to be.

Looking down I could see that the only decoration in the reception hall was an enormous black circular table. On it was a huge gold vase. It had been filled with gladioli which, to me, seemed more beautiful than the paneled walls or floor of inlaid marble.

We finally reached the second floor, at which point my aunt sighed audibly.

I said, "You mustn't think of starting our return tomorrow, Auntie. This journey has taken far more out of you than me."

Her smile was weary. "You've made a remarkable recovery. But my concern for you is still great. Promise me you'll not go on any expeditions in the gardens. You're not familiar with them, and you might fall and injury yourself."

"Have no fear. I'm as weary as you. I believe I'll have just a tray tonight."

"Rest, then, and when you wish sustenance, go downstairs. There are twin dining dooms. You may dine in the one of your choice."

"Twin dining rooms." I couldn't help smiling.

"Don't laugh, *ma petite,*" my aunt cautioned. "There are also twin drawing rooms, twin sitting rooms, twin tea rooms."

"How many rooms are in this palazzo?"

She shrugged daintily. "I've never counted. But be assured of one thing—you'll never lack for space." We finally reached the landing, and my aunt paused. "Your suite is in the wing opposite mine. Melisse will escort you there."

The maid my aunt had designated as hers had followed us and at my aunt's motion started to lead the day to my suite.

"Isn't it the third door down?" I asked my aunt.

She looked astonished. "How did you know?"

It was my turn to shrug. "I just knew."

"Melisse will unpack for you. Then send her to me."

Martin was ascending the stairs with part of our luggage. However, since our trunks had already arrived, everything I needed would be there. Melisse could attend to my aunt. I wasn't used to a personal maid and saw no reason to have one now.

Melisse had already opened the door of the room and stood back for me to enter. I did so after I excused her and asked that she attend to my aunt's needs. She was an attractive girl with a pleasant smile, and her pale green uniform was a fitting complement to her dark skin.

I evidenced no surprise when I entered the room, for I knew it would be the one I'd come to in my dream. I glanced over at the french doors. They were the ones I'd used to make my exit from the house the night of the masked ball. At least, in my hallucination. The furnishings were duplicates of those in my dream. Dainty pieces of white and gold. The large mirror on the wall was the same. I turned, half expecting to see Mrs. Leloude and Adrienne trailing behind her, carrying her mother's shoes.

I moved on to the bedroom. A pair of large canopied beds occupied one side of the room. An *étagère*, glassed on four sides, occupied the area between the windows. A dresser, highboy, dressing table, and writing desk were tastefully placed about the room. The rug was thick and luxurious. Every object in the room was a treasure. I imagined some were so old as to be of immense value. I could admire it, but I didn't feel comfortable in it. It was overly ostentatious and meant to impress. I preferred furnishings of quiet elegance and a home that radiated the warm personality of the owner.

But I didn't dwell on my likes or dislikes. I was glad we'd reached our destination, though I doubted I'd remain here. Once my aunt was rested, I'd ask that we return to New Orleans. While Flagton or its people didn't frighten me, Olympus did. I had no desire to linger here any longer than necessary.

With that decision made, I undressed and prepared myself for my bath. I was weak from exhaustion, and my muscles were stiff from so much sitting. Nonetheless, I bathed quickly, then donned a nightdress and slipped into bed, not even pausing to lower the shades against the waning daylight. No sooner had my head touched the pillow than I was lost in sleep.

I awakened to bright sunlight and the muted sounds of someone in my room. I stirred myself and slitted my eyes against the glare. It was Melisse, and she was approaching my bed cautiously. I shaded my eyes with my hand and greeted her.

She returned my greeting, saying "I have brought you a *café noir,* Miss Julie. Your aunt suggests you drink it hastily, then dress and come downstairs for breakfast. She has business in town and wishes you to accompany her to visit Dr. Manning."

I sat up and accepted the miniature cup and saucer. "I can't believe I slept the night through."

She smiled. "Your aunt did also."

"Is she rested?"

"Oh, yes. She looks quite beautiful again."

"Good."

I was glad to hear it. I'd never seen her features so drawn with fatigue as yesterday. It was as if she'd aged ten years in an afternoon. I wondered whether it had all been because of the journey or because she'd returned here with trepidations she'd been careful to keep concealed from me. I couldn't believe it was the latter. Her love for Olympus and the pride she took in its beauty were evident as she spoke of it, even though she'd not been here in many years. And I sensed her sole desire to come here was to acquaint me with it and instill in me the same pride for it that she had.

Melisse departed and I sipped my *café noir* as I dressed. I'd chosen a pale violet cotton, minus frills, but with a wide purple velvet waistband that accented my waistline. I carried my hat and gloves downstairs and set them on the large circular table in the hall. Martin escorted me around the stairway to a door that led into the dining room. Rather, I should say, one of the twin dining rooms, for the second was just beyond, and they were connected by a large archway.

The surface of the table was covered with gold leaf, protected by a glass top. Mirror-paneled walls alternated with bronze helmeted figures in bas-relief. They'd been freshly polished and gleamed with the richness of the metal.

My aunt looked refreshed and regal in a dark green silk suit. Her diamond earrings sparkled brilliantly, and they were matched by a pin which was fastened to the frilled front of her blouse. She studied me carefully as I took my seat, her brown eyes revealing their concern. Once reassured, she gave me a warm smile, which I returned.

She said, "Melisse told me you also slept the night through."

"Yes. And I feel wonderful."

"So do I, and if you wish to start the return journey, I will do so. Otherwise, I'd like to delay it a day."

"Suppose you do," I replied enthusiastically. "Perhaps by then, I'll become as enthralled with Olympus as you and won't wish to return."

"Perhaps. Though I'm not certain I want you to remain. I don't want a worry of any kind to impede your recovery."

"The way I feel this morning, I don't think anything will."

"I have business to attend to at the bank, and while I'm there, you may pay a visit to Dr. Manning. That *is* the name William Tanney gave to me."

"I'm so glad," I said. "He seems most competent."

My aunt raised a cautioning finger. "He left no bill for his services, and I know he spent the night at your bedside. Please ask him to send me one."

"I will, Auntie. Frankly, though I'll be pleased to see him and thank him for his care, I feel no need to go."

"You must, though. For my peace of mind. Also, Dr. Tanney allowed you to make the journey away from New Orleans only on condition I would see that you remained under the care of a doctor of his choice."

"It won't be a hardship, I assure you," I said, thinking back to those deep-set gray eyes studying me professionally. "But I don't like to take up a doctor's time when there's no need of it."

"I'll strike a bargain with you, *ma petite*. We'll let Dr. Manning be the judge of that."

"Very well," I acquiesced. "You're right, of course."

"Now let us eat and be off. You know how greatly the heat of day bothers me, and we have an hour's drive into town."

"Can't you postpone it until another day? It's almost noon. I don't have to see Dr. Manning today."

"Oh, yes, you do."

"Then let me go alone."

"Not today. My business can't be postponed. Now do get on with your breakfast, child."

We started with fresh strawberries covered with powdered sugar and resting in a white mound of softly whipped cream. Then came eggs, bacon, and potatoes, with hot raised rolls and strong coffee.

Henry again drove us, but this time in a carriage which,

though of an earlier vintage, was far more luxurious than the one my aunt had gifted me with. The inside was completely upholstered in silk damask, and the padding of the seats was so thick, it was almost like a bed.

My aunt had not ordered the shades drawn, for the carriage was still cool and the sun sent a welcome warmth through the top and glass sides. Henry urged the horses along at a brisk pace and I sat back, glorying in the beauty of the countryside. The road was well-shaded, but here and there I caught a view of a plantation house with a wide driveway leading to it. One particularly beautiful one had weeping willows framing the drive leading to the white-pillared dwelling. Several people were visible on the porch. A party of some sort, I thought. Or perhaps even a wedding. Certainly it was a beautiful day for one.

"Where is the Leloude home?" I asked.

"Next to ours. Just beyond. That's why you didn't see it. It's a beautiful plantation house. Zaffery Leloude has been fairly successful. After the war his father had the foresight to purchase land in North Carolina, where he planted acres and acres of tobacco. Here he grows cotton. However, the weather for the past two years has not been conducive to good crops."

"Poor Adrienne." I said it without ever meaning to.

"What do you mean?"

"You should have seen the first glimpse I had of her. She looked ten years older than she was. And she was dressed in a style of at least a decade ago."

"She looked rather attractive when she came into the dining room," my aunt said.

"I dressed her hair and showed her how to do it herself. She was quite entranced with the result and left to alter her dinner dress, which, she said, had a bustle."

"Good heavens," my aunt exclaimed. "What *is* the matter with Louisa? But then, she was always a harridan. The servants are terrified of her, and she used to have a time keeping them. Apparently she hasn't changed."

"Do you think she would harm me?" I asked. "I know she has a terrible temper, but . . ."

"How well I know," my aunt broke in. "And that's the reason for my trip into town today."

"I don't understand," I said.

"I'm going to see an attorney who is also a friend of long standing. I've already mentioned him to you—Louis Taylor."

"What can he do?"

"I'll tell him how Louisa accosted you at the inn and how she threatened you. At least she'll know you told me. But if an attorney has been informed of the threat she made against you, I doubt you will be troubled by her further. However, I suggest you remain away from Adrienne."

"But I like her, Auntie," I exclaimed. "And I see no reason why we can't be friends."

"Perhaps you and I see no reason, but Louisa will not countenance her daughter socializing with you in any way, no matter how minor. You know that."

The thought disturbed me, yet I saw no solution. However, I'd not need to worry about it. We'd not be here more than another day or so.

We reached the town and drove along the main street, though Henry slowed his pace because we didn't know exactly where Dr. Manning's office was located. The business street was long and wide and separated in the middle by a wide green, heavily shaded. A few townsfolk lounged on the cast-iron benches that were placed along the paths. A cannon graced the very center of the path. A bronze statue of a Confederate soldier stood on a marble pedestal a few feet away. My aunt informed me that her papa had presented the statue to the town, but the cannon was one used in the Civil War.

On the opposite side were large homes, in one of which Louis Taylor resided. But first, my aunt stated, she had business to attend to at the bank. Henry rounded the green and again moved slowly down the opposite side of the street so we might find the office of Dr. Manning. My aunt was certain now it was in one of the homes.

She was correct. A signboard bearing his name and profession hung from a post at the edge of the lawn. I left the carriage and waved a farewell after my aunt assured me she would return for me when her business was completed.

I went up the path to the door, which was open. I was about to push the bell when I noticed a sign on the open door bidding one to enter. The screen door opened and closed noiselessly behind me.

There was no one in the waiting room, but I could hear muted voices beyond a closed door to my right. It was a pleasant room, the walls painted a soft green, with a matching rug. Bowls of flowers lent added cheer. On a long table in the center of the room were several magazines of interest to both ladies and gentlemen. There were even some children's books, which proved Dr. Manning was thoughtful as well as competent.

I picked up a magazine and scanned the pages while I waited, but I found it difficult to concentrate. Somehow I couldn't believe I was seated in a doctor's office in the town of Flagton. I suppose that wasn't so strange, but the manner in which I came to be here certainly was. Or if not strange, at least unnerving.

Eventually, his door opened and he appeared, escorting an elderly gentleman to the door. He saw me immediately and flashed a smile of recognition. After the gentleman left, I stood up and he motioned me to the inner room.

"You look remarkably well," he complimented me.

"I feel guilty being here taking up your time," I said.

"Don't. You had a slight recurrence of fever two nights ago, and you must guard against any relapse. Dr. Tanney was right, you know. You should have supervision for a while. Your aunt gave me a letter he wrote telling me of the severity of the illness you suffered. You're a lucky girl."

"Yes," I said. "There were a few days when I remembered nothing."

"More than a few days were involved," he replied with a knowing smile, "but you've made a miraculous recovery. I'll write Dr. Tanney that the rigors of the journey left you untouched." He paused and regarded me anew. "At least, I'd like to write that to him, except that I felt you weren't completely honest with me at the inn."

I felt my face flame with color.

He nodded. "I was right, wasn't I?"

"It isn't anything that concerned my health. I was very fatigued when I went into the garden."

"Then why did you go?"

I regarded my gloved hands clasped primly in my lap. "I couldn't sleep. Perhaps I was over-fatigued."

"That would do it," he agreed. "But not in your case. You're being evasive. I heard you cry out that night. Your words were blurred, yet you sounded terrified. Am I correct?"

Without looking up, I nodded.

"And you won't tell me?"

"It's so fantastic you'd think me bereft of my senses."

"Let me be the judge of that, Julie. I'm not being bold in using your first name. I did it that night to reassure you. Your pulse was throbbing wildly, and it gave me cause for alarm. That's why I remained with you through the night. I feared you might doze and have a nightmare."

At the word, my head darted up and I regarded him with fear-filled eyes. "Did I? Did I talk in my sleep?"

"No. But you're a deeply troubled young lady, and unless you tell me about it—in confidence, of course—I cannot continue to regard you as my patient."

To myself I thought I had little need of a doctor, yet I knew he meant he was as concerned with my mental well-being as with my physical. The fact that he sensed I'd been less than honest with him was proof of his competence and interest in his patients.

"Very well, Doctor," I said, "I will tell you my story, but remember, I warned you."

"Just tell me, Julie."

I went back to my hallucination and told him about everything including my seeking Adrienne and her mother in the garden. I told him all about Mrs. Leloude's threats and how she'd gripped my wrists, then flung me from her when I cried out for her to release me. I added that I didn't know whether I'd fainted from weakness, or from striking my head against the arbor.

"I've only been here a year," he said when I finished, "and I know little of the story. Though I am familiar with Olympus, and I know that your aunt left with you after the death of your mother, whose end was sudden."

"Do you think that makes me a witch—or made my mother one? The fact that she could foretell events that subsequently happened?"

"No. If I could manage such a thing, I'd consider it a gift."

"I don't want to be the possessor of such a gift."

"Did you ever dream anything that came true before?"

"No. And I don't want to. I saw myself lying dead at the foot of the Apollo statue. I saw the twin staircases with the fountain waterfalls between, and each with a statue of a god or goddess. I didn't know of their existence until I arrived there."

"I understand you lived at Olympus until you were three. Without knowing it, you could have retained a picture of it. It's most impressive."

"You've been there?"

He nodded. "Mr. Louis Taylor, your aunt's attorney, took me there one day. He supervised the care of the grounds and occasionally checked the interior of the house. It's impressive, to say the least."

"Overwhelmingly so. I don't believe I want to stay there. My aunt has agreed to return to New Orleans in a day or two."

He said, "It would be wise, since you're convinced that the figure in your hallucination was you."

"I was dead, Doctor!" I exclaimed.

"You were in coma when you hallucinated, and very near death," he said quietly. "I would say that is why you saw yourself dead. It's happened to people before who doctors thought couldn't survive an illness. They, too, saw themselves dead."

"Murdered? Don't forget, I had a silken cord around my neck."

"Of course I can't explain that. Dreams aren't easily explainable, and they're always distorted. However, I can readily see how this has upset you, and understandably so, with Mrs. Leloude's behavior. I'm going to pay her a visit."

"Oh, please don't," I pleaded. "We're not remaining, anyway. And you might turn her against you."

My statement annoyed him, and his voice became stern. "I'm not the least bit concerned about that. You happen to be my patient. At this particular time, and after the severity of your illness, you need peace of mind. I'm going to see that you get it."

"I beg of you not to. I don't know why I'm asking this, but I am."

His fingertips lightly tapped the desk as he mulled over my request. "Very well. I'll remain quiet, but against my better judgment."

I smiled my relief and stood up. "Thank you, doctor. Oh, I almost forgot. My aunt said you didn't leave a bill for your services at the inn. She asked me to request one of you."

"I'll not bill you for that," he said. "I'd have done that for anyone, and you were not officially my patient. Now you are, and as such you'll be billed. As for the treatment I'll prescribe for you—plenty of rest and freedom from worry. And I believe that can only be realized by returning to New Orleans, though it's much too hot for you there."

"We'll probably go north." I said. "My aunt favors New York City or Boston. She really should have been a Yankee."

He smiled. "I'm a Connecticut Yankee. I hope you don't mind."

I laughed. "No. I spent several summers in New England, and I like it. My aunt kept me away from here deliberately in the hope that the troubles of the past would be forgotten."

"I know little about them," he said. "Doctors have no time for idle gossip. And as for witches, such talk is stupid."

Further conversation was cut off by a voice raised in greeting, which came from the waiting room. It was followed by a brisk tapping on the door, done by an object of some kind, probably a cane, since the voice was that of a male.

Dr. Manning excused himself and went to the door. Before he could say a word, the gentleman on the other side entered and looked around, talking as he did so.

"I know you have Miss Julie Moniere here. Her aunt, the beautiful Miss Yvonne, has asked that I bring her niece back to Olympus. Ah," he pointed a gold-tipped cane in my direction, his eyes speculative, "so there you are."

Dr. Manning, resigned but tolerant, turned to me. "I wasn't aware you knew Armand Bergeron."

"I don't." My manner was courteous but cool. And with reason. The gentleman was blond, fair, and possessed of such handsomeness, it seemed a waste in one of the opposite sex. I could think only that his conceit matched his good looks. He was tall, slender, with perfect features. His blue eyes were regarding me with interest. The same interest, I was certain, with which he regarded every female of my age. He was elegantly dressed in a fawn-colored morning suit, he gave off the scent of men's shaving cologne, and yet his skin was so smooth, I doubted it had need of a razor.

I stood up. Dr. Manning, sensing my annoyance, moved over to stand beside me. Before he could introduce us, Mr. Bergeron stepped forward, reached for my gloved hand, and brought it to his lips.

"Miss Julie, I will admit quite frankly I am the terror of Flagton. Mothers seek me out because I am a bachelor. At the same time, they warn their daughters to maintain strictly formal behavior when in my presence."

"We have not been introduced," I said stiffly. I'd not let him think I was overwhelmed by either his rakish manner or his handsomeness. Nor impressed by his popularity because he was unmarried.

He looked his astonishment. "A lady of spirit and the utmost decorum." He bowed. "I apologize. Please, Bruce, introduce us."

Dr. Manning did, and I thought I detected a fleeting glance of admiration directed my way. I was glad, for I didn't want to be thought a prude.

I said, "Whey my aunt left me here, she stated she would return. What caused her change of plan?"

"I met your aunt at the bank. Of course, it's been some years since she was here, and I was a mere boy at the time. About ten, I would say. I remember the beauty she was and still is. She was a guest in our home many times."

I eyed him coldly. "Mr. Bergeron, you haven't answered my question."

"Forgive the digression, Miss Julie, but I merely wished to assure you I was acquainted with your aunt. Anyway, Mr. Duvall, the banker, introduced us. We reminisced a little, and then she said she was on her way to see Lou Taylor. It so happened I'd already stopped at his residence and learned from a servant Louis had left for Olympus to pay his respects to the gracious Miss Yvonne. Naturally, your aunt became flustered. She said it was most important that she see him and told us why, adding she wished to return to Olympus immediately, but you were visiting Dr. Manning. I asked if I might bring you back—with your permission, of course. And hers. She gave hers willingly. Now I am your humble servant, hoping you will honor me by allowing me to escort you back to Olympus."

I didn't see where I had any choice, though I hoped Dr. Manning might protest and ask if he might. But he didn't, so I accepted graciously, though with still a touch of formality. If Mr. Bergeron noticed, he gave no sign of it.

Dr. Manning accompanied us outside. "When will you be leaving Olympus, Julie?"

"I doubt we'll be here more than two days," I said.

"I'd like to see you again before you go," he said. "Perhaps tomorrow afternoon at Olympus, if you have the time." For some reason, his statement pleased me. Was it because I felt it might prick the ego of Mr. Bergeron, who seemed to be regarding us both with interest as if he wondered whether there might already be a romantic attachment? I was letting my imagination run away with me, and I caught myself up quickly.

"Very well, Mr. Bergeron, we had better get started."

"Oh, your aunt suggested I drive you around and point out various places of interest. She mentioned specifically the Leloude plantation."

"That's not necessary," I said. "If I were going to remain here, I'd appreciate your gracious offer. But I'll be leaving."

"A pity." Mr. Bergeron seemed genuinely sincere. "You shouldn't let anyone drive you from Flagton. Olympus is too beautiful to be allowed to lie fallow and go to rot. The place deserves better than that. Laughter and gaiety and music. Life and excitement."

"There couldn't have been very much there, from what I hear."

"There was at one time," Mr. Bergeron said. "Your aunt loved parties, and from what I hear, she knew how to give them."

Dr. Manning said, "You know, Julie, Armand is right. Olympus would be an ideal place to convalesce."

"Are you implying I'm a coward in leaving?"

"Not at all," he replied. "You've been a very sick girl, and your recovery will certainly not be hastened by living in fear."

"Fear of Louisa Leloude?" Mr. Bergeron said.

I flashed him a look, wondering how much he knew about me. "She *is* formidable."

"She is indeed," he agreed. "I think I'm the only one in town not in awe of her, so I can understand your feelings. After all, that terrible frightening dream you had, and then to see the two figures in your dream come to life."

I was as astounded as Dr. Manning. "How did you know about that?"

"Your aunt related to Gene Duvall and me your illness and ravings while in coma, followed by your meeting with Louisa at the inn."

"I wasn't aware I raved."

Mr. Bergeron shrugged. "Perhaps she didn't say exactly that. But she said you saw Olympus in that dream and described it perfectly to her."

"I did," I said quietly. "I also saw myself dead at the foot of the Apollo fountain."

"I know, and I'm sorry," Mr. Bergeron said. I was surprised at the compassion in his eyes.

Dr. Manning's hand rested lightly on my shoulder. "Don't dwell on it, Julie."

I assured him I wouldn't, adding, "May I look forward to seeing you tomorrow, Doctor?"

"Unless I have an emergency, I'll be there."

Mr. Bergeron's carriage was open, and I could sit back and view the countryside with ease. Once we were on our way, I was glad of his company, for he pointed out various homes and informed me briefly of the occupants and their backgrounds. We came to the large, pillared home my aunt and I had passed on our way into town, and much to my dismay, we turned into the drive. I looked at him, aghast.

"Why are you bringing me here?" I asked.

"I want my friends to meet the beauteous Miss Julie Moniere."

The drive circled up to the house and continued on to exit at the far end. "Please don't stop at the porch. It will be an intrusion and most unseemly."

But he would not be deterred. "To do other than stop would be ruder. They're going to like you. I do. Besides, if you're not treated kindly, I'll not come to their socials."

"Don't you think it's conceited of you to use yourself as a bribe for them to accept me?" I was revolted by his reasoning.

"Calm down, Julie." The sternness in his voice startled me. "I like you. And I have good reason not to. But you have just as good a reason not to like me."

"What are you talking about?"

"Your father and mine engaged in a duel. A duel your mother predicted no one would win. She was right. They died as a result of the wounds they inflicted on one another."

I covered my face with my hands.

"Please don't cry," he urged. "Nothing unnerves me like a woman's tears."

I lowered my hands. "I'm not crying, Mr. Bergeron. I'm shocked by the manner in which they died. My aunt told me of it. Although I hadn't connected the names."

"It's over. I'd not have mentioned it had you gone along with this spur-of-the-moment idea I had. When you didn't, I said the only thing I could think of to bring you to your senses. I'm sorry I hurt you. I like you, Julie. As for your aunt—she's so beautiful it's unbelievable. I want you to stay here. Don't ask me why. I just do. Perhaps because I feel the town owes you an apology for the way it treated your mother."

"How did it treat her?"

"As a social outcast."

"Do you think I'll be treated any differently?"

"You'd better be, or they'll answer to me."

My smile was bitter. "You may lose your popularity with the matrons."

"I doubt that. This is my plan. You're my friend. If they want to be my friends, they must accept you."

"I'm not sure I like the terms."

"No more do I, but it's a start."

"You're being foolish, Mr. Bergeron. I'm not even going to remain here, so why waste your time?"

"I shan't consider it wasted. There's no more time for talk. You have a lovely smile. Use it."

A servant came forward and held the horse while Mr. Bergeron alighted and assisted me down. There were four or five girls on the porch engaged in lively conversation, which ceased when the carriage stopped. They eyed me openly and were plainly puzzled, seeing a stranger here.

One of the girls disengaged herself from the group and met us as we stepped onto the porch. She greeted Armand, though her eyes never left my face.

He said, "Julie, this is Lizbeth Guthrie. Liz, this is Julie Moniere. She's returned with her aunt to Olympus."

"Indeed," came the caustic reply. "And why, may I ask? To make predictions of evil as her mama did before her?"

"Miss Moniere is my guest, Liz." Mr. Bergeron's tone was as cold and sharp as ice. "And yours when she's on this property. Have you forgotten your manners?"

Her face flamed, but whether in anger or embarrassment I didn't know until she spoke. "I apologize, Miss Moniere. I should have asked immediately what terrible end you predict for me."

After a moment's shock, I found my voice. "I don't make predictions, Miss Guthrie. At least, I've never made one before, but it wouldn't take a seeress to predict that one so steeped in venom as you are will get little good out of life."

Her smile mocked me. "I have everything my heart desires."

"Everything?" Mr. Bergeron asked.

The other girls had approached and were now standing on either side of her as if to show their loyalty. Their hostile manner quickly changed to astonishment at his reply.

Miss Guthrie seemed momentarily unsure of herself, for she too had been taken aback by his boldness. Then I knew. She loved him, and from the looks they exchanged, I gathered she'd believed he returned her affection. But she quickly regained her poise, and her eyes regarded him spitefully.

"Everything," she repeated, making it a statement. "And so do my friends, including the right to extend invitations to guests. It was presumptuous of you to bring this girl here without consulting me first. Do not repeat the mistake."

"I knew you were spirited, Lizbeth. At least that's what I thought you were. Now I learn you're also very rude."

"Why should I be polite to someone who says I'll get little good out of life? Is she saying in so many words that I am to die soon?"

"I told you, Miss Guthrie, I do not make predictions. But I was taught that the heart is nourished by love. With some, giving a warm glance or a friendly smile comes easily. Others have to cultivate it."

Her smile was contemptuous. "What are you saying?"

"Merely that none of us have the right to be scornful of another. Nor should we wish to, lest we be dead before nightfall and remembered only for our last unkind deed."

"You *are* threatening me."

She stepped back and her eyes became fear-filled. "Get off this property. You are despicable. You too, Armand. I don't ever wish to see you again."

"Julie did not threaten you," he exclaimed. "She merely . . ."

Miss Guthrie, followed by her coterie of friends, turned and fled into the house, the screen door slamming behind them. Mr. Bergeron's unfinished sentence hung in mid-air.

He turned to me, his features contrite. "I'm sorry, Julie."

"So am I," I said, feeling as guilt-laden as if I really had called down a curse on Lizbeth Guthrie. "Please take me to Olympus."

Mr. Bergeron left me at the door, at my request, for I needed the sanctuary of my room to regain my composure. He apologized profusely and begged that I not dwell on Lizbeth's display of temper and rudeness. There was no need to remind him I'd not have been on the receiving end of it had he taken me directly back to Olympus. His motive had been none other than noble, but it had also been in vain. I would never be accepted here.

I would rest in the sanctuary of my suite and then repack. I couldn't depart from Olympus soon enough.

However, I wasn't to be so fortunate as to be alone for a while, for I had no sooner entered the hall than Martin told me that my aunt wished to see me in the second drawing room.

Despite my nervousness I couldn't help smiling. "Where is the second drawing room?"

"On the right off the reception hall, Miss Julie."

I went directly there, thinking it was just as well. I wanted to talk with her about my parents. I knew so little. Not until Mr. Bergeron had informed me about the duel was I aware of any details of Papa's death. I recalled Dr. Manning's comment that he knew little about the gossip other than the fact that my mother's death had been sudden. I hoped not in violence, like Papa's, yet I wondered.

The drawing room was huge, high-ceilinged, and furnished with delicate French furniture. The fireplace was pink marble, as was the floor. The wall panels had paintings showing the sack and destruction of Troy. However, I had too much on my mind to be overwhelmed by such magnificence, and I was fast becoming accustomed to it. Tea service was set on a table before the fireplace, and my aunt and a gentleman were seated on one of the twin settees flanking the table.

My aunt exclaimed happily at sight of me. "Julie, *ma petite*, this is Mr. Louis Taylor."

He set down his cup and saucer and arose to acknowledge the introduction. He was of medium height, with curly gray hair and a face that beamed kindness. Certainly, I thought, not the type one would expect a lawyer to be.

He said, "How closely you resemble your mother! She was a lovely lady."

"Thank you," I replied.

My aunt, quick to sense all was not well with me, said, "What is it, Julie?"

"Mr. Bergeron brought me home as you requested," I said.

"He *offered*, Julie," my aunt corrected. "I felt it important to see Louis. We have just finished discussing your encounter with Mrs. Leloude. He is going to pay her and her husband a visit and have a quiet but frank discussion with her."

"There's no need for that," I said. "They aren't the only ones who wish me away from Flagton."

"Was Armand rude?" my aunt asked.

"On the contrary, he was most gracious."

My aunt poured a cup of tea and offered it to me. I took it and sat on the opposite settee.

"Then, what happened? You're very pale."

"He insisted on stopping at the Guthrie plantation. He wanted me to meet Lizbeth and her friends."

My aunt nodded. "That's where we saw the young ladies on the porch as we drove past this morning."

"Yes. I was not acceptable either to her or to her friends. And I was informed of that fact. She expected me to call down a curse on her. When I made a simple statement, she insisted I had foretold her life would be cut off soon."

"How dreadful!" my aunt exclaimed, her dismay evident.

Mr. Taylor resumed his seat beside my aunt. "It is indeed. And such enmity directed against you must be stopped."

"It will never be stopped," I said. "I wish to leave Olympus as soon as you feel up to the journey, Auntie."

"Of course, my dear," she agreed. "I'm sorry you had to endure such a snub."

"It's more difficult to endure since I had no knowledge of any of this until my encounter with Mrs. Leloude. I didn't really know about Papa and Armand Bergeron's father until yesterday.

My aunt was about to pour herself another cup of tea, but set the silver pot down. "I'm sorry, Julie. I should have told you about it, but I didn't want you burdened with such knowledge. I feared it would prey on your mind. That was my only reason for not telling you."

"I suppose you were right. It's just that it has all come so quickly that it's a shock."

Mr. Taylor said, "I apologize, Miss Julie, for those who have hurt you. However, do you feel you're doing the right thing in running away?"

"I'm left with no choice," I said. "You know of my hallucination, of course."

"Your aunt has told me everything, and I can understand your fear of living here since you saw yourself dead at the foot of the Apollo fountain. But it was just a dream."

"Yes," I agreed. "But I have many enemies here because of Mama. Perhaps some, who suffered in some way because of her predictions, wish to do me harm."

"Is it because you're afraid that you don't wish to stay?" he asked. "Don't be embarrassed. I wouldn't blame you."

"That may be partly my reason," I admitted. "Though I think it would be more accurate to say it's because I dislike the ill-feeling I've aroused by my return."

"I had hoped," my aunt addressed Mr. Taylor, "the ill-feeling would have been dissipated by now and that the town would accept Julie on her own. I want her to have Olympus."

"No, auntie. I don't wish to seem ungrateful, but while this is beautiful," I looked around the room and moved my head negatively, "I don't need such magnificence."

Mr. Taylor gave a brief nod of understanding. My aunt looked hurt.

"Louis," she said, "after we leave, please put the place up for sale."

"I will do that," he assured her. "And I'll place advertisements in the New Orleans newspapers and nationwide periodicals. We'll have no difficulty disposing of such an unusual property. Especially with its history."

I looked about me. "Was some of this booty taken by Lafitte and his band of thugs?"

"I'm sure it was," Mr. Taylor said, and my aunt concurred with a nod. "I'll say one thing. They knew quality."

"I wonder whether, if Mama and Papa had lived elsewhere, happiness rather than tragedy would have ruled their lives?"

"That's something we'll never know, my dear." Mr. Taylor set down his cup and saucer and arose. "I must be off. It was good of you to come back, Yvonne. I will stop at the Leloudes' and inform them you have told me of Louisa's encounter with your niece. I will add that should any harm befall her, we will make public the threat Louisa made against your niece's life."

"Auntie, can't we just return to New Orleans and forget the whole thing?"

"I would, my dear, except that I wouldn't feel you were safe even there. And you did express a wish to live in these parts."

"That is still my wish."

"Then you must let Mr. Taylor judge as to what is best for you. My main concern is your well-being. You've been very ill. I don't want you to live in fear of your life. Nothing must upset you that will slow your recovery and the return of your strength. We'll leave Olympus tomorrow. The sooner we do, the better."

"I'm not entirely in agreement," Mr. Taylor said, "but I'll not attempt to dissuade you. In view of your niece's recent illness, her peace of mind is all-important."

My aunt said, "On that we are agreed."

Mr. Taylor arose, thanked my aunt for the refreshments, assured her he would attend to the Leloude matter and the sale of Olympus, and added that should any further disagreeableness arise she would need only to send for him. My aunt thanked him and accompanied him to the door. I remained in the room and poured myself a second cup of tea and munched on a sandwich. I was too emotionally upset to be hungry, but I knew nourishment was all-important to regain my strength.

My aunt rejoined me and half filled her cup, but remained standing as she sipped it. "I hope you aren't angry with me because I accepted Armand's offer to bring you back."

"No. I just wish you hadn't told him about my hallucination during my illness."

"I meant no harm, Julie," she said. "But I am frightened for you. And I felt a great urgency to discuss the matter with Louis. That's why I had Henry drive me back immediately, once Armand offered his services. Of course, I didn't realize he would take matters into his own hands and increase your mental turmoil by bringing you to the Guthries'."

"And yours," I said.

"Yes." She sipped thoughtfully at her tea.

"I know how Papa died. Mama's death was also sudden. Are you sure it was a natural death?"

My aunt regarded me thoughtfully, but made no comment until she'd emptied her cup and set it back on the table. "I've already told you, your mama was found in the formal garden unconscious. There was a bruise on her brow. It was believed she may have felt faint and come into the garden to refresh herself."

"You told me she suffered a heart attack and fell."

My aunt nodded. "Her head struck the marble bench alongside which she was found lying. She never regained consciousness. It was believed she suffered a fatal heart attack."

"Had she been ill?"

"I'd say no. She never recovered from the death of your papa, and she did speak of shortness of breath and mild chest pain, but wouldn't see a doctor. Perhaps it wouldn't have been so bad if that town hadn't hated her so. But she'd predicted the deaths by violence of two people—a man and a woman—even before your papa dueled with Armand's papa."

"Why did she do so? Particularly when she was disliked."

"She wasn't disliked at first. Only after she made those predictions that came true. And it wasn't as if she was trying to gain popularity by doing so. It was in the form of a warning. The lady, Mrs. Stout, was going on a journey to visit her parents. She wished to show off her newborn son. Your mama asked that she postpone her trip for a week because of a dream your mama had in which she saw the carriage in which they riding overturned. She also saw Mrs. Stout and her newborn lying still at the side of the road, only she didn't tell that part of the dream. But Mrs. Stout scoffed. Your mama's dream came true. Though Mr. Stout survived, his wife and son were killed. Thrown from the carriage when an axle broke."

"What was the other instance?"

"The drowning of a gentleman. He attended a soirée at which your parents were also present. Without any ado, your mama went up to him and told him he'd been invited to cruise on the yacht of a Northern gentleman visiting in New Orleans. She asked that he refrain from accepting the invitation. He too derided her and went. He was tossed overside during a violent storm and lost at sea. When word came back, your mother's warning was recalled. She was called a witch in public and scorned by the entire town."

"What was the name of the gentleman?"

"Oh, Julie," my aunt pleaded, "we're leaving here tomorrow. Please don't concern yourself about it."

"I must," I said. "I'm terribly confused and I must know the entire story of Mama and Papa. Perhaps then my dream will make more sense. Perhaps I do have the gift—if such it may be called—of being a mystic. If, in that hallucination, I foretold my end, then perhaps I can foretell others. For purposes of good, rather than evil."

My aunt looked highly agitated by my statement. "I beg of you not to think that way, *ma petite.*"

"Why not?"

"Because even when your mother foretold, she never prevented any of the tragedies. Not even that of your papa."

"What was the name of the man lost at sea?"

"Stuart Bergeron, Armand's uncle."

I was astounded by the revelation. "Then Armand—Mr. Bergeron could have deliberately brought me to Lizbeth Guthrie's, knowing I'd not be accepted. He pretended to be my friend, yet let me be deliberately humiliated."

"I can't believe he would do such a thing," my aunt exclaimed.

"I don't know what to believe," I said. "Was it Armand's papa who challenged Papa?"

"No. Your papa challenged Lester Bergeron. Lester had called your mama a witch in public. No gentleman of honor would let such an insult go unanswered."

"More's the pity," I said.

"Julie!" My aunt was shocked.

"I mean it, Auntie. Two lives ended because of violence."

"Your mama's good name was at stake."

"I never knew her—or at least I can't remember her. But if I were to put myself in her place, I'd rather have my husband and his love, than widow's weeds and years of loneliness. I'm sure Mama felt the same way."

"I understand, my dear. But in the South, and especially in New Orleans, where a gentleman's code of honor was involved, it could only be satisfied in a duel. A duel which your mama predicted neither would win. Everyone thought she meant each would wound the other and that would be the end of it. Instead, they died from wounds inflicted by gunshot. From that day on, your mother was avoided and scorned by all."

"Yet you brought me back!" I exclaimed in dismay. "Surely you must have realized such ill-feeling would be passed on to me."

"Such a thought never occurred to me. You were merely a toddling child when I took you from here. Why should you be hated for what the town considered the sins of your mother?"

"Even if the town were to give me the benefit of the doubt, they never will, now that the story of my hallucination is out."

"No one knows that," she said.

"Mr. Taylor and Armand Bergeron know if it," I said. "And Mr. Duvall."

"Certainly Mr. Taylor would not wish you ill. And as for Armand, I'll not believe it of him. Mr. Duvall is in my employ."

"Armand would certainly have reason to."

"Yes," my aunt admitted reluctantly. "But he's a gentleman."

"I must say he behaved like one today. He apologized for bringing me to Lizbeth Guthrie's home. But he'd insisted on it, stating he was held in such high esteem by mothers because of his bachelorhood that they'd accept me. I begged him not to bring me there, but he was adamant. Of course, he realized his mistake immediately. At least, he appeared contrite, but he could have been playing a game."

"I'm sorry you were subjected to that." My aunt pressed her hand to her brow.

"I'm sorry it brought on one of your headaches."

"I'll lie down. It always helps. I wish you would, too."

"I will, but I've a lot of packing to do."

"Leave that for the servants. We'll go on ahead. The trunks can follow."

"Thank you, Auntie. In that case, I will lie down."

I did so and went down to an evening meal which I ate in solitary splendor. Afterwards I took a brief walk about the estate and sood at the top of the stairway leading down to the Apollo fountain. It was a setting of beauty and artistic splendor. I didn't attempt the stairs, as dusk was setting in and I had no wish to have night fall and have to make the ascent in darkness. However, I did count the landings, each with its pool and waterfall spilling into the one below, finally culminating in the Apollo fountain, which was circular and by far the largest. I counted the steps between the landings above. There were ten. And as many landings, each with its own fountain and statue. And at the bottom, I saw myself as I was in the dream. I turned and walked back to the house.

I awakened to the sound of my name being called over and over. Someone gripped my shoulders and shook me lightly. I struggled, trying to push away whoever had a hold on me.

"Julie, Julie," the voice exclaimed, though in a whisper. "It's me—Adrienne."

There was no light in the room, but I didn't doubt the identity of the girl, and I relaxed.

"What are you doing here?" Irritation tinged my voice. Not only because she'd somehow gained entry into the house, but that she had wakened me so brusquely.

"Hush," she exclaimed, but released her hold on me. I heard her move about softly, then strike a match the light of which made me blink. She touched the flame to a candle set on the mantel and brought it over to my bedside. She set it on the night table, pulled aside the mosquito netting, and propped herself at the foot of my bed.

I was already sitting up, still bewildered by her presence and curious as to how she got into the house.

"Is something wrong?" I asked.

"Everything's wonderful," she exclaimed.

"Not for me," I said, thinking back to my encounter with Lizbeth Guthrie, but Adrienne was too filled with her own thoughts to notice.

"You predicted a young man would fall in love with me, and he has. And what's more, I love him."

"You must, to come here at this hour to tell me."

Her admonishments for me to be quiet seemed to be forgotten, for her laughter filled the room. "I couldn't sleep. I had to talk to someone."

I settled back on my pillows. "Tell me about him."

"When we arrived in town yesterday, Mama let me off in town, as I wished to purchase some ink. We'd been abroad for two months, and in that time, the general store was sold by Widow Lynn to a gentleman with fiery red hair, a million freckles, and a smile that sent my senses spinning."

"Young?"

"Twenty-eight."

"What's his name?"

"Jeb MacDowell. Isn't it beautiful?"

I looked impressed. "Very. Go on."

"There was no one in the store at the time, and we talked for about an hour. He expressed a desire to see me again. I consented, and told him how strict Mama was, but I'd be in town the following day for a fitting. I knew Mama had to attend a meeting of ladies regarding a social at the church and I'd be alone. Anyway, I went there yesterday afternoon. Jeb had another gentleman working in the store, so he was able to take me for a drive in the country. And guess what he asked me?"

I'd not spoil her surprise. "I can't imagine."

"He proposed. I accepted."

"And your mother?"

Her voice rose with emotion. "She'll be difficult, but I'll marry him if I have to elope. I love him."

"Hush!" I exclaimed. "You'll waken my aunt."

Her voice lowered. "Aren't you lucky she isn't so strict with you?"

"In that respect, yes, I'm lucky."

"I know what you mean. Mama's already heard about what happened at Lizbeth's. She's very mean. And jealous," she added. "Armand didn't help your cause when he brought you there. She considers him her very special private property."

"And he?"

"He's a flirt. A *bon vivant*. He must have liked you, though. I understand he put Lizbeth in her place."

"*Lizbeth* put me in my place."

"She's so cold. Except when she's with the opposite sex, and she's as big a flirt as Armand."

I wasn't nearly as curious about Lizbeth and Armand as I was regarding the manner in which Adrienne had found entry into this house.

"Can't you see the difference in me?" she asked.

"The light is so dim in here, Adrienne," I said. "But your voice radiates happiness."

She picked up the candlestick, holding it so closely to her face I feared the flame would singe her hair. I sat up and regarded her.

"Your eyes are sparkling," I said. "Yes, you're in love."

"And do you know what made it all possible?"

I smiled. "Your needing a bottle of ink."

"No such thing. It was your kindness and the things you said to me at the inn. You made me feel young, and when you dressed my hair so prettily and showed me how to keep it looking that way, it did something magical to me."

"I'm glad. Tell me, Adrienne, how did you get in here?"

Again her laughter trilled, but she quickly covered her

mouth and pointed to the adjoining room. "The french doors in there lead out onto a balcony. Completely hidden by wisteria vines is a stairway that leads to the grounds. I often used to explore them during the years when the house was empty. One day I found the stairway, ascended it, and turned the knob of the french door. To my surprise, it opened. No one knows I came here. But I know of someone who did come here, and more than once."

"Who?"

"Armand Bergeron"

"He entered the house?"

"He did. And through the same door as I."

"Did he know you came here?"

"Oh, no. But one day I came here and I was in this room looking around. It was fun exploring the place. There's so much to see."

"Please tell me about Armand," I urged. At any other time, I'd have been astonished at the change in Adrienne, but just now Armand was my concern.

"Well, as I said, I was in this room, admiring the furnishings. I heard the latch click on the french door, and I ducked under the bed. It was dusty, and it was all I could do to keep from sneezing. But I heard footsteps in the sitting room, then someone came in here and moved about. I knew it was a man because of the heavy footsteps, and anyway he walked out of here and went into the corridor. I lay under that bed so long I was sure night must have fallen, but I didn't dare get out. I began to wonder if the intruder might have left through another door. But I doubted that because the doors downstairs were all bolted, with the exception of the large front door. Mr. Taylor has a key to that. He came here from time to time, mostly to supervise the men who kept the grounds up."

"I know about Mr. Taylor. Tell me about Armand."

"Finally, I heard the footsteps come back into the sitting room. They paused at the entrance to this room. It was as if the intruder sensed someone else was in the house. My heart was pounding madly because at the time I didn't know who it was. Anyway, the steps finally moved to the french door. I heard it open and close, and after about two minutes—I didn't dare wait any longer, as I wanted to see who it was—I slipped out from under the bed, went cautiously to the door, and peeked into the room. Of course, if anyone had been in there, it would have been silly to peek. Unlesss his back was to me, I'd have been seen."

"Go on, Adrienne."

"Anyway, I went to a window and moved one side of the drapery enough to give me a view of the grounds. Armand was going down the steps to the Apollo fountain. He went all the way down them, walked about restlessly, then sat on one of the marble benches. I stopped worrying then, because I knew I could be out of the house and off the property before he came up the stairs, and he had to come up them to leave."

Adrienne's information that Armand came to this house gave me pause for thought. I wondered what there was here that attracted him. I also wondered if his attention to me had a motive other than the one he professed when he brought me to Lizbeth Guthrie's.

Adrienne broke into my thoughts. "Will you meet me in town tomorrow, so I can introduce you to Jeb?"

"I'm sorry, Adrienne. We're returning to New Orleans tomorrow."

"Oh, no!" Disappointment edged her voice. "I wanted us to be friends."

"I'd like that, too, Adrienne. But Flagton doesn't want me here, and after my humiliation at Lizbeth Guthrie's, I have no desire to remain."

"But to leave this beautiful house!" she exclaimed woefully. "It's like a palace."

"But has it ever known happiness? Could it ever know it, considering the manner in which the wealth to build it was acquired?"

"You had nothing to do with that," she argued.

"Nor did my parents, but they didn't know happiness here, either. No, I want no part of Olympus."

"Are you angry with me because I came here when the house was empty?"

"Goodness, no," I exclaimed. "I'm sure you thought of it as a sanctuary."

"How understanding you are, Julie. And what a good friend you would have been to me."

"Yes," I agreed, "we would have been good friends. But when you come to New Orleans, you must visit me."

She brightened at the thought. "I will. I swear it."

"And you know I wish you and your Jeb happiness."

"Thank you, Julie. I must go now, but I had to come and tell you your prediction came true. And a beautiful prediction it was. You *must* have the gift your mother had."

I couldn't help but smile, for I could see how useless it would be for me to attempt to persuade Adrienne or anyone in this town that I was not clairvoyant.

"I have no gift, Adrienne, but if you think I have and if I've somehow been the means of making you happy, I'm content."

"I must go now. Good night, Julie. And I'll come to see you in New Orleans."

She embraced me and slipped off the bed, pausing at the door to wave a final farewell. I heard the latch of the door snick shut, and I settled back on my pillows, but had to rise again to blow out the candle flame.

I was glad she had come, and pleased she had found happiness. I only hoped she'd have the courage to stand up to her mother. I doubted Mrs. Leloude would be pleased at the prospect of her daughter marrying the owner of the general store in town. But I was just as certain that her hold on her daughter was broken and I'd been the catalyst who'd done it. I knew Mrs. Leloude would be a formidable enemy. And now the Guthries were aligned on her side.

I didn't belong here. Nor did I wish to stay. The picture of myself lying cold and lifeless at the foot of the Apollo fountain made me shudder. I propped myself on my elbow, fluffed my pillows, and let my head sink onto their softness. I breathed slowly and deeply and eventually drifted off into sleep.

THREE

I had no recollection of descending one of the stairways leading down to the Apollo fountain, yet here I was. Even in the moonlight, the statue of Apollo gleamed golden, and the water spraying in arches from the edge to almost reach the statue was filtered with moonbeams. It was a fairytale setting, but I didn't feel like a princess awaiting her prince, for I was not alone.

Adrienne and her mother were on the stairways a few steps above the landing. One on either side. I smiled in recognition, but both regarded me somberly. I started to move toward Adrienne, but my way was blocked by a shepherd's staff. Not pointing at me, but held horizontally, as if to block my path should I try to ascend. And indeed that was her intent, for as I started toward her, her head moved slowly from side to side in negative fashion.

I turned to her mother, who also held a shepherd's staff, and in the same manner. Her smile was bitter but triumphant. Then I heard my name called, and I looked up to see my aunt at the very top, her arms extended toward me in a gesture of supplication. She needed my help. I tried to move around the staff Mrs. Leloude held. When she prevented me from doing so, I attempted to grasp it, but she struck me with it across my middle with such force I was thrust back.

I looked up at my aunt again. She still maintained the gesture of one begging for help. Then I saw, above her head, a cemetery with tombstones and the figures of a man and woman, hands joined. I called out her name again and again, and I screamed when—no matter what ruse I tried—I could not get past Adrienne and her mother.

Someone was shaking me, speaking my name over and over.

"Julie, Julie, *ma petite,* wake up. You're having a nightmare."

As I wakened, weak cries were still emanating from my throat. Soft lamplight filtered through the room. I heard my aunt say, "It's all right, Melisse. My niece is awake. You may go back to bed. Just set down the lamp."

"Yes, Miss Yvonne." Melisse's voice was barely audible.

I struggled to wakefulness, but made no attempt to sit up. My heart was pounding wildly, and I was bathed in perspiration. I looked up at my aunt, who was bent over me, open concern in her eyes.

"You had a nightmare, Julie. You were screaming."

I pressed a hand to my brow, as if to ease the throbbing in my temples. "I was trying to get to you. I was at the foot of the Apollo fountain. You were at the top, your arms extended to me, beseeching me to come to you."

She patted my shoulder. "I came to you instead, *ma chérie*. It was just a dream. There's nothing to worry about."

"There is," I said. "I'm sure you're in danger."

"Julie, you've got to forget that awful hallucination you had. Otherwise, you're going to make yourself ill, and I don't mean physically. I'm concerned about your mental attitude."

"And I'm concerned about you," I said. "I saw a cemetery. There were tombstones and the marble figures of a man and woman holding hands and looking at each other, as if not even death could part them."

She straightened, and even in the dim light, I saw her pale. "I had those statues made after your mama died. They're standing at the entrance to the crypt that holds their earthly remains. You must have gone there when you took a stroll and seen it. It's not too far from the house."

"I've not seen it, Auntie."

My statement disconcerted her, but only momentarily. "You must have, my dear."

"No." I sat up. "And certainly, I'd not have retained any memory of that from my childhood."

She said, "The statues weren't placed there until after we left. I've never seen them. I'm going to have a glass of sherry. Please join me."

I moved aside the mosquito netting, sought out my satin slippers, and pushed my feet into them. My aunt picked up one lamp, I took the one Melisse had left, and we went to her suite. It was feminine, though not as pretty as mine. The draperies, a soft rose taffeta, must have been newly made for they were crisp and alive with color. The chairs matched. The rug was a dove gray, and the furniture had the graceful S curves of Louis XV. Vases of flowers were placed about the room, and two bowls of roses were set on either side of the mantel. Their scent filled the entire room, but it was not overpowering.

My aunt was already at a long table at one side of the room, pouring wine from a cut-glass decanter into two glasses. I put my lamp on a table near the chaise longue that was set before the fireplace. I figured she would stretch out there. Though she'd made light of my dream, I knew she'd been unsettled by it. So was I, and I relished the wine she handed me, for I was trembling as

I eased myself into a chair. She stretched out on the chaise, holding her almost full glass carefully as she did so.

We sipped the beverage slowly and thoughtfully, my aunt finally breaking the silence.

"I don't like to believe in dreams," she said. "But I'm beginning to fear you have the gift your mother had."

"Did Mama consider it so?"

My aunt set down her glass and settled back on her pillows, her eyes thoughtful. "I think it frightened her. It had reason to, once the town turned against her."

"Did you suffer, too?"

She frowned. "As I told you, our family was never popular here. My grandfather, your great-grandfather, was hanged. But of course he'd already accumulated great wealth, and so the family did not suffer financially. Socially, we were tolerated, but only because we could contribute large sums to charitable causes. And we saw to it we contributed."

"How was Papa regarded?"

"No one could dislike your father. He had a high sense of ethics. So much so, he would have no part of the family estate."

"How did he support Mama?"

She smiled. "He was a scholar and historian of note. He wrote and sold articles to periodicals and had several books published. However, though he and your mama lived within their means—even here—he left you nothing but his books."

"I'm proud of him, Auntie," I said. "A pity my parents didn't go elsewhere. Particularly since he would not accept any of this."

"He was as devoted a brother as he was a loving husband. He lived here because he felt he owed it to me. He was concerned because of the ill-feeling the town bore me. Not that he feared for himself, but he did for me."

"Did you love it this well?"

The way her eyes took in the beauty of the room assured me more than words that she did. "I've always loved it here. That's why I was so pleased when your schooling was completed. I was hopeful we could come back here and live in peace. I wanted to die here, and I felt that by now, the town had forgiven the sins of my grandfather. Particularly in view of what had happened to my brother."

"They'll never forgive." I took another sip of my glass and set it down. "Auntie, we must leave tomorrow. If I have Mama's gift, then I've seen death hovering over both of us. I saw myself dead. I saw the cemetery over your head."

"Oh, no!" she exclaimed. A sob escaped her, and she pressed a hand over her mouth. I stood up, picked up her glass, and handed it to her. "Please drink it, Auntie. I wish I hadn't told you the entire dream."

She said, "I'm glad you did. Forewarned is forearmed, as the saying goes. We will leave this place promptly in the morning."

I sat there until she finished the wine, then saw her to her bed. I adjusted the netting and put out her lamp once she assured me I needn't sit by her bedside. She said the wine had relaxed her and she felt better. I picked up the lamp I'd carried into her bedroom and returned to my suite. Needless to say, I lay sleepless until dawn crept into my room, bringing into silhouette the various pieces of furniture. Once I thought I heard a movement in my sitting room, but attributed it to nerves.

Melisse's soft voice speaking my name awakened me. Her features were blurred by the mosquito netting, but her words were painfully clear.

"Please dress at once and come downstairs, Miss Julie. Dr. Manning is here."

"Is my aunt ill?" I was already out of bed and reaching for my wrapper.

"She's upset."

"About what?"

But she had already turned and moved hastily from

the room, as if avoiding my question. I bathed my face and dressed quickly, catching my hair in a snood that fastened in a bow at the top of my head. I could think only of my dream of the previous night, and I wondered whether my aunt had discovered something or had had some sort of mishap after I left her.

I moved swiftly through the sitting room and was about to enter the corridor when I noticed one of the french doors ajar. I went over and closed it. As I did so, I noted that the drapery which framed one side had slipped from its fastening. I caught it between my hands and looked for the tieback that would hold it. It was missing. I glanced at the one framing the other half of the door. A thick golden cord held it. I checked again to make certain it wasn't still on the hook, or had fallen to the floor, but it was nowhere in sight. The cord was a duplicate of the one in my dream—which had been used to strangle me.

Was that why my aunt had wished to see me. Had she seen it somewhere? Or had it been she who removed it from the drapery, and if so, why? Questions crowded my mind as I made my way downstairs. In the reception hall, a somber Martin bade me good morning and told me my aunt was in the east sitting room.

Dr. Manning, grave-faced, was seated on the settee alongside my aunt, who was standing by the mantel. She looked tired and strained, and was pacing back and forth before the fireplace. Her arms extended at sight of me. I went to her, more puzzled than ever when she smothered me in an embrace.

I said, "What is it, Auntie?"

Dr. Manning said, "Sit down, Julie. I want you to have some *café noir* before we talk."

I'd not noticed the service on the table between the settees. And for the first time I wondered about the hour. A glance at the clock on the mantel showed me it was almost eleven. I'd slept the morning away. I wondered why my aunt had let me, since we were to start our return journey today.

Dr. Manning was already pouring the black liquid into a demitasse cup. I had no desire for it, but his features were stern, and I knew I'd hear nothing until I'd partaken of the hot beverage. I took it from him, but remained standing.

"Sit down, Julie," he repeated. "You too, Miss Moniere."

"I can't," she exclaimed, wringing her hands. "I just can't."

"You can and you will," he said. I liked his manner. Quiet and professional and determined. "Otherwise, I'll take Julie into another room. She has to remain calm."

I sat down obediently, and my aunt sat opposite me. I spoke with growing impatience. "What's wrong?"

"Drink the *café noir* first," he ordered.

I did so, knowing to do otherwise would delay my getting the news. He waited in silence until my cup was half empty, then, without preamble, stated his reason for being here.

"Lizbeth Guthrie was killed this morning. I know you're planning on leaving today, and in view of what happened, I feel you should."

I was too stunned to speak.

My aunt stated agreement, adding, "I only wish Armand hadn't said you predicted an early end for her."

"I did no such thing!" I exclaimed.

Dr. Manning said, "Armand told me about bringing you there yesterday. He should never have forced you on those people. I told him so in no uncertain terms. He told me why he did, but it still doesn't excuse his action. However, he stated you predicted her death."

"That isn't so," I said. I set down my cup and saucer.

"Just what *was* said?" Dr. Manning asked. He sat down beside me and took one of my hands in his. The gesture was professional, and so was his manner. He wished only to reassure me he had confidence that I spoke the truth. His eyes told me that, and I was grateful.

I pressed the fingers of my free hand to my temple. "I don't remember exactly. I think it was something one of the nuns once said to us in class. I—can't think."

"Sit back, Julie." He released my hand and pressed a hand lightly against my shoulder, urging me back onto the settee. I hadn't realized until then that I was sitting stiffly on the very edge of it.

I forced myself to think of the few brief words that had been exchanged between Lizbeth Guthrie and myself. Slowly I recalled them and repeated, as best I could, the thought I'd expressed. That one so steeped in venom would get little of good out of life. That it ill behooved us to be scornful of another. That we should let our heart rule us, for the heart is nourished by love and we should be kind rather than unfeeling, lest we die before nightfall . . .

"Oh, dear God," my aunt exclaimed and began to sob.

"Don't give way to hysteria, Miss Moniere," Dr. Manning spoke sternly. "Julie needs you now."

She pulled a handkerchief from the waistband of her skirt, dabbed at her eyes, and stifled her sobs.

Once Dr. Manning was assured my aunt was quieted, he turned to me and nodded for me to continue.

"Lest we die before nightfall," I repeated, "and be remembered only for our last unkind deed. When I said that, she insisted I was threatening her."

"Ridiculous," Dr. Manning said, much to my relief. "However, Armand apparently believes it, and so do the girls who were there during your confrontation with Lizbeth."

"Was she strangled?"

Both my aunt and Dr. Manning regarded me with shock. Before they could reply, I added, "With a golden cord that could be used to hold back a drapery?"

"No," Dr. Manning said. "She was not murdered. Her neck was broken in a fall from a horse last night. Armand called on her, and they quarreled. After he left, she went riding. She was an expert rider, but to go at night and over the fields was reckless. Apparently the horse lost his footing, and she was thrown. She wasn't found until this morning. When she didn't come down to breakfast and the servants found her bed unused, a search was instigated for her. As soon as I received the news I went to the Guthries. There was nothing I could do for the girl, and I came here."

"Have you been here long?" I asked.

He nodded. "Your aunt told me about your nightmare, and she asked that you be allowed to sleep. I was in agreement. You could do nothing for Lizbeth, and you need rest. Certainly your stay here has been anything but tranquil."

"Dr. Manning wishes me to take you away from here immediately. I think he's wise."

"I can't think of our safety now, Auntie. Not in view of what happened to Lizbeth Guthrie. I'm shocked because I never wished that girl ill."

"Of course you didn't," she exclaimed indignantly. "But everyone in town will say you put a curse on her. They'll say you're a . . ."

Her voice trailed off, and she dabbed at her eyes.

"A witch." I finished her statement. "But I'm not, Auntie. You know it, and I know it."

"And so do I," Dr. Manning said. "It's unfortunate you came back to such unpleasantness."

My aunt said, "It's my fault. I should have known better than to bring her back."

"What do you mean?"

My aunt related in detail the history of the family and of the town's antagonism toward the family.

Dr. Manning listened, his features inscrutable. When she finished, all he said was, "What's done is done. My desire now is to be assured of Julie's safety. She's my patient, and Dr. Tanney entrusted her to my care. I intend to see to it that nothing happens to her."

"We must leave at once," my aunt said.

"No," I replied.

They both regarded me with shocked disbelief.

"I'll not go. I've done nothing wrong. I believe it was wrong of you, Auntie, to flee with me years ago after Mama's death. I'm sure if I'd grown up here, the townsfolk would have realized there was nothing abnormal about me. But to come back an adult, closely resembling Mama" my aunt nodded, though reluctantly—"has brought a flood of memories and revived ancient gossip. I must bear the brunt of it."

"Don't forget the Leloudes," my aunt cautioned.

"I'm well aware of them."

"I told Dr. Manning about your nightmare last night," she said.

"I place no credence in dreams," he said. "Neither in the one you had while in coma, nor in this recent one."

"In this one, I felt my aunt's life was threatened. I described to her two statues which are in the cemetery behind the palazzo. I've never even been to the cemetery."

"She told me about it," he replied, "and I'll admit I can't explain that. My entire concern is for you. I don't want hysteria to sweep the town. Or if it does, I want you away from here."

"If I run, they'll be certain they were correct when they say I placed a curse on Lizbeth. I did no such thing. Therefore, I'll not leave Olympus. You must go, Auntie, but I will not."

She regarded me with incredulity; then slowly her features relaxed, and the semblance of a smile touched her lips. "I'm proud of you, my dear. I'll not leave, either. If you have courage to brazen it out, I can do no less. If there is a risk attached to our remaining, we will take it."

"It's foolhardy," Dr. Manning said.

"Perhaps," I agreed. "But they must learn for themselves I'm not gifted with supernatural powers. I didn't know Lizbeth would fall from her horse. I predicted no such thing. I did not predict death in any form for her.

I have no such power. If I had, I'd have told her not, under any circumstances, to mount a horse."

"I agree," Dr. Manning said. "But how can we make the people of Flagton believe?"

"We must," I said. "At least, *I* must. Not to preserve Olympus. I have no affection for it. Nor did I have any memory of it, though I must have stored a picture of it in my brain since it became part of my hallucination, but it's too awesome for me."

My aunt was regarding me with shock. "How can you speak so deprecatingly of this magnificent edifice?"

"Forgive me, auntie, but it's the way I feel. You grew up here. I did not. And when I think of my parents, I wish it had never been built. Perhaps that's childish, but it's the way I feel."

"It *is* childish—and ungrateful." My aunt's face flamed with indignation.

"You mustn't take offense, Miss Moniere," Dr. Manning stated in his quiet but firm manner. "Julie has been under a severe strain. In the brief time she's been here, she succeeded in arousing the enmity of the entire town, through no fault of hers."

"Doctor, I hope you're not stating I brought this on my niece."

"I'm afraid I am," he said. "You knew how the town regarded her mother. How did you think they would be any different toward her daughter? Does she really have a close resemblance to her mother?"

"Very," my aunt replied. "But she has no gift, as her mother had."

"I agree—if her mother had such a gift, which I strongly doubt."

"You shouldn't," my aunt said. "I'd like to think she didn't, but I know differently."

"We won't go into that," he said. "However, since Julie is determined to remain, and you state you will do the same . . ."

"Be assured I will," my aunt said, her tone almost belligerent.

"Then I ask that you come into town and live at my residence. I live alone, but with you there, Julie will be properly chaperoned."

"You'd antagonize the entire town," my aunt said.

"I'll risk that," he replied. Then, smiling, he added, "Somehow I doubt I will, since I'm the only doctor around."

"Where are you from, doctor?"

"New Haven, Connecticut."

"And how, in heaven's name, did you come to Flagton?"

"I spent summers here with my uncle, Victor Holt. He had a home in New Orleans also. He and my mother were brother and sister. My parents are deceased, as is my uncle. I became attached to Dr. Barnes, who used to take me around on his calls. He suggested the town could use a good doctor as could the region for many miles around. When my uncle passed on and left me his properties, I decided to settle here. I like it."

"Perhaps," my aunt said stiffly, "you have a medicine you could give people that would eliminate their hatred for us."

"If I had, be assured I'd put it in every dish on their tables," he said. "But let's get serious again. I must make some calls, but I'll return this afternoon. I want to talk with Julie. If you've changed your mind about remaining here, or will accept my invitation to live in town at my place, I'll bring you back."

"Thank you, Doctor," I said. "But we'll stay here—for the time being, anyway. If our lives are endangered, here is where the risk is."

He was annoyed.

"Why do you suppose I want you in town at my home?"

"It's good of you," I replied, ignoring his pique. "But if we're in danger, I want to know who is behind it."

"Even if you get murdered trying to find out?" he asked sarcastically.

"I'll be on guard," I said.

"Do you have a gun, or know how to shoot one?" he persisted in his questioning.

"No."

"Would you fire one if you had to?"

"No," I replied. "At least, I hope I wouldn't."

"I thought as much. I don't like your being here, Julie." His hands caught mine and held them in a firm grip. "Please come back with me. You and your aunt."

I smiled in appreciation. "It's good of you, but I must refuse. I'm not going to run. I'm sorry for what happened to Lizbeth. She was so young and very beautiful. But I did not foresee or foretell her death."

"Don't dwell on it," Dr. Manning said. "I wish you hadn't had to know, but since you did, I wanted to be the one to tell you. Now I must be off. I'll return this afternoon."

"I'll walk you to the door, Doctor," I said.

Dr. Manning said his farewells to my aunt, cautioning her to have breakfast and urging me to do the same. I assured him I would.

His buggy was outside, and I stood on the marble terrace to wave a farewell. He picked up the reins, but before urging the horse into motion he looked at me, and for the first time, his manner was not professional. I knew, because his smile was admiring and his eyes regarded me with more warmth than the social or professional code dictated.

He said, "You look beautiful standing there, Julie. You must have left behind a host of swains in Europe and New Orleans." When I smiled, but made no comment, he added, "Is there someone special?"

To that I said a mere "No."

His smile widened. "I'll return as soon as possible. Take care."

I nodded assurance that I would. He slapped the reins

lightly on the horse's rump, and the animal started a brisk trot around the house. Just before the doctor passed from view, he waved. I returned the salute.

I felt a warm flush suffuse me as my heartbeat quickened, and not from weakness. I only wished his reason for coming here had been different. I wanted to tell my aunt I was developing a fondness for Dr. Bruce Manning. A fondness that I felt he might well reciprocate.

During breakfast my aunt asked me again if I was certain I wished to remain at Olympus. When I assured her I did, she said to think about it and if I should change my mind not to hesitate to tell her and we would go to Dr. Manning's, where we could spend the night, and from there begin our journey back to New Orleans.

"I'm not certain," she went on, "you should remain here. I know Dr. Manning doesn't approve of it."

"Do you think our lives are in danger because of Lizbeth Guthrie's tragic accident?"

"Apparently Dr. Manning does. Living in town, he's in a position to know."

"What you're saying and what Dr. Manning probably implied to you was that the entire town could rise up against us."

"Against you, my dear," she amended my statement.

"But you own Olympus, and isn't that what the town resents?"

"I don't believe they do any more. However, they did harbor great resentment toward your mother."

"Do you really think Mama's death was the result of her injuring herself in a faint?"

My aunt looked surprised. "The possibility of violence never occurred to me. Once again, I doubt that the relatives of those who met death after she predicted it would have sought vengeance against her person."

"But you say they hated Mama. That they've carried the hatred through the years and passed it on to their children was painfully evident yesterday when Armand brought me to Lizbeth Guthrie's."

My aunt sighed. "I prefer to think Lizbeth's attitude was caused by jealousy. The plantations do not have the easy time of it they once had. Don't forget, you are a very wealthy young woman. Armand also is well off. That makes him greatly in demand."

"Auntie, I haven't a dime."

"Have I ever denied you anything?"

"Of course not, and I didn't mean to suggest I'm ungrateful since I'm dependent on your bounty, though it's the truth."

"Yes," she said. "But now that your education is completed, you are to have a weekly allowance and a bank account on which you may draw for whatever you need."

"I can't do it, any more than Mama could," I said.

"My dear," my aunt's tone was patient, but it was evident the subject was becoming painful to her, "I have no other relatives. Half of what I have should have gone to your mama on your papa's death. It's very fine to be an idealist, but it's far from practical."

"Then I fear I'm not a practical person," I said.

"Certainly you couldn't expect to go out in the business world," she exclaimed in dismay. "You were educated to be a lady."

"I'm sure ladies manage quite well in the business world," I said. "I would appreciate it if you'd allow me to take a business course. The idea of earning my way appeals to me."

She was becoming exasperated. "It's preposterous. You owe it to me to take an interest in Olympus. To carry on after I'm gone."

"If you were so concerned that Olympus should live after you've gone, you should have married and had an heir."

For a moment, she was shocked into speechlessness. "Julie, you've never spoken in such a fashion to me before."

"I'm sorry," I said contritely. "But try to understand. I don't want to stay here. Olympus is much too grand for me. My parents would not accept any of the wealth, and I will not. I love you and respect you, Auntie, but I wish to make my way in the world."

"And when do you propose to start?" We'd had minor disagreements before, but this was the closest we'd ever come to a quarrel. "If I remember correctly, about an hour ago, you refused to leave Olympus."

"I know. And I want to stay for a few days, anyway. If I run, the people in town will believe I did make a prediction."

"It might be better if you did run. I may as well be frank, since this is the moment for unburdening our minds. I agree with Dr. Manning that you should not remain here."

"With your permission, I would like to stay a few days."

"With my permission! You have no idea how it hurts to hear you speak that way."

I slipped my arm through hers. "Forgive me. I am being difficult—and contradictory."

She managed a smile. "Indeed you are. Suppose we not discuss your future plans until after we've returned to New Orleans."

"Thank you, Auntie. I appreciate your understanding."

"I'm not so sure I do. But be assured I'll make the effort."

With that settled, I turned the subject to my reason for remaining. "Can you name one person here who'd wish to harm me?"

"No one," she said quietly. "However, your mama did kindle a tremendous amount of ill feeling. I think the only person in Flagton who thought kindly of her was Louis."

"Louis?" I questioned. "Oh, yes. Mr. Taylor. The gentleman who manages your affairs here."

"And in New Orleans, too, my dear." My aunt's smile was reflective. "He loved Daphne, though he never made his feelings known to her until after your papa's death."

"Did Mama know him before she met Papa?"

"Oh, no. Your mama was a seamstress in New Orleans. She was only seven when her parents died. She was raised by an aunt. One day your papa came with me for a fitting at Madame Lucy's. He fell in love with Daphne on sight. But she gave him no encouragement. Finally, he asked me to help him. I invited her here on the pretext of needing a fitting, but pretending illness. Once here, Thomas was able to convince her of his love. When she protested their backgrounds were too dissimilar, he offered to tutor her in studies that would be helpful. As for the qualities that go into making a lady, she had them. They were married in the formal garden. It was a beautifull wedding with over one hundred guests."

"Then Mama wasn't always despised here," I said.

"She was liked until she revealed that she was a sibyl." While describing Mama, my aunt's manner had been light, almost gay. But as a sudden thought came to her, she sobered. "Tell me, Julie, why you asked if Lizbeth had been strangled." In the shock of hearing the news of Lizbeth's sudden demise, I'd forgotten about the cord I'd discovered missing before I came downstairs. As quickly, I made a sudden decision not to mention it, fearful my aunt would insist we leave.

"Didn't you hear me?" she prodded.

"I suppose it was because of seeing myself lying at the foot of the Apollo statue in the hallucination I had."

"And when you heard of Lizbeth's death, you thought she was the one to be strangled and not you."

"Oh, no!" I exclaimed. "I don't want to talk about Lizbeth. I only wish I'd protested more strongly when Mr. Bergeron turned into the drive. But I had no idea of what he was up to."

My aunt's tone registered her disapproval. "As Dr. Manning said, Armand shouldn't have taken it upon himself to do such a thing. It was unfair to you. He must have been aware of how your mama was regarded."

"Probably he wouldn't have if you hadn't told him about my hallucination."

My aunt nodded agreement. "I just wish he hadn't been at the bank when I talked with Gene Duvall."

"Well, he was, and there's nothing we can do about it. I'd like to see the cemetery."

My aunt stood up. "I'll take you. I want to see the statues. Since I never came back here from the time I took you away until we returned the day before yesterday, a tour and inspection of the grounds is in order."

"From what I've seen of them, you did well to trust Mr. Taylor as overseer."

"He's a gentleman of splendid character. A pity he never married, but once he met your mama, he never had eyes for another woman."

"Did Mama show any interest in him after Papa's death?"

"Not the slightest. She devoted herself to you. I sometimes think if Thomas hadn't been buried in the family cemetery at the rear of the grounds, she's have returned to New Orleans and resumed her trade as seamstress. She was not a person who could be idle, and she insisted on sewing for me in order to pay for the roof over her head. She would accept no part of the estate; as she told me quite frankly, her feelings were identical to those of Thomas."

Hearing that made me feel guilty that I was living here on my aunt's bounty. It was the first I knew that Mama had insisted she pay her way for residing at Olympus, but I made no comment. It would only upset my aunt and cause her further agitation.

I matched my steps to my aunt's, and we moved briskly over the grass. The grounds were vast, and no matter in which direction I looked, they were well-manicured. We skirted shrubbery and moved on into an area of conifers. Trees became thicker and taller here, and in some places shut out the sun altogether. But it was still beautiful and tranquil, the silence broken only by our voices and those of songbirds trilling happily.

We finally reached the cemetery, which was surrounded by a tall, heavily scrolled iron fence. In the center was a large crypt, in front of which stood the two statues I'd seen in my dream. I was startled, for both the features and the pose were identical.

My aunt's mouth opened to ask a question, but the expression on my face told her there was no need.

"That's what you saw," she said, and made it a statement.

"Yes. The features on the statues are the same as they were in my dream."

My aunt looked pleased rather than fearful. "It could be you have the gift. You're a sensitive, as was your mama."

"Please don't say that." Her statement unnerved me.

"I'm not frightened. Nor do I want you to be."

"You should be. Didn't you tell me everything Mama predicted came true?"

"Yes."

"I told you I saw myself lying beneath the Apollo fountain. There was a silk cord around my neck. I'd been strangled. In my dream, I saw you, arms extended, pleading with me for help. I was prevented from reaching you. You were standing in the cemetery—or perhaps that was symbolic. If so, it was an ominous symbol."

"I'll not be frightened," she said quietly, "nor must you be. I still say your hallucination was the result of your illness. As for the dream with the statues of your parents, I may have, at one time, discussed them with you."

"I don't recall your ever doing so," I said.

"Nor do I," she admitted. "But it is highly likely I did. Or you may have seen sketches of them that were sent to me by the sculptor for my approval. In any case, I refuse to be frightened by your foolish dream. I'm just sorry you're frightened by it, and I repeat that if you wish, we can spend the night at Dr. Manning's and set out on the morrow for our return to New Orleans."

"So long as you're not disturbed by my dream, I want to remain. I want to convince the people of Flagton I'm as normal as they. That I have no gifts for foretelling anyone's future."

She looked pleased by my decision. "In that case, I suggest you not dwell on either of those figments of your mind."

"If that's all you think they are, why do you say I'm a sensitive?"

"You do weary me with your questions, Julie. But then, it's a logical one for you to ask. I know I sound contradictory."

"Indeed you do, Auntie. Please answer my question."

She eyed me tolerantly. "I suppose because you became so agitated when you related what you dreamed. It was only one dream, and I was not lying dead."

"But I was," I asserted firmly.

"Do you believe anyone in Flagton would honestly wish to kill you?"

"I can't answer that, since I don't really know anyone in the town—except Dr. Manning."

"Then you must make a decision—either we will return to New Orleans tomorrow, or you must stop talking about your dream and hallucination."

"We'll strike a bargain," I said. "I'll not refer to it again if you'll refrain from calling me a sensitive."

She nodded agreement. "I give my word."

"Hello, Yvonne."

Startled, we turned to confront a tall, slender gentleman dressed in riding apparel. He was carrying a short crop, and he slapped it slowly but methodically against his thigh. His other hand held his wide-brimmed hat.

He was swarthy in appearance, with black hair and sideburns and eyes so deep-set it was difficult to ascertain their color. Yet I thought I detected a certain sadness in them.

My aunt quickly regained her composure. "Hello, Zaffery. Julie, this is Mr. Leloude, Adrienne's papa. As I told you, they live on the plantation adjoining ours. Zaffery, this is my niece, Julie Moniere."

He nodded. "Pleased to make your acquaintance, Miss Julie. And I want to thank you for what you did for my daughter."

"I like Adrienne," I said. "I had hoped we might be friends."

His smile was apologetic. "I fear Mrs. Leloude has other ideas. And for the present, I must agree, particularly after Louis Taylor's visit."

"I had no recourse other than to protect my niece," my aunt said stiffly. "I'm sure you know Louisa threatened her."

"I'm just as sure my wife didn't mean it," he said. "Naturally, she's upset by your return. Our life has been tranquil up to now. She fears it will change."

"What you are saying is that I have come back to make trouble for you."

"That's what I'm saying, Yvonne. But I'm here to repeat, just as before, I'll fight you with every breath in my body. No one is going to take my land away from me."

My aunt's fair skin colored with embarrassment. "My dear Zaffery, I want no trouble. I want no more land. I came home to live in peace, and I want that understood. Your wife Louisa must understand that also. I don't like threats made against my niece. She's an innocent party to the past."

"I know what you mean," he replied, and I was struck by the compassion in his voice. It was deeply masculine, but he was soft-spoken and I could see weariness in his eyes. It was as if life had deflated him, but he was making a desperate effort to hold on. "But when you send your attorney to my home with a warning you will hold us responsible should any harm befall your niece, I feel you are really threatening all I hold dear. In this case, my family."

"And your land, Zaffery." My aunt also spoke softly but her shoulders had stiffened and there was a defiant glint in her eyes.

"I worked hard for that, and my father before me. I'll not see it taken away. Not as much for me, as for my wife and daughter."

"Did you come here to quarrel with me?" my aunt asked.

"No. To intercede. Let us alone. I have a feeling your brother and his wife would be alive today except for you."

"What?"

"There's no need to repeat it," he said.

"Nor is there need to repeat your wife's threat to my niece."

He glanced at me, but his eyes quickly shifted back to my aunt. "Louisa's frightened, or she'd not have behaved in such a common fashion. My apologies to you, Miss Julie, for my wife's bad manners that night at the inn. After Louis Taylor left, I had a confrontation with her. She confessed what she did and admitted she behaved in abominable fashion. You'll have no further trouble from her. But I advise you not to reveal any dreams you may have or make any foretellings of someone's death by violence to anyone while you're here."

"I assume you are referring to poor Lizbeth Guthrie," I said. "I made no prediction of her dreadful accident."

"Her friends say you did, Miss Julie. Armand Bergeron backs them up."

"I fear Armand took unfair advantage of me," my aunt said. "Unfortunately, he was at the bank yesterday when I was. I didn't remember him, of course. But Gene Duvall told me who he was. Armand seemed quite friendly, and I felt no reluctance in discussing my niece." My aunt gave me an apologetic glance. "When I stated I was going to pay a visit to Louis Taylor, Armand informed me he'd already called at his home and was told

Louis had set out for Olympus. Armand offered to take Julie home."

"I don't know the exact circumstances," Mr. Leloude replied.

"I have just told you," my aunt retorted. "Julie was at Dr. Manning's. She needed medical attention after her confrontation with Louisa at the inn. Fortunately, Dr. Manning was spending the night there. Also, it so happened, his name was given me by Dr. Tanney of New Orleans. Julie has only just recovered from a grave attack of yellow fever."

"I'm sorry to hear it." He addressed me, then turned to my aunt. "I really came here to make an apology for Louisa's behavior."

"That's good of you," my aunt replied, "but Louisa's the one who should have come."

I felt thoroughly uncomfortable and wished my aunt had not sent Mr. Taylor to warn Mrs. Leloude to issue no more threats against my person.

My aunt addressed me. "Go back to the house, Julie. I'll join you shortly."

But Mr. Leloude hadn't finished. "As for you, Yvonne, I hope you haven't come back to try to wrest my land from me. The last two years have been bad. As you know, the cotton crop wasn't good because of the weather, but I feel I can hang on."

"I have no wish to make trouble for you, Zaffery. And good luck. Briefly and in truth, I repeat, I came back to live out my days here. You know the love I bear this place. But I want peace of mind, both for me and for my niece."

"If that's the truth, it's good news."

Somehow I had a feeling he was at my aunt's mercy, yet he wasn't begging, nor would he do so. He stood tall, and he looked my aunt in the eyes when he spoke. He had pride and courage, but I had a feeling he distrusted my aunt.

"Good day to you both." He turned and moved with

long, leisurely strides from the cemetery and disappeared from view among the trees. My aunt and I stood motionless, our eyes following him until he was no longer visible. We heard the sound of a horse's hoofs move at a trot along the ground and slowly fade. Only then did we regard one another.

"Well," my aunt said pensively, "now you've met the Leloude family."

"I liked him," I said. "I sensed a sadness in him, as if life hadn't been easy for him, but he'd not let it defeat him."

"You're very discerning, my dear. Now let us return to the house. I'm expecting Mr. Gene Duvall."

"The banker?"

"Yes. If he's already arrived, I will introduce you, and then I would like you to excuse us. I have business to discuss with him. There wasn't time yesterday, and Gene has certain matters he wishes me to know about."

"Does one of them concern Zaffery?"

My aunt looked surprised. "It's possible. I do hold a large mortage on the property. But I have no intention of taking it from him. Be assured that after what happened to Lizbeth Guthrie, I shall be most discreet. But you must also remember, I'm a business woman."

I regarded her with uncertainty. This was a side to my aunt she had never before revealed, and I sensed she would be unyielding to anyone in her debt.

Mr. Gene Duvall *was* awaiting us, pacing back and forth on the terrace.

My aunt's features lifted at sight of him. "How good of you to come, Gene, and my apologies for not having been inside to receive you."

"No hardship, Yvonne," he said genially. "It's a privilege to come here and feast one's eyes on such beauty."

His compliment made my aunt beam, and I could see how taken she was by Olympus. Mr. Duvall was of medium height and rather distinguished in appearance, for his dark hair was winged at the temples with white. His skin was browned by the sun, but not in the least leathery. A thin mustache across his upper lip gave him a rather dashing air. I had the feeling that his glance, though cursory, had thoroughly categorized me. He was the banker. As such, he knew I was a pauper, dependent on my aunt's bounty, though from my apparel he could only gather she was quite generous with me.

We went inside and after exchanging a few pleasantries, I excused myself and went upstairs.

I paced my suite restlessly, for the encounter with Mr. Leloude had left me uneasy. I hadn't forgotten that Dr. Manning had stated he would call on me unless he had an emergency. I prayed there would be none, though that was far from likely. I reminded myself he had his patients to see and calls to make on those too ill to come to him. But only by thinking of him was I able to forget the concern etched on the face of Zaffery Leloude. And I couldn't help but think my aunt was, in large part, responsible for it.

The thought disturbed me, for I'd always felt she was gentle and compassionate. At least, she'd always been that way with me. Today, however, I'd seen another side of her. She was shrewd and could, no doubt, should the occasion warrant it, be cruel. I tried to thrust such thoughts out of my mind, but they kept recurring. I went over the conversation between her and Zaffery Leloude and paused in my pacings as I recalled the statement he'd made regarding my parents. That he believed they would be alive today were it not for her.

How shocking! And how could I feel even a trace of compassion for him after he made such a statement? I told myself my aunt would not have devoted herself to raising me had she in any way been responsible for my parents' demise. Even indirectly! Her conscience would have smitten her.

And hadn't she shown great concern for my safety when Mrs. Leloude threatened me on the grounds of the inn? As soon as we returned, she'd made it a point—even leaving me behind in Flagton—to have a meeting with her attorney Louis Taylor and have him warn Mrs. Leloude that should any harm befall me, she would be held responsible. Why should I feel compassion for Mr. Leloude, when it was my aunt who was concerned about my safety?

Nonetheless, I continued to do so. I remembered him thanking me for what I'd done for Adrienne, and I wondered if he knew about Jeb MacDowell. I hoped so. I hoped Adrienne had her father as a confidant. And yet I doubted it, else why would she have come to me in the still of night to tell me of her happiness?

Voices drifted through the open window, and I ran over to it. It was Mr. Duvall and my aunt. The lace curtain was so filmy it was almost non-existent. Yet it concealed me from view and I spied shamelessly.

My aunt's voice lowered, but even so, a hardness crept into it as she said, "I will issue the invitations and will expect an acceptance from everyone. You will see to it."

"You're asking a lot, Yvonne," he said. "Almost too much."

"For me, almost too much is never enough. You know what I expect."

His head moved slowly in a gesture of defeat. "I can't promise."

"I issued an order, not a request. You have no alternative but to carry it out."

He made her no answer—merely got into his carriage, urged the horses into motion, and moved slowly down the drive. It was as if he hated the journey to end.

I had to know what this was all about. Somehow I felt I was involved. I went to the bathroom, washed my hands, and bathed my face with cold water. I changed to a fresh blouse and put on the pearl necklace my aunt had presented me with as a graduation present, knowing the sight of it would please her. Then I went downstairs, only to be confronted by Melisse, who told me my aunt had a headache and had asked that I not disturb her.

When I asked if she would come down for dinner, Melisse replied in the negative, adding she had asked that a tray be brought to her. That meant I'd not see her until the following day.

I went out and strolled the estate until it was time for my evening meal. Not until I was in my bed did I realize I'd still not inspected the stairways and the fountains that separated them. Was it fear that kept me away, especially from the fountain at the bottom, which encircled the huge statue of Apollo? I was asleep before the answer came.

I came awake suddenly and lay motionless, aware something had broken into my slumber. I thought I heard someone in my room, and I slitted my eyes. The shades were raised halfway, and though no moonlight filtered into the room, after a while I was able to make out the various pieces of furniture. I heard nothing. No surreptitious sound, no cautious footsteps crossing the sitting room, no sense of someone being in this room, standing motionless lest some careless gesture on his part had broken the silence of the house.

I tried to dismiss my uneasiness, but I was tense now, and I knew I'd not go back to sleep until I investigated the house. Perhaps my aunt was astir, or she might even be in danger. I had reason to believe neither Zaffery Leloude nor Gene Duvall had any special liking for her. I slipped from bed, pushed my feet into soft-soled slippers, donned my negligee, and moved cautiously into the sitting room. I disdained a candle and stood in the doorway looking about and studying the room, particularly the french doors. I suddenly realized I'd not given a thought to locking them. I went over to them, felt for the key, and found it missing. I turned a knob, and it opened. I knew the key had been there when I discovered the missing portiere cord. Who could have taken it, and why?

I closed the door quietly and moved out into the corridor. Looking down, I saw a candelabrum burning on the large table. Someone was about. I moved on to my aunt's suite. The door was ajar, though the suite was in darkness. I felt my way cautiously to her bedroom and whispered her name. There was no answer, and I went over to her bed.

My hand touched the bedclothes and felt that they'd been thrown down. I moved around to the other side of the bed, and again my hand explored the bed. It was empty. Perhaps it was she who's awakened me. She might have been restless and disturbed by her conversations with Zaffery and Gene Duvall. I left her suite and went downstairs. I had no idea which room she might be in—or even if she'd left the house. But I felt a search of the first floor would be in order, though I couldn't do it in darkness.

I picked up the candelabrum and inspected both sitting rooms. Neither was occupied. I returned to the hall and moved on to the first of the dining rooms. It was startling in its mirrored wall to regard myself approaching, candelabrum in hand. Then I saw someone else's reflection and slowed my steps. Whoever it was, was just inside the door. Someone who held an object above his head, ready to strike a blow at whoever entered the room.

I'd only reached the arched entrance of the room when I became conscious of that, and just as I was about to step into it, the person started to lower the object. At that instant, I identified her. It was my aunt.

I called out her name. She cried out in shock and dropped the object. It fell with a dull thud attesting to its weight.

She stepped into view and faced me. "Oh, my dear, I could have killed you!"

Though my heart was beating madly at the thought of

my narrow escape, I couldn't help smiling. "You almost did."

"I thought I heard a prowler and came downstairs to investigate. I'd checked your suite first. You were asleep."

"Then it *was* you who wakened me. I too thought I heard someone. I checked *your* suite, found your bed empty, and came downstairs. I was going to search the house before I went outside."

"Whatever would I be doing outside?" she exclaimed.

I thought of my dream of seeing her in the cemetery, but refrained from mentioning it. "I don't know. Perhaps we'd better investigate further."

"There's no need for it. I checked the entire floor. The upstairs rooms that aren't used are kept locked."

"Which reminds me," I said, "the key to the french doors in my sitting room is missing."

"Why didn't you tell me before?" she asked in alarm.

"It was there yesterday morning. I know because I noticed the drapery framing one side of the door had slipped its moorings. At least, I thought it had. Instead, I found the cord that held it back was missing."

Her hand went to her throat. "But who . . .?"

"I haven't the faintest idea." I couldn't bring myself to mention Adrienne's nocturnal visit of the previous night. And when I didn't tell of that, I couldn't mention the fact that Armand Bergeron was familiar with Olympus and had paid more than one visit to it. Though Adrienne had told only of that specific visit, she had said he was also a visitor. For what purpose, I wondered? Or was it merely curiosity?

"Perhaps it was missing when I came," I said. "I couldn't say for a certainty it was not, though it seems I'd have noticed."

"I think you would have, too, my dear," my aunt agreed. "You're a very orderly person. Let's go upstairs and check your doors. They must be kept locked. I presume it *is* locked."

"It is not. I've already checked it."

"Then I shall take the key from mine, which opens only onto a balcony, but it should work. And do keep the doors locked."

"Be assured I will."

My only thought was that if there had been an intruder, he'd have left.

At the landing, my aunt left me briefly to get the key from her suite. Once in my sitting room, she checked the french doors and after finding them unlocked made a brief search of the carpeted floor for the key. Satisfied it was nowhere about, she slipped hers into the lock, turned it, and left it there.

"If someone not connected with this household took the key from those doors to gain entry, he'll be foiled. This is the only exit above the first floor that leads to the grounds."

She lifted the drapery that hung loose on one side of the window, regarded it thoughtfully, then let it drop. She made no further comment, nor did I, yet I noted the determined set of her jaw as her glance switched to me.

"Do you still wish to stay, Julie?"

"Yes."

She motioned to the french doors. "We'd be fools not to realize someone either means us harm or is attempting to frighten us away. I'm sure I heard someone in the house. I believe now the cord to that drapery has been stolen. So far as I know, no one has access to Olympus—legitimately—other than Louis Taylor, and I have the utmost trust and confidence in him. However, he must be told about the cord and the fact that someone has appropriated the key to the french doors of this room. Would you like another suite? Or perhaps we should switch. No one could possibly have a grudge against you. After today, you know Zaffery Leloude dislikes me. Louisa hates me."

"Why?"

She sighed. "I hold a large mortgage on their property. I could have claimed the land years ago. It was your father who would not allow me to do so. I fear you have inherited the idealism of your parents." She shrugged. "No matter. My main concern is your safety. I will not tolerate the town rising up against you as it did against your mama. If they want to fight, then it shall be with me."

"I'm staying for just one reason, Auntie—to convince the town I'm not a sibyl. Nor do I have any kind of supernatural power. Once they realize that, I'll leave."

"You don't like it here."

"Its beauty is breathtaking. Overwhelming, perhaps. But it lacks warmth."

Her features shadowed. "With art objects from every corner of the earth?"

"They belong in a museum. I'm sorry, Auntie. I must be honest."

"I would want you no other way." She embraced me. "Now go to your bed and get some rest. You've had precious little since you came. When do you see Dr. Manning?"

I glanced at the mantel clock. It was after three. "He promised to visit this afternoon unless he had an emergency."

"Good. Sleep late if you can, so you'll have no telltale shadows under your eyes. I have a feeling I'll be reprimanded if you do."

I laughed and walked with her to the door. I leaned against it after I closed it and let my thoughts drift once again to the good doctor. I spoke his name aloud and liked the sound. I also liked him; the rapid beat of my heart gave assurance that my feelings were more than a mere liking.

I went about the room and blew out the lamps. Then I returned to my bed, got between the covers, and slipped blissfully into a sleep that left me rested and eager for the new day.

FOUR

Dr. Manning called promptly at two o'clock. He commented favorably on my appearance and expressed the hope there had been no further unpleasantness for me. My aunt mentioned Zaffery Leloude's visit, relating it in complete honesty.

Dr. Manning said, "He's a hard worker. I'm pleased you gave him an extension on his mortgage."

My surprise matched hers, though for different reasons. "I told no one about that," she said.

Dr. Manning smiled. "Zaffery told me. I insist that he drop in to my office whenever he comes into town. His heart isn't strong, and I like to keep a check on him."

"I didn't know," my aunt said.

"I doubt anyone does, other than his wife. I felt it my duty to inform her, believing she would see to it he didn't overextend himself."

My aunt said, "I'm sure she will."

Dr. Manning turned to me. "I'd like to take you for a drive. It would do you good."

"Are you sure you have the time?" I asked.

He smiled. "I made the time. Are you ready?"

He bade my aunt adieu and we went out to the buggy. The large folding top was up, giving ample shade. I felt quite elegant seated alongside him, listening contentedly as he made idle chatter regarding the town. But once we were on the road, he turned the conversation to me, inquiring again about my health, whether I was sleeping, whether I was eating sufficiently to ensure my gaining strength. Once assured, he commented favorably on my appearance.

I was wearing a gown of pale green voile spotted with pink dots. He told me I looked as refreshing as a summer breeze and that the color of the dress accented the color of my eyes. He looked quite dashing in a white suit that, despite the heat of day, was unwrinkled.

"Have you encountered any further unpleasantness?" he asked.

"No." Perhaps my reply came too fast. If so, it was because I wanted nothing to mar the afternoon. In any case, he wasn't fooled.

"You have," he disputed. His keen eyes regarded me so intently I lowered my gaze. "Tell me about it, Julie."

"There's little to tell. At least, I know of nothing that can shed light on a little episode that left my aunt and me unnerved last night."

"I'd like to hear about it."

I related how we had been awakened and what we'd done. He listened quietly, his features showing concern only when I told how my aunt, unaware of my identity, had almost struck me.

"If you could see yourself in the mirror, couldn't she have observed you also?" he reasoned. "Particularly since she was in the dining room."

"She may not have looked at the mirrored wall. If so, I'm sure she didn't recognize me. I saw her, though I didn't know it was she, at first. A single candle doesn't shed much light."

He didn't look convinced. "I doubt that an intruder would prowl a house with a light of any kind."

I was puzzled by his reasoning. "Are you insinuating you think my aunt would have harmed me?"

"Suppose we wait to discuss this. There's a lake about a third of a mile down the road. It's cool there and a good place to talk."

Once there, I related everything that had happened since my arrival at Olympus. I hadn't intended to, but the setting, combined with his gentleness and genuine concern made the telling easy, though I first made him swear not to reveal a word. Once he gave his promise, the words came easily.

He'd guided the horse to the very edge of the lake, which was tree-shaded and cool. There were picnic tables and benches placed strategically, but the area was deserted, affording us complete privacy.

I told him of Adrienne's visit to me and of her newfound happiness in the person of Jeb MacDowell.

Dr. Manning smiled. "She was with him today. I hope her mother won't confine her to the house once she learns of it."

"Why is her mother so strict with her?"

"I don't know. Louisa's a very devoted wife to Zaffery. He, in turn, loves his family."

"After his visit yesterday, I'm aware of that." And so, I was certain, was my aunt.

"And Adrienne told you Armand Bergeron also visited Olympus."

"She said he entered the house through the french doors she also used."

"And that's through the sitting room of your suite."

I nodded. "Doctor, when I stepped into the room the first time, I was astounded to see it was a duplicate of the one I had hallucinated."

"It's possible your mind retained a picture of it."

"Yes," I agreed. "But Adrienne and her mother were also in that hallucination, looking exactly as they do today. I'd never seen them before."

He looked pensive. "I can't explain that. But I'm sorry your aunt chose to talk about it to Gene Duvall and Armand Bergeron. Armand has repeated that story at the local tavern, and it's common knowledge by now."

"Armand mentioned the duel my father and his fought. A duel that killed them both."

"I still can't believe he resents you because of what happened. Or that he'd try to kindle the anger of the townspeople by spreading the story around of your hallucination."

"The fact remains, though, he has done it. Either he or Gene Duvall."

"I'm sure Gene didn't. He's a typical banker. Discreet and close-mouthed. So it would leave only Armand."

"I wonder what his interest is in visiting Olympus?"

"Why not ask him?" Dr. Manning said. "Let him know he's been observed."

"I couldn't without involving Adrienne."

"I suppose not," he said.

"There's something else," I said. "It doesn't involve me, though I'm concerned about it."

"What is it?"

"I don't feel I have the right."

"I'd like to feel I have the right to insist you tell me everything."

His statement, though startling, also pleased me.

"I mean it, Julie. My interest in you extends beyond the professional. Though we've met only briefly, I've fallen in love with you."

A warm glow encompassed me, and when our eyes met, he knew the depth of my emotion matched his. He took my hands in his, and his lips touched mine.

"I love you, Julie," he said.

"And I love you," I replied. He released my hands, and

his arms moved about my waist, but I slipped free of his embrace.

"Please, Doctor . . ."

"Bruce," he corrected, "Say it. Say my name."

"Bruce," I obeyed, pleased I could now say it freely. "I *do* love you, but until I have peace of mind, I don't feel I have the right to love. I'm not frightened for myself now as much as for my aunt. You know the dream I had. The one in which she was pleading with me for help and Adrienne and her mother prevented me from going to her."

"I told you I place no credence in dreams."

"But I had never laid eyes on them before my hallucination, and yet I saw them even before I knew of their existence. I'm beginning to wonder if I *am* gifted—cursed would be a more likely description, for certainly it's brought nothing but mental agitation. I fear I'll probably bring misfortune to all around me."

"Don't you think such a gift would have made itself manifest before now?"

"I don't know what to think."

"You had nothing to do with Lizbeth Guthrie's fatal accident. She went out for a ride to cool her anger. She and Armand had quarreled bitterly over you. Perhaps you didn't know this. Armand is fickle where women are concerned, but Lizbeth had her sights set for him. I believe eventually he would have married her. However, he wasn't ready to settle down. I could see the moment he set eyes on you, he was impressed."

I couldn't accept that. "His subsequent behavior hardly bears out your statement, since not only Lizbeth's friends, but Armand also, insist I predicted her tragic end."

"I disputed that, not only to Armand but to Lizbeth's parents. And to others who have brought up the subject. Please give me your permission to tell him his visits to Olympus are known. I'll not mention Adrienne's name."

"No. But I will do it."

"When do you expect to see him?"

"I have no idea. Perhaps I shan't. It may be he'll avoid Olympus, now that it's occupied."

"You say the key to the french doors is missing."

I nodded. "There's another in it now, and the doors are kept locked."

"Good. You started to tell me there was something else that troubled you, but you didn't feel you had the right to discuss it. I asked for that right. Please tell me."

I didn't hesitate. I had to discuss this with someone. "It's about my aunt and Gene Duvall. He visited her yesterday. I met him, but excused myself as my aunt had asked me to do beforehand, stating she had private business with him. I went upstairs to my suite, but I was restless, and after a while, I heard voices outside. I could see both of them from my sitting-room window. He was highly agitated. It seems my aunt had made some demands on him which he said he wasn't certain he could carry out. She insisted he do so, stating it was an order, not a request. Have you any idea of what it might be?"

Bruce sobered. "No."

"Now you're holding back," I chided.

He said, "Give me twenty-four hours. Flagton is a small town. No secrets are kept beyond that time. Be assured, as soon as I know, you'll hear from me, either directly or through a messenger."

I said, "I have the feeling our return has stirred up a hornet's nest."

"Perhaps it's as well. I want your name cleared of the charge of being a witch."

"So do I," I said. "I told my aunt I was remaining at Olympus only until that has been done. She was hurt."

"Is it Flagton you want to get away from? If so, that will present a problem for me. I can't court you miles away from here."

"I don't want to talk about that now, Bruce. But I'll say this—it's not Flagton. It's Olympus. Its magnificence is evident, but it's a museum, not a home. It's impressive but cold."

He said, "I'm glad you feel that way. I could never give you anything like it. Now I have a request. I'd like you and your aunt to dine with me tomorrow night at my home. It won't overwhelm you, but I hope it will enchant you. It's always had that effect on me."

I was charmed by his invitation. "Thank you, Bruce. I'm honored."

"Then you'll accept?"

"Of a certainty. And I'm sure my aunt will."

Before I could protest, his arms enclosed me and he drew me close. Our lips touched, and the embrace became fervent. Nor did I withdraw. So enraptured was I, I forgot the tension and trouble that had engulfed me since I arrived in Flagton. I knew there was happiness for me here if I could get the townspeople to accept me as one of them. Still holding me, Bruce assured me of it. We remained in that enchanted spot a little longer, giving further assurance of our love and murmuring sweet nothings lovers have whispered to one another through the ages, but which always seem fresh and new to those involved.

The ride back was made in silence. There was no further need for words. Bruce held the reins with one hand. His other enclosed mine, and when we exchanged glances, our eyes were warm with love.

There was a carriage in front of the entrance when we returned. Bruce informed me it belonged to Ned Parks, who ran the local smithy. He rented out that carriage and another which was closed.

He accompanied me to the door and expressed regret he could not come inside, but he reminded me of our dinner engagemeent for the following night. I assured him we would be there. I was certain my aunt had no prior commitment, for our return had been completely ignored by the town.

I waved farewell to Bruce and watched him until he disappeared. I was reaching for the knob when the door opened and a gentleman and my aunt came outside.

She brightened at sight of me. "Ah, my dear. I'm happy you're back. You look a little tired. I suggest you go upstairs and rest."

I wasn't the least bit fatigued, but I knew it was her way of dismissing me. The gentleman I judged to be about thirty. He was of medium height, without any outstanding features. I don't mean to imply he was ugly, but rather that one wouldn't remember him one minute after having met him. His features were quite ordinary, his expression bland. After giving me a cursory glance, he turned his attention back to my aunt.

I continued on into the house, having no excuse to stay. Nor could I slow my steps once inside, for Martin hovered about in the reception hall, in case he might be wanted by my aunt.

I was aware that the gentleman carried a flat leather case, which probably contained papers of a business nature involving my aunt's many interests. I went upstairs so she'd not think I was attempting to snoop or pry into her business. Somehow, the thought of inheriting all her wealth was fast becoming as distasteful to me as it had been to my parents.

Suddenly I became aware that I'd not seen a picture or painting of my parents. Surely, with such wealth, there must have been an artist in the vicinity to paint a likeness of Mama and Papa. I would question my aunt about it at the first opportunity.

I stretched out on the chaise longue and let my mind dwell on Bruce. I gloried in the fact that all tension left me just thinking of him. I could well believe he was held in high regard in these parts, and I wondered if I dared hope that once the people of Flagton knew about our love for one another, their antagonism would end.

During our evening meal I brought up the subject of my parents and the lack of family portraits. "There isn't even one of you, Auntie," I said. "At least, not in the rooms I've been in."

"There is a portrait room, my dear," she told me. "It's the ballroom, and it's locked, but I'll take you on a tour of it after we've had our demitasse. Now I have something else to discuss."

"So have I," I exclaimed, eager to tell her about Bruce and me.

She smiled. "You're in love. With your doctor."

I returned the smile. "Is it so obvious?"

"It is."

"Bruce has invited us to dine with him tomorrow night."

"I hope you accepted."

"I did. I knew you wouldn't mind."

"I'm looking forward to it." She sobered. "But doesn't it present a problem?"

"You mean my living in Flagton?"

She nodded. "I'm assuming marriage will follow the courtship."

"I wouldn't let him discuss marriage. Not until people here realize I'm not a witch. That I have no powers to foretell the future."

She patted my hand reassuringly. "Perhaps your doctor is the answer. I'm sure he is well-liked here."

"He's very dedicated to his profession."

"I will expect him to be just as dedicated to my niece. Come along, my dear. Let me show you the portrait room. It's also the ballroom and will be opened for your wedding reception."

"That's being premature, particularly since he hasn't asked for my hand in marriage."

"Only because you wouldn't allow him to," my aunt said airily. "Anyway, I'll expect him to come and discuss such a step in your future with me."

I couldn't help but smile. "He may discuss it with you, Auntie, but the decision will be mine, since it happens to be my future."

Her laughter filled the reception hall. Martin was there, and she requested that he light two candelabra, then unlock the doors of the portrait room.

He lit the candelabra and went to carry out her order. We each appropriated one and I followed my aunt, who led me beneath the stairway and along a wide corridor, on either side of which were closed doors. Our destination was at the very end, where pale light beckoned us. The doors were opened wide and when we stepped into the room, I was astounded by the enormity of it. It seemed doubly so because one side was completely mirrored. On the opposite side hung the portraits whose images were reflected in the mirrors.

Martin had already lit the lamps which were mounted on high pedestals. Chandeliers hung overhead, and I could well imagine the beauty of the room when they were lighted. At the very end were several french doors opening onto the terrace which was evident around most of the palazzo, but my interest concerned the portraits of my parents.

My aunt, ever discerning, realized that and led me directly to the center of the room and faced the portraits. On my way, I noted those, I presume, of ancestors. Their features were coarse, attesting to their way of life. Their eyes bore a mocking look, as if they were scornful of the world. I turned away from them and paused beside my aunt.

She pointed to two framed oils directly before us. "There are your parents, Daphne and Thomas, my brother."

It almost seemed as if I was looking at myself, except that Mama was in costume. The costume of a shepherdess. A duplicate of the one I was wearing when I hallucinated.

I exclaimed in dismay.

"What is it, Julie?" My aunt's arm enclosed my waist.

"It's so like . . ." I couldn't go on.

"The way you looked when you hallucinated?"

I nodded, too overwhelmed to speak.

"Don't be frightened, *ma petite*. I think I know the answer."

"Then tell me, please."

"Before you get too upset, please observe your papa is also in costume. That of a shepherd, though of a rather well-dressed one. You see, they had those costumes made —or rather, I did—just before your papa fought the duel. They were so pleased with them, I suggested they have their portraits painted in costume. They agreed. You played at their feet while it was being done Though *you* have no recollection of it, your mind retained it."

"That part makes sense, Auntie," I acknowledged. "But not to have seen both Adrienne and her mother as they look today . . . I find that highly disturbing. Just as disturbing as the dream I had of you beseeching me for your help and both of them preventing me from going to you."

"You are a highly imaginative young woman," she replied, as calm as I was uneasy. "But in view of what happened to Lizbeth Guthrie, I can understand why your nerves are on edge. Would you like to see my portrait?"

I wanted to leave the room, but to do so would have been rude. "Yes, Auntie."

We moved a few feet along. I gasped aloud at the beauty gazing down at me. My aunt was dressed in queenly garb, her fingers and bodice bejeweled, her posture, as always, regal, her astonishing beauty breathtaking. A diamond tiara topped her black hair. I'd seen it on her before.

I said, "I'm glad an artist was available who did you justice. You will turn heads wherever you go."

"I have been fortunate in retaining my beauty," she admitted. "But I have been more fortunate in having you. I give thanks for that each day. And now, my dear, I *am* fatigued. But before I retire, I must write invitations for a soirée which will be given here Saturday night."

I couldn't believe my ears. "Surely you're not serious. Who will come?"

"Everyone I invite," she replied serenely.

"You can't believe that."

"I do, and so must you."

"They might come for you, but not with me here."

My consternation amused her. "They dare not refuse me. I hold a mortage on almost every piece of property in this town. The last two years were bad ones for the crops. Most of the plantations sought additional loans from the bank. I instructed Gene Duvall to grant them. Though I've been away from here for years, the landowners have been treated kindly by me. Even the Guthries will come, if only to pay their respects."

"Surely you wouldn't expect them to. They're mourning their daughter. She's not even been laid to rest."

A coldness crept into her voice. "I *will* expect them. And they will come."

"Auntie, I don't want to be forced on them. It's wrong for you to do that."

"I want them to meet you. To converse with you. Only then will they realize you are as normal as they. It is my way of doing it. I'm tired of what this family has had to put up with. I've been most generous with Flagton—both the people and the town. Now it's time for them to show their appreciation. Come along, my dear."

I followed her from the room, too sick at heart for further argument. We set our candelabra on the table and moved on to the stairway.

"Should you wish to see your parents' suite, it is the one directly at the end of the wing you occupy. The door is unlocked. You will find informal pictures of them. And of yourself as a baby."

"Thank you, Auntie."

"My dear, try to understand. I'm doing what I feel is right for you. You're far too imaginative—too terrified of a foolish dream and a hallucination when you were close to death. You're becoming obsessed with thoughts of them. I'm sure Dr. Manning—or Bruce, if I may—will approve thoroughly of what I am doing."

"In that case, will you refrain from sending out the invitations until you discuss it with him tomorrow evening?"

"I have no doubt he will agree, and I have set the soirée for Saturday night."

I was defeated and knew further argument would be useless. I was in thorough disagreement with my aunt, and I was certain Bruce would be. One didn't make friends by holding a gun at someone's head. I knew they would have no recourse but to come, and my sympathies went out to them.

At the door of my suite, I paused and regarded the closed one used by my parents. I had no wish to enter it just now. My heart felt heavy with guilt and remorse. I only wished I could think of an argument to dissuade my aunt from carrying out her foolhardy plan. I felt it could only result in defeat, if not in disaster. I opened my door, went inside, and closed it behind me. It was as if by doing so I had closed the door on my carefree girlhood.

I was so filled with thoughts of what my aunt was doing that sleep was out of the question. I knew now the cause of Gene Duvall's concern when he left here. I knew, too, what my aunt had meant when she said she wasn't requesting, she was ordering. And I knew the order was to inform those on whose properties she held a mortgage to make certain they attended the soirée. Otherwise, my aunt would be ruthless.

I got up, dressed, lit a candle, and carried it from my suite to that of my parents. I opened the door softly, for I had no wish to disturb my aunt, and closed it behind me. I had to stand motionless for a few moments until I could make out the various objects of furniture. I moved to a table in the center of the room, set down my candle, and struck a match, touching it to a five-armed candelabrum. I saw another on a table alongside a chaise longue set before the fireplace. I touched flame to the wicks and soon the room glowed with soft light.

I looked around me then and was scarcely able to believe I was still in the palazzo. The furniture here was ample and appeared to be hand-hewn. For some reason, I knew Papa had made it himself. The rug was braided, probably by Mama, and colorful cushions covered the chairs and benches that lined one wall. Pillows of every size and description were tossed carelessly on chairs and even on the floor on either side of the fireplace. I could see Papa lounging there with Mama stretched out on the chaise. What a lovely picture they must have made!

I picked up a candelabrum and moved on to the bedroom. Here again, the room bore no resemblance to mine or my aunt's. The bed was a four-poster of maple, the rug braided in cheerful colors, and the bedspread a patchwork quilt. Twin rockers flanked the fireplace. I noted small pictures on the mantel and investigated. There were two of Mama and Papa together and one of Papa seated, holding me. Mama stood alongside him, her hand resting on his shoulder. Papa's eyes were on me, and his features glowed with pride. Mama regarded us both with love.

These two rooms gave me a better picture of my parents than any spoken words could have. I noticed a basket on a low stool beside one of the rockers. It contained a half-finished child's sweater, the knitting needles still holding the stitches. My eyes filmed with tears as I regarded it, but I quickly brushed them away. I knew that, despite what the town had done to Mama, she'd known true happiness in these two rooms with Papa.

My attention was drawn to a wardrobe. I went to it, opened the door and gasped in amazement. The shepherdess costume Mama had worn in the portrait was here, along with Papa's. Without further thought, I set down the candelabrum, slipped out of my dress, and tried on the costume. It fitted me perfectly. Even the shepherdess's staff was there, covered with ribbon, topped with a large bow. To complete the picture, I put on the wig. Everything was a duplicate of what I was wearing when I'd hallucinated. I went over to the standing mirror and regarded my reflection. Now that I'd seen pictures of Mama, I realized I was the image of her.

I picked up my dress and the candelabrum, and returned to the sitting room. I blew out the candles and picked up the one I'd used to guide me here. Despite being encumbered by the staff, I managed to close the door and return to my suite.

I tossed my dress on a chair, left my candlestick on the table and, still carrying the shepherd's staff, went to the french doors. I unlocked them, opened one, closed it behind me, and moved without the slightest hesitation to the stairway leading to the grounds. I knew where I was headed—the Apollo fountain. I'd not even brought a candle, and the night was only partially lit by a quarter moon that drifted in and out of the clouds. But I carried the shepherd's staff.

Did I want to duplicate my hallucination? I didn't know why I was doing this, or even what propelled me, though I was aware that I wasn't sleepwalking. I reached the head of the stairway and paused. The white statues of the gods gave an eerie air to the setting, but the water splashing from fountain to fountain lent a cheerful note.

I started down one stairway, staff in hand. The setting was the same as in my dream except there were neither strains of music drifting from the house nor fog. I paused and looked back. The palazzo was in darkness except for a faint glow slipping through my sitting-room window. It was the bedside candle I'd placed on the table.

I looked skyward to make certain the quarter moon was still evident. It was and, reassured, I continued my descent. I was behaving in a ridiculous fashion, I told myself. Rather like a schoolgirl who'd accepted a dare. Yet my reason for coming here hadn't been a gesture of defiance. Nor had it been an attempt to overcome my fear of the place. Or had it? I'd left my suite so spontaneously, I couldn't be sure. Perhaps that was it. Perhaps I felt that if I came here, dressed in the costume I'd worn in my dream, circled the fountain of Apollo, then returned to my suite, my mind would throw out the picture of me lying dead there. And so I continued my descent, my movements leisurely, holding the staff aloft.

I finally reached the bottom and moved slowly around the large circular fountain, in the center of which was the statue of Apollo. It was a magnificent piece of sculpture, larger than any of the other statues that looked down on him. I regarded the place where I'd seen myself lying cold and still. I felt not a trace of fear. In fact, I was beginning to find it amusing, and I tossed my staff aside. The sound it made was muted, for beneath the ribbon covering was soft cotton padding.

I rested my hands on the marble edge of the fountain and looked into the water. My reflection was distorted because of the slight movement of the water. Then a shadow fell across the water next to mine with a suddenness that was startling. I started to turn, but strong hands enclosed my throat. My hands raised to free myself, though the gesture was useless, for I was already choking as the fingers pressed more firmly against my windpipe.

I no longer doubted that I was a witch and could foretell happenings of good and evil. I'd seen my manner of death. What matter if it was by a cord or by hands? Either means could accomplish the evil deed. I couldn't even warn my aunt to flee this evil place, for she would be next. My shocking dream of seeing her arms extended in an imploring gesture with the cemetery above her head meant only one thing. Her days were also numbered.

I managed to cry out "Let me go!" as I struggled. I raised one foot and thrust it hard behind me. I was rewarded by a grunt of pain. I did it again, with less success. My fingers got hold of skin at the wrists and pinched as hard as I could.

The hands released their hold on my throat, though I was certain it was not because of any great pain I'd inflicted. I was spun around, and the huge white wig of curls was pulled from my head. My hair fell to my waist, and I was thrust against the fountain with such force that I cried out in pain. But I was free.

I looked at my attacker. It was Armand Bergeron. "So it's you," he said.

"What are you doing here?" I demanded. I massaged my throat gently.

"What do you think I'm doing here?" came the insolent reply. The anger in his tone matched that in mine.

"I haven't the faintest idea. After what you did to me—the lie you told about me—I should think you'd avoid Olympus."

"I hate it," he declared.

"Yet you seem to have a liking for coming here."

His hands were clenched as if only in that way could he restrain his anger.

He refuted my statement with a slow, negative shake of his head. "I thought you were Yvonne. A good thing you cried out and I recognized your voice. Otherwise you'd be dead."

"You admit you're here on a mission of murder?" I asked indignantly.

"She isn't fit to live," he said.

"You're disgusting—and dangerous. I intend to report this attempt on my life."

"If I let you live to do so," he replied.

I couldn't argue that point and decided not to pursue it. "I've been told you came to Olympus—I should say trespassed, for such it was—when the place was unoccupied."

An icy smile touched his lips. "So Adrienne's been chattering."

"I didn't say where I learned of it."

"You didn't have to. I didn't fear her. The palazzo was a refuge for her from that harridan of a mother of hers. I knew she'd tell no one she saw me that day."

"So you knew she'd seen you."

"She hid under the bed, only she forgot to pull in

her skirts. Also, her terror of discovery caused her heart-beat to quicken and her breathing become rapid. It was plainly evident in the silent room. I didn't fear Adrienne in any way."

His brazenness astounded me. "You've made it evident you hate my aunt. Do you hate me also?"

"If I did, you'd not be alive to ask the question."

"Then why did you say I'd foretold Lizbeth Guthrie's death?"

He shrugged. "I suppose I was getting even with your aunt through you."

"How childish."

"For the first time, we agree. You see, I blame your aunt for my father's death."

"That's preposterous. I'm as appalled as you at the way your father and mine met their deaths. To me it was a foolish waste of life."

To my surprise, he agreed again, adding "However, to them it was the only honorable way of redeeming the good name of a member of the family."

I said, "Since you took it upon yourself to move freely through the house, did you see the suite my parents used?"

"Yes. And when I observed those rooms, I felt as guilty as if my hand had fired the shot that killed your father. Though you'll probably not believe that."

"I'm more puzzled by you than I am skeptical."

"I'd like you to call me Armand."

"I'm sorry," I replied stiffly. "But I don't care to be on a first-name basis with a gentleman who only minutes ago tried to strangle me."

His tone softened. "I asked your forgiveness."

"That I might grant, except that you still might murder my aunt."

"No," he replied. "I have my emotions under control now, and it won't happen again. I went berserk. I thought you were your aunt and she dressed up and came down here to flaunt her . . . oh, I don't know. I only know your aunt deprived both of us of a father."

"Why do you keep saying that? The duel was fought because your father called my mother a witch."

His voice sharpened. "That's not the truth."

"My aunt told me the story," I exclaimed heatedly.

"Oh, your mother was considered a witch in these parts just as you now are. But my father did not call your mother any names. The duel had nothing to do with your mother."

"What are you saying?" I exclaimed.

"Merely that your father challenged mine to a duel to avenge the good name of your aunt."

My head moved slowly from side to side in bewilderment. "I don't understand."

"Do you wish to?" he asked.

I nodded, and he led me over to a bench. It was a relief to sit down, and yet I was more frightened now than when he had tried to murder me. Frightened without knowing why. I remained silent. There was nothing for me to say.

Then he started to speak, so softly I could scarcely hear him. "Your aunt told your father that my father seduced her. It was a lie. Though I'm certain your aunt is the essence of discretion with you, she's a worldly woman whom I doubt could be faithful to any man."

I was shocked by what he'd said, and my mouth opened to deny it. Yet there was such a note of sadness in his voice I couldn't help believing he spoke the truth as he knew it. I also knew he was not much older than I when the duel occurred and could not have known of such things.

"Who told you this?"

"Adam Corning, my father's attorney, who was also his second. My mother had been an invalid since my birth. My father was handsome, young, and vulnerable. In fact," Armand motioned to the statue of Apollo, "it's his face that graces that statue."

"Did your father's friend tell you that also?"

Armand nodded. "There was another statue there, but it toppled and broke during a hurricane. Your aunt had that one made. Since none of the townspeople came down those treacherous stairs to this fountain, she was able to do so without causing gossip."

"I have always considered my aunt to be a woman of high character."

"She took great pains to create that impression when she had you during vacations and holidays."

"Suppose what you say is true, how would you know about her behavior in subsequent years when she never returned to Flagton or New Orleans?"

"There are many wealthy people in these parts who travel abroad. Also, many have relatives who live abroad who also happen to be acquainted with your aunt. They wrote of her. However," he added, "that does not concern me. What does are some letters my father told his attorney he had written to your aunt. She threatened to send them to my mother if he broke off the affair. He broke it off anyway. Enraged, she went to her brother and convinced him she had been wronged. Your father had no recourse but to avenge her honor."

"And Mama was blamed."

"No one knew of the reason for the duel other than the two involved, except Mr. Corning and your mother. Because of my mother's frail health, your mother accepted the blame for the tragedy."

"Did you know my mother predicted neither would win in the duel?"

"Yes," he replied. "And her foretelling was correct."

"What about the letters?" I asked.

"From the time I heard the true story from Mr. Corning —and I did not hear it until after my mother passed away—I have come here, endeavoring to find those letters. Needless to say, my efforts have been to no avail."

"But there *are* letters?"

"There are. Papa admitted his indiscretion to Mr. Corning, stating your aunt was his mistress. She became enraged when his conscience forced him to break off the affair."

"Is that why you tried to kill me tonight?"

"No. My rage blotted out my reason. Your aunt called in the mortgages on my properties. Her move leaves me penniless."

"When did that happen?"

"Gene Duvall informed me this evening. I came directly here, but left my carriage on the road. The place was in darkness, and I came down to the fountain to try to contain my rage. Unfortunately, you also chose that time to come here. I thought, in the half light, it was your aunt and she was play-acting."

I said, "I'm sure you know that what you've told me comes as a complete surprise. I find it difficult to accept your story and yet, in a way, I want to. It absolves Mama of being responsible for the duel."

"I've been quite a rotter in regard to you."

"After what you've told me, I can understand."

"It doesn't excuse my behavior. I apologize, Julie. If you'll allow me to call you that."

"I will if I can count on you as a friend."

"You can," he said. His anger had abated, and his manner was relaxed. "After poor Lizbeth's funeral, I will assure her family I lied when I stated you predicted her death."

"Please don't say anything now," I urged. "Perhaps in time, I can assure them I am as normal as they."

He managed a smile. "If they give you half a chance, I'm sure you will."

"I'm going to search for those letters. It won't be easy, for I'll have to be cautious. But I suggest you not come here again. One thing I've learned about my aunt since we arrived—she'll go to any length to have her own way."

"You'll search for those letters?" He seemed to find it difficult to believe.

"I will, Armand. Now suppose you leave before my aunt wakens and finds me missing."

"The only way out is go back up the stairs."

"Julie!" The voice was shrill, but identifiable. It was my aunt.

We were both startled by the sound of my name being called. We were still seated on the bench, in shadow and on the opposite side of the Apollo fountain, making us invisible from the top of the stairway.

I said, "Conceal yourself behind the trees until we go inside. *Now*—before she comes down."

He obeyed quickly, just as my aunt called my name again. I answered, replying that I was all right and would come up.

I retrieved the staff and wig and ascended the stairs far more rapidly than I'd gone down. My aunt's astonishment at my apparel was such that she didn't notice the nervousness I evidenced. I only hoped Armand wouldn't lose control of his temper again and come up and confront her. I hoped she would mention what she'd done to him so I might persuade her to reconsider such drastic action.

"Where did you get that costume, and why did you put it on?"

"I found it in the wardrobe of my parents' suite. It's the one Mama was wearing in the portrait."

"And, I suppose, the one you were wearing when you hallucinated." There was rising impatience in her manner.

"Yes. I put it on and went down to the Apollo fountain to see if I might rid myself of the fear I've had since I hallucinated."

"And did you?"

"I think I did."

"Don't you know?"

"I know you're irritated with me, Auntie, and I don't blame you. But I just had to do it. I was down the stairs and heading for the Apollo fountain without weighing the pros and cons of such a step."

"For all you know," my aunt said testily, "Louisa Leloude might be prowling this estate."

I wondered what she'd have said if I'd informed her Louisa's daughter Adrienne not only had prowled the estate, but had entered the house. But that I would keep to myself, though I'd advise Adrienne not to be so indiscreet from now on, particularly since I was keeping the door locked.

My aunt regarded me with disapproval. "I must say, Julie, you have sorely tried my patience."

"I'm sorry, Auntie. I shan't do it again."

"Come, *ma petite.*" Her voice softened as her arm enclosed my waist. "It's damp out here. We'll have a glass of sherry, and I'll tuck you in. This time, no more prowling."

"I promise," I said dutifully, and we returned to the house.

But I wondered how she would have reacted if she knew I'd learned the real reason why Armand's papa and mine had fought the duel.

FIVE

Dinner at Bruce's was a delight. The home he'd inherited from his uncle was large and pleasantly furnished. Much to my surprise and certainly to that of my aunt, Armand Bergeron was also a guest. His greeting was friendly, though, and soon my aunt was her charming self.

The table was moderate in size, making conversation easy. The room was candlelit, and soft light was reflected in the sterling service and sparkling crystal. The food was served by a manservant and everything, from the first course to dessert, was delicious.

Bruce asked if he might show me the garden and invited my aunt and Armand to join us. However, they were engaged in a spirited conversation concerning the social life of New Orleans. He regaled her with lively anecdotes and answered her questions regarding the various individuals they both knew. He also informed her about changes that had occurred during her absence, never once giving a hint of the ill feeling he bore her. Yet I wondered why he had accepted Bruce's invitation. I also wondered whether Bruce was aware of what my aunt had done and what she was thinking. But she was as good at pretense as Armand.

Outside, I learned that what I had thought would be the rear of the house was actually the front, with a huge porch and a gallery supported by several columns. Wicker furniture decorated the porch, and there was a medium-sized dog of no particular breed who wagged a welcoming tail when we emerged. Bruce informed me his name was Rags and he'd found him on a country road, starved and mangy. He'd brought him home and restored him to health, and now he accompanied him on his rural calls. I petted Rags and he trotted ahead of us as we traversed the garden paths, one of which led down to the river, which was a narrow, winding stream. Weeping willows lined the banks, and hanging from the trees was Spanish moss, which gave a decorative and lacy effect to the trees.

We chatted idly until we were out of earshot of the house. Then I asked the question uppermost in my mind. "Why did you invite Armand Bergeron?"

"Before I answer that question, let me ask one of my own. Did he hurt you last night?"

"So he told you."

Bruce nodded. "He came to me after he returned from Olympus. He related how he'd almost strangled you. I was furious, but managed to contain myself until he'd completed his story. Did he hurt you?" Bruce repeated his question.

"No."

"He told me he mistook you for your aunt. Why did you dress up in that costume?"

"I don't really know. The costume was Mama's, and it was a duplicate of the one I'd worn when I hallucinated. As soon as I put it on, I headed for the Apollo fountain without giving a thought as to why I was going there."

"Do you know now?"

"I felt that if I went down there, perhaps I could rid myself of the morbid thought that I would meet my death there. Needless to say," I said wryly, "when Armand's hands enclosed my throat, I was certain I was a sibyl and I thought of my poor aunt who, I was certain, would be his next victim. At the moment, I didn't know it was Armand intent on strangling me."

"I was sorry to learn about what your aunt did to him. He told me the entire story. He was fearful he might have harmed you and wished me to pay you a visit. I told him what I thought of him for doing such a thing, but I felt when you were able to sit and converse with him afterward, you'd not been injured."

"He gave me a bad fright. There isn't even a bruise on my throat. I took pains to look this morning, lest my aunt notice."

Bruce led me to a bench beneath a willow, pushing aside the lacy leaved branches. When they dropped, we had complete privacy with just a glimpse of the river. The leaved branches formed a soft green lacy curtain.

Once we were seated, his arm enclosed my shoulders. "An invitation arrived from your aunt this morning for a soirée at Olympus Saturday night."

"Anyone whose mortgage my aunt holds received one."

"That would include almost everyone in town, and many on the outskirts."

I nodded. "It's her way of showing the power she wields in this town. I begged her not to do it. But she's determined and stubborn, stating she is doing it for me. She feels once they get acquainted with me, they'll accept me. I don't agree—not that way, for it's like holding a gun at their heads."

"True."

"Did Armand get an invitation?"

"No."

"Does he know about them?"

"Yes. I went to see Armand after my invitation was

delivered. Gossip was already running through the town regarding the step your aunt had taken, and indignation is high, though they'll have no recourse but to go. I persuaded Armand to come here tonight. He can be as persuasive and charming as your aunt. I have a feeling that before the evening is ended, she will have invited him to the soirée."

"But will he accept, after what she's done to him?"

"He'll accept and she'll not foreclose on his property."

"How can you be so certain?"

"More than anything else, your aunt wants the goodwill of this town. For herself as well as for you."

"If the true story regarding the duel ever comes into the open, her efforts will be for naught."

"For the present, I hope the truth does not come out. The people in this town need time. Only she can give it to them. Most of them know this. The others are busy persuading the stubborn element to forget their animosity and attend the soirée."

"Will you be there?"

He brought my hand to his lips. "At your side every moment. You won't find it too difficult. The gestures of friendship will, of course, be false, but eventually I'm sure they will accept you. I would like to ask your aunt to announce our engagement. That would further ensure your acceptance, but we're not going to do it that way. They'll grow fond of you. You're a lovely young woman with a great capacity for gentleness and compassion."

"I hope so. I'm certain of one thing. My love for you is boundless. But I'm still not certain if I have Mama's gift. There is still the dream I had of my aunt. I saw the statues of my parents in the cemetery and my aunt standing before me. You know the dream I had."

"Yes. But I still don't believe you're a witch or have the gift of foretelling."

"My aunt isn't concerned about the dream. But then, she's so happy to be back at Olympus I don't think anything would frighten her. Not even Louisa Leloude, and certainly she's a forbidding woman."

"This will work out," Bruce said. "It has to. We have to get on with the business of our future. I waited a long time for you to come my way. I was almost beginning to despair of ever meeting the girl I wanted to share my life with. But my patience has finally been rewarded."

His words warmed me, and I wondered if I could endure the hatred of the town to be with him. All doubt left me when his lips closed on mine.

It wasn't until breakfast that my aunt informed me of what she had done to Armand. "It was cruel of me, I know, but it was no more cruel than what he'd done to you. Stating you'd foretold the death of Lizbeth Guthrie." She gave an indignant toss of her head.

I had to pretend ignorance. "I'm surprised to hear it, seeing how gallant he was toward you last night."

Her smile was reminiscent. "So much so, I told him he needn't worry. To forget what I'd done. That I'd made the decision to ruin him in the heat of anger. Needless to say he thanked me, then admitted he had lied to the Guthries about you. He said he was going to tell the truth after poor Lizbeth's funeral. That will be today. I would like to send flowers, but I know better."

"Since they believe I'm a witch, they would feel it was adding insult to injury."

She regarded her reflection in the mirrored wall and fussed with the pins in her hair until it was rearranged to her satisfaction. Then, giving a contented nod, she turned her attention back to me.

"I have already received notices of acceptance for our affair Saturday night. There will be two musical groups to play, both from New Orleans. I've already sent telegrams for them. One at each end of the ballroom. They'll spell one another. Besides, it will give us variety. We'll have every kind of dance from a Viennese waltz to folk-dancing."

"I hope you're doing the right thing, Auntie," I said soberly.

"I'm certain of it," she replied airily. "Don't you fret, *ma petite,"* she said.

But my concern didn't lessen. Her gesture was not only defiant; it was brazen.

My aunt excused herself then, stating she had business in town.

"May I come with you?" I asked, hoping I might catch a glimpse of Bruce. He'd not been able to tell me definitely last night if he would be able to see me before the soirée. He had several very ill patients and two women who were expecting babies momentarily.

"I'm sorry, Julie. It's business."

"I'm the one to apologize," I said.

"Explore the house," she said. "There is so much to see."

"Of what I've seen, I like my parents' suite the best."

Her dismay quickly changed to understanding, and she embraced me. "I know. They were two very loving and lovable people. I fear I've not been able to give you the kind of love they would have. But I've done my best. Try to believe that."

"I do." I touched my cheek to hers. It was more a gesture of obedience than affection, and she sensed it.

"What is it, Julie?"

"Nothing."

"Something's troubling you," she insisted.

"Very well. This affair you're giving. It's not the right way to go about it."

"My dear, I've been on this earth many more years than you. I know the ways of the world, and I know the power of money. Don't be scornful of it."

"I'm not, Auntie. Just scornful of what it does to people. What it's done to you."

"Try to remember I'm acting in your best interests."

"I disagree."

"You question my motives?"

"No. Only your method of getting your own way. I don't want people to smile at me when they despise me."

"If they do, they'll never let you know it. But they won't. Perhaps my methods are questionable, but my motive is honorable. I love you, as I did my brother. He died defending your mother's honor."

I covered my ears to blot out the lie. I wanted to confront her with what I'd learned from Armand, but I couldn't. She had granted him an extension on his obligation to her. Despite the little time I'd known him, I could imagine how it must have galled him to have to accept. Yet I could visualize him doing it, even bowing slightly, smile gracious, his manner gallant.

"I don't want to hear about it," I exclaimed.

"You've never used that tone of voice to me before."

She was regarding me carefully, her manner puzzled, and yet I sensed a growing suspicion, as if she wondered whether I could have learned something. However, unless she had seen me with Armand at the fountain, she could not imagine I would know the true reason for the duel. I had to allay her suspicions, yet I would not condone her behavior.

"I had no idea when you brought me here that I would be regarded with such hatred."

"It's because of your mama," she said.

"I can't believe it's entirely because of her."

"What are you saying?" My aunt's voice rose in anger, but I, too, was angry, though not to the point where I would be indiscreet.

"Surely you don't think you have endeared yourself to the townsfolk by forcing them to attend this soirée."

"I'm not nearly as concerned by what they think of me as what they think of you."

"I want them to like me, Auntie. But a liking based on respect, not threat."

Her voice took on a note of restrained patience. "As I've already told you, once they meet you, they will take to you. You're a lady, with all the requisites of a lady. And you're in love, my dear. You're glowing."

"I'm in love," I admitted, "and I've made up my mind that no matter what I have to contend with in this town, I will."

She smiled. "Because of Bruce?"

"Yes."

"Has he proposed?"

"In so many words, but I feel this is not the time to make our intentions public."

"In heaven's name, why not?"

"You know the answer to that."

"I do not."

"What you did to Armand, you will do to others if they do not attend the soirée."

"I will." There was no hesitancy to her reply.

"You're only feeding the fires of hatred."

She gave an impatient shake of her head. "We're getting nowhere with this argument. I will not rescind the invitations. What's done is done. The townspeople must go along with it, and so must you."

It was my turn to evidence surprise. "You never spoke that way to me before. It's as if you're ordering me to pretend I'll not notice their forced courtesy."

"I am." Her features were stern, her voice harsh.

"I'll do my best, Auntie," I said.

"I'll expect you to. And now I must go into town. A matter of grave urgency has been brought to my attention, and I must attend to it. I may be gone all day. If so, we'll have a talk tomorrow. I feel one is long overdue. You have the stubbornness of your mama—a fact I hadn't the slightest suspicion of until today."

"Did you like Mama?"

Her face flamed with indignation. "What a question!"

"You didn't answer it."

"Nor will I," she retorted, making no attempt now to hide her anger. "Think back to your childhood, girlhood,

PLATTERS

with French Fries and Cole Slaw

FRIED SHRIMP	2.50
HADDOCK	2.35
VEAL CUTLET	2.65
CRAB CAKE	2.70
OYSTER	2.65
CHUCK WAGON	2.35
SHRIMP SALAD	2.90
TUNA SALAD	2.55
CHICKEN SALAD	2.55

SHRIMP IN A BASKET	1.95

SINGLE HAMBURGER	.90
SINGLE CHEESEBURGER	.95
CRAB CAKE	1.05

SALADS	½ PINT	PINT
COLE SLAW	.40	.65
MACARONI SALAD	.40	.65
POTATO SALAD	.40	.65
TOSSED SALAD		1.05
ANTIPASTO	for 1 2.35	for 2 2.85
ONION RINGS		.65
GARLIC BREAD		.80
FRENCH FRIES		.60

STORE HOURS

Tues. thru Sat. 10 A.M. to 1 A.M.

Sunday 3 P.M. to 11:00 P.M.

Monday 10 A.M. to 3 P.M.

Phone Orders Call 242-2515

MIKE'S PIZZA HOUSE

Fresh-Dough Pizza Pies and Submarines

No Waiting-Call In Your Order And It Will Be Ready For You.

Phone: 242-2515

HOURS:
Tues. thru Sat. 10 A.M. to 1 A.M.
Sunday 3 P.M. to 11 P.M.
Monday 10 A.M. to 3 P.M.

1306 LINDEN AVE. ARBUTUS

SUBS

HAMBURGER	1.45
CHEESEBURGER	1.55
STEAK	1.45
STEAK & CHEESE	1.55
STEAK & GREEN PEPPERS	1.60
STEAK & MUSHROOMS	1.65
SHRIMP STEAK	1.50
SHRIMP SALAD	1.80
CHICKEN SALAD	1.50
TURKEY	1.60
TUNA	1.60
COLD CUT	1.40
POLISH HAM	1.65
HAM & CHEESE	1.70
IMPORT	1.70
BAKED PEPPERONI	1.75
SAUSAGE	1.75
MEAT BALL	1.75
HADDOCK	1.45
OYSTER	1.45
FOOT LONG	1.15
WITH SAUCE	1.30
CHUCK WAGON	1.60
VEAL CUTLET	1.60
BAR-B-QUE	1.50
MEAT BALL PARMIGIANO	1.90
BAKED CHEESE	1.40
VEAL PARMIGIANO	1.90
ITALIAN PROVOLONE	1.60

SUBS CONT.

PIZZA SUB	1.25

FRESH DOUGH PIZZA PIES

	12"	16"
REGULAR	3.20	3.60
MEAT SAUCE	4.15	4.65
PEPPERONI	4.15	4.65
MUSHROOM	4.15	4.65
SAUSAGE	4.15	4.65
GREEN PEPPER	4.15	4.65
ANCHOVIES	4.15	4.65
BEEF & ONION	4.15	4.65
PROVOLONE	4.15	4.65

.95 extra: for each added item on 12" pie
1.05 extra: for each added item on 16" pie

MIKE'S 12"' SPECIAL $7.00
with all the ingredients

MIKE'S 16"' SPECIAL $8.15
with all the ingredients

SPAGHETTI

PLAIN SAUCE	2.45
MEAT SAUCE	2.80
MEAT BALLS	2.80
SAUSAGE OR MUSHROOMS .50 EXTRA	
SHELLS	2.50
RIGATONI	2.50

MEAT SAUCE .75 EXTRA

HOME MADE MACARONI

RAVIOLI CHEESE	2.80
RAVIOLI MEAT	2.80
LASAGNA	3.50

(2) Meat Balls .75 Extra

VEAL CUTLET ***Parmigiano*** 3.25
Includes Tossed Salad

SAUCES

PLAIN SAUCE	1.60
MEAT SAUCE	1.80
MEAT BALLS	.80 each

and young womanhood. Ask yourself whether or not I devoted my life to the proper rearing of you."

"You *didn't* like Mama!" I exclaimed.

She had risen and started from the room, but paused at my accusation and turned slowly. I watched her reflection in the mirrored wall opposite.

"You ungrateful wretch!" Her face paled, but not from dread of discovery, as I thought. It was anger, and her parting words assured me the relationship between my aunt and me would never be the same again.

She advanced into the room to stand behind my chair, and we regarded each other in the mirror. "I will expect you to remain here until after the soirée so as not to humiliate me. If you choose instead to leave before it takes place, I will call in the mortgage on every piece of property in this town. I'll make paupers of the residents and destroy Flagton. Your precious doctor will be without a practice. Not that he'll suffer. I have already had his background and finances checked. He's very wealthy and practices his profession because of his dedication to the sick."

I made no reply. The victory was hers. She was a worthy though unscrupulous adversary.

I said. "You wouldn't want me here now, would you?"

"Not unless you could change your attitude toward me."

"My attitude could change only if yours would. By showing compassion to the people in your debt."

Her smile was bitter. "They're lucky I haven't made their lives miserable before now." She glanced at the watch pinned to her bodice. "I've wasted too much time already. Do I have your word you will stay? Or will I give my bank—I do own it, you know—orders to foreclose?"

"I'll remain until after the soirée." I had no choice but to submit to her demand, though it galled me as much as I knew it did Armand.

She turned and left the room, her stride brisk and her head high, as always. It was only her pride which had suffered. I knew now she was devoid of any emotion except one of self-adulation. She'd always had her own way. She was a schemer, a liar, a woman who by a mere word could destroy a life or a reputation. She'd not feel the slightest compunction about ruining individuals who had spent a lifetime working hard and diligently to make a decent living and who, through adversity due to mother nature, had been forced to risk what they held dear in order to have another opportunity to retrieve their fortunes.

I heard my aunt's voice, still high with anger and imperious, order Martin to carry out some function or other. His reply was soft and assuring. Then the door closed. It was followed by the sound of wheels, mingled with that of horses' hooves beating a retreat down the driveway.

I'd scarcely touched my breakfast, but I had no desire for food. I went to my room and paced restlessly. I wanted to go to Bruce, but I couldn't break into his day. There were sick people who needed his attention far more than I. The problem was mine, and only I could resolve it.

I remembered Zaffery Leloude the day he confronted my aunt and me in the cemetery. He bore my aunt no resentment then, but thinking back, I recalled that her expression which I'd thought brave at the time, was defiant. Even then, she was feeling a secret triumph. These people were at her mercy. She hated them. I wasn't certain how she regarded me. Probably not with hatred, but certainly not with love.

She had educated me in the best schools, but had done so with the thought that one day I would be mistress of Olympus. *Never!* My appreciation of the beauty these walls held was as great as hers. Probably more so, since to her it represented only wealth and power. But I disliked it because of the manner in which it had been acquired. And that's why Papa would have no part of it. Nor Mama. I admired them for it, and though I could remember neither, my heart warmed at thought of them.

Once again, as I strolled about the room, I thought of Zaffery Leloude. Certainly, he had evidenced none of the bitterness toward my aunt that his wife had shown toward me. As for Adrienne, we'd become friends—or we could if her mama would permit.

Impetuous as always, I picked up my straw hat, slid a pin through the crown, put on my gloves, and went downstairs. Martin met me in the hallway. I told him I wished my carriage brought around to the front, and I went outside to wait. I was astounded at the swiftness with which Henry appeared, driving the coupe my aunt had given me.

He looked pleased to see me again, but when I asked him if he knew where the Leloude residence was, he informed me he did not.

"I've never been there," I informed him, "but when you turn onto the road, make a left turn inside of the right, which leads to town."

"Yes, Miss Julie." He assisted me into the carriage, climbed into the driver's seat, and we were off.

My behavior was as impetuous as last night when I'd donned Mama's shepherdess costume and went down to the Apollo fountain. Until minutes ago, I had no idea I was going to the Leloude residence where I was certain to be given short shrift. But if I had to plead, I would. It was Mrs. Leloude I wished to see. I wanted to hear, from her lips, why she had hated Mama, and now me. I knew she had no liking for my aunt, either, and I wanted to know why. Certainly if she was in possession of her mental faculties, she had to have a reason for such hatred. I wanted to know that reason.

It was a goodly drive from Olympus to their impressive plantation. An ornate cast-iron fence with an arch also of cast iron formed the entrance to the grounds. Cast-iron letters spelled out *THE OAKS* and formed part of the arch.

Henry drove through, directly up to the porch, and helped me alight. Once I'd stepped onto the porch, he guided the animal over to a watering trough set to one side. The animal eagerly slupped up the refreshing liquid.

I used the knocker on the closed door and stood decorously, waiting for it to open. A servant admitted me, but when I gave my name, she eyed me with open fear.

I pretended not to notice and said, "Please tell Mrs. Leloude I wish to speak with her. I'll take little of her time."

She nodded, still too stunned and, perhaps, too fearful of a scolding to make a verbal reply. She retreated to the back of the house, and I was left standing in the reception hall. I was tempted to step into the parlor, but refrained from doing so lest it be considered too bold a move. However, I was determined not to leave until Mrs. Leloude granted me an audience. I was tired of mysteries, guile, and hatred directed at me without knowing why. I had the feeling there was more to it than the fact that my mama had been regarded as a witch. Perhaps I was wrong, but I was going to find out.

Strange as it seemed, I felt no regrets because my aunt and I had had words. Despite what she said, I believed she educated me only because of guilt feelings regarding Mama. True, she had no living relatives except me, and I would fall heir to her vast inheritance, but she now knew I cared no more about it than had my parents. And so I had nothing to lose. But if I could, I would clear Mama's name. How that would affect Armand and the rest of the town, I had no idea, but I could not let Mama's earthly remains lie in the cemetery, knowing she was an innocent victim of a woman who had destroyed her good name in order to conceal wickedness.

The quiet of the house was broken by footsteps above. Apparently the maid had used the servants' stairway at the rear of the house to reach her mistress. The steps were not the brisk ones of my aunt, but Mrs. Leloude was a heavy-set woman. I scanned the hall briefly, noting that the furniture was old, but highly polished, the rug spotless, but worn so thin in trafficked areas that the design was no longer visible. Yes, the Leloudes had fallen on hard times, but pride, determination, and hard work had sustained them and, I felt, would continue to do so.

I wondered how I could defy my aunt without harming the people of Flagton and the surrounding countryside. I had no answer, but I felt I had an obligation. I reminded myself that Mama wouldn't be helped now by revealing her innocence. It still didn't deter me. I would get at the root of the matter, or die trying. The recklessness of my deliberation gave me pause for thought, but I had no further time to dwell on it, for Mrs. Leloude had started to descend the stairs.

I moved to the wall farthest from the stairway and caught a glimpse of myself in a mirror. My face was flushed with color, but not from the heat. Now that I'd forced a confrontation, I was frightened, and it was apparent in my tightly clasped hands and my stiff posture. I told myself she could do no more than order me from the premises—that she'd certainly not do me bodily harm in her own home. Particularly since I'd come in a carriage and with a driver who could give an account of where he'd brought me.

Mrs. Leloude had almost completed the descent now. She was wearing a lacy negligee, heavily beribboned. It had once been a pretty shade of lavender, but was now faded almost to white. But it had been freshly laundered and the ribbons carefully pressed. Here again, the pride of the Leloudes was clearly evident.

Her gray hair was braided and bound about her head, and a faint scent of rosewater was evident when she approached. Her features were as stern and forbidding as on the night we met in the garden, yet her eyes lacked the scorn that had filled them the night she came upon my aunt and me in the dining room of the inn.

"Don't you feel it was presumptuous of you to come here, Miss Moniere? Particularly after our meeting in the garden?"

"Yes, Mrs. Leloude. I only hope you will bear with me. I must speak with you."

"After the *invitation,*" her lips curled disdainfully around the word, "from your aunt, I have little choice but to receive you. Come into the parlor, please. It's cooler there."

She motioned me into the dimly lit room. The jalousies were closed, and my eyes had to adjust before I could make out the furniture. It was heavy, and here again, though old, it was covered with colorful paisley shawls, probably to hide the fact that it needed recovering. I sat down in a straight-back chair and Mrs. Leloude sat opposite.

We were no more than seated when the maid who had admitted me entered with a tray containing two tall glasses filled with lemonade. Ice tinkled gently against their sides, and I must have smiled at the thought of liquid refreshment because Mrs. Leloude said, "It's a long hot drive at midday. You must be overwhelmed with thirst."

"I am, and I'm most appreciative."

There was no friendliness in her voice, but neither was there animosity. As she'd said, she had no choice but to receive me. After I'd had a few refreshing sips of the liquid, I got to the point.

"I'm sorry my aunt decided to have the soirée."

"It will do no good, you know," Mrs. Leloude said. "The townspeople will not accept you."

"Why not?" I asked.

She was taken aback by my question, but only momentarily. "Because of your mama."

"That's difficult to accept."

"She was a witch. As her daughter, you have inherited her power."

"I have no power, Mrs. Leloude. As for my mother, perhaps she was a sensitive, gifted with a sixth sense which, to my knowledge, she used only twice."

"Three times, and each time her prediction came true."

"In two cases, her predictions were given as warnings

in the hope those involved would refrain from going on a planned journey. If they had, they might be alive today."

"So might your father and Armand Bergeron's. Her third prediction which came true."

"Yes," I agreed, adding, "it was a foolish waste of life. However, we can't undo the past. So it's the present I'm interested in. I want to know why you hate me."

"Because of your mama."

"Her powers as a witch?"

She averted her eyes, raised her glass to her lips, then set it down on the table as if she'd developed a sudden dislike for it.

"Yes," she replied.

"I don't believe you, Mrs. Leloude."

Her eyes widened in startlement and her mouth opened to make a retort, but quickly compressed.

I repeated my statement, adding, "You have another reason for hating me. You hated my mother, yes—and you hate me because I resemble her and whatever distasteful memories you have of her have been fanned back to life by my presence."

"You're talking nonsense, Miss Moniere."

"I'm speaking the truth, and you know it. Has it ever occurred to you your hatred for my mother could be unjust?"

"Never." She spoke the word quietly, as if all anger had drained out of her. Or was it because she dared not let her temper get the better of her lest I return to Olympus and wreak vengeance on the family through the power my aunt held over them?

"I believe you. Would you speak if I gave you my word I would never repeat what you say? If it's something concerning my mother, it's over now. She's been dead many years. I can't even remember her. But I saw the suite my parents occupied. It isn't like the other rooms at Olympus. It's simple and warm and gives evidence it was once filled with the love they bore one another."

"Your mother loved your father?" Her tone was one of disbelief.

"Of course she did. How could you doubt? How could anyone doubt?"

She again lowered her gaze and looked away. I wondered what thoughts were going through her mind and how I could get her to voice them.

"Your mother was unfaithful to your father."

"That's a ghastly lie."

"It's the truth. I know."

"Who said so?"

"Your aunt."

I exclaimed aloud. "You're lying."

"I'm not. Your mother—and my husband . . ."

My voice raised angrily. "That's not true. *That is not true!*"

"I have evidence," she said, unmoved by my outburst.

"What kind of evidence?"

"A letter written by your aunt to my husband, begging him to remain away from Olympus and Daphne, your mother. The letter stated that Louis Taylor was your mother's lover and suspected her infidelity. She reminded Zaffery that Louis's jealousy could lead him to challenge my husband to a duel. And she reminded him that he had a family."

"How did you come into possession of the letter?"

Even in the dim light of the room, I saw her face color. "The letter was brought by messenger. My husband was away at the time. I had been suspicious of his unexplained absences sometime prior to the time of the letter. But they stopped as quickly as they'd started, and our marriage resumed its former happy state. However, when the letter arrived with the Olympus crest on it—which was the Apollo fountain—I thought it might be of an important or serious nature. I opened it and discovered the reason for my husband's unexplained absences. It destroyed our marriage. We have lived together for the sake of Adrienne, but nothing was ever the same again. We merely kept up appearances."

I was shaken by the revelation. "I will never believe Mama was guilty."

"You cannot prove her innocence."

"Your husband could."

"We never discuss it."

"Please do. I beg of you."

"I will not bring up the subject. We have fallen into a way of life agreeable to us. We want no scenes or torment in front of our daughter. It may seem strange to you, but I do love her. It was wrong of me to deprive her of a girlhood, but I feared her falling in love with a man who would be unfaithful to her. I want to thank you for helping her at the inn—fixing her hair and putting the thought of rebelliousness into her head. I was terribly angry at the time because she looked so pretty and desirable. But I'm over my anger."

I finished my lemonade and stood up. "Mrs. Leloude, I beg of you to talk with your husband."

"It's not that simple. Please sit down. I have a confession to make."

I resumed my seat and waited hopefully, believing she had changed her mind. It took her a few moments to compose herself, or perhaps to arrange her thoughts. I didn't mind. I wanted the truth and I felt it was in this woman's means to relate it.

She said, "I'm responsible for the death of your mother."

"What do you mean?"

"Your aunt gave a costume affair. The townsfolk went. They dared not refuse an invitation from Olympus because, as you probably know, your aunt held mortgages on all the properties in these parts. Anyway, your widowed mother was in the costume of a shepherdess. She looked like an angel. Seeing her standing there, knowing her seeming innocence and purity were hypocrisy, maddened me. I followed her outside, confronted her with the note I'd received which had been sent to my husband—I kept it. She insisted she was innocent, but I laughed at her. I told her I was going to kill her. She turned and ran from me. I was thinner then and pursued her. I heard her cry out. I thought she'd been startled by someone. But when I reached her, she was lying on the ground. I thought she had fallen and went to her side, my anger replaced by trepidation. She was still. There was a terrible bruise on her head. She had fallen and struck her head on a marble bench."

She paused and covered her face with her hands, as if to blot out the picture still so clear in her mind. "I started to cry, knowing I'd been responsible for her fall. Your aunt was outside. She heard me and came running. I told her what had happened. She insisted I dry my tears, go back inside, and say nothing. I did so, not wanting to anger Zaffery. I felt that he'd hate me if he knew I'd been responsible for her death. I've lived with this secret all these years. It's made me a frightened, embittered woman."

"Thank you for telling me what happened." I couldn't doubt her story. Nor could I wholly believe it. "It was good of you to see me. I'll go now."

She made no move to see me to the door. I thought of Adrienne and paused. "Is your daughter here?"

"No. She's in town seeing Jeb MacDowell. Oh—she told me how she used to visit Olympus. She made a clean breast of everything, once she told me about Jeb and their love for each other."

"I hope you'll not interfere."

"I shan't. Good afternoon, Miss Moniere."

I said, "I shan't repeat what you told me, Mrs. Leloude."

"Then you believe me." Her surprise was evident.

"No," I replied quietly. "However, I have no wish to cause further unhappiness. I'd say you have suffered enough."

She arose and approached me. "If it will give you any

consolation, I've not known a moment's happiness since that night."

"I feel no bitterness toward you," I said. "I'm grateful for what you're telling me. My aunt never mentioned your part in Mama's death, other than to say it was the result of an accident."

"She visited me later, after your mama was buried, and asked exactly what had happened. I told her I opened her letter to Zaffery because he was away, thinking it might be a matter of urgency. She was shocked and saddened that I'd learned about the affair. She expressed regret that she'd written the letter, but said she did so because she feared Louis Taylor would find out about Zaffery and your mama. Louis had engaged in a duel once before and emerged the victor. Though it did not involve the honor of a—lady."

"You mean, Mr. Taylor and my mother . . ."

"He worshipped her, though there'd been no gossip of a romance."

"My aunt did mention it, but said Mama had no interest in him." When doubt clouded her eyes, I said, "I'm telling the truth, Mrs. Leloude."

She nodded slowly. "I'm sure you are, Miss Moniere. And so have I."

"Once again, thank you for seeing me. If Mr. Leloude and Adrienne aren't here, there's no need for them to know I came."

She appeared relieved. "Thank you. I will say that since I relaxed my discipline on Adrienne, a lot of the tension has left this house. I'm hopeful, in time, it will once again know contentment, if not happiness."

"If you work for it, Mrs. Leloude, I'm sure it will come to pass."

"Thank you, Miss Moniere." The merest hint of a smile touched her lips. "I can understand Adrienne being so taken with you. She's eager to attend the soirée. She would have liked it even better if Jeb had been invited."

I smiled. "I shall ask my aunt to do so. I'm sure she will."

"Thank you, Miss Moniere."

I wasn't at all certain my aunt would comply, but I hoped she would.

"One thing more, Miss Moniere. I hope you won't mention to your aunt what I told you."

"I shan't. I'll tell her only that I called on you to pay my respects, that you were most gracious and informed me you were attending the soirée."

She stood in the doorway until I was in the carriage and waved a farewell as we started off. I returned it and settled back in my seat, my mind a jumble of thoughts. I'd learned from Armand how ruthless my aunt had been. I'd learned that Mama had died from a fall while fleeing from the rage of Mrs. Leloude. And yet I found it impossible to believe Mama had been seeing Mr. Leloude. If I'd not seen the suite my parents had occupied, I might be saddened by doubt. But I had seen those two rooms, and even though they'd been empty for many years, they still bore evidence of radiant happiness.

I felt a growing puzzlement regarding my aunt. I was more bewildered now than I'd been before I saw Mrs. Leloude. Mama and Louis Taylor! How could I learn the truth about the two of them? I was certain Bruce couldn't help me. Loyalty to Mama would prevent me from going to Armand Bergeron to see if he could enlighten me. My aunt could tell me no more than she had. There was but one other—the gentleman supposedly involved. Louis Taylor. It was mid-afternoon, too late to journey to Flagton. But I would lose no time seeing him tomorrow. Though I'd met the gentleman but once, I was impressed by his gracious manner. I felt that from him I would learn the truth regarding him and Mama. I hoped I could get the information I sought without mentioning the letter my aunt had written to Zaffery Leloude. But if I couldn't, then he would have to know about it.

The fact that Mr. Taylor was my aunt's attorney didn't

deter me. If he had loved Mama, he'd respect my confidence. If he hadn't and informed my aunt, it would make no difference. I intended to leave Olympus after the soirée. Life with my aunt was no longer tolerable.

My aunt saw me only briefly that evening. It was late when she returned, and I'd already dined, but she stopped by my suite. Her manner was restrained, but polite.

I told her I'd paid a visit to the Leloude plantation and had been graciously received by Mrs. Leloude. Her surprise at my revelation was quickly replaced with relief.

She said, "I'm glad to know that Louisa has come to her senses. It will make things much more bearable. You see, my dear, I was right. You will be accepted."

I ignored that. "She apologized for her behavior at the inn."

"She should have."

"She was the only one at home. Oh, yes, she told me Adrienne is pleased at the idea of coming here, but she'd be more so if Jeb MacDowell were invited."

My aunt's brows raised questioningly. "Who is he?"

"He bought the general store."

"You mean Louisa doesn't mind?"

"Not a bit. She even thanked me for helping Adrienne."

"Helping her?"

"I told you I dressed her hair differently at the inn. I'm afraid I also encouraged her to rebel at the strict discipline of her mother."

She smiled. "I'll see to it Mr. MacDowell is invited to the soirée."

"Thank you, Auntie."

Her smile was reflective. "I can remember when you'd embrace me for doing something I knew you particularly wanted."

"I'm grateful," I said. "And I'm sorry we quarreled this morning."

"So am I," she said. "Regardless of what you think,

I'm more than fond of you, Julie. I hope you've changed your mind about leaving."

"I haven't. I'm just not comfortable here."

"We could live elsewhere," she said.

"I can't allow you to continue to support me."

"What will you do—marry your doctor?"

"If he asks me."

"He'll ask you." She spoke with quiet assurance. "I met him in the town village. After he greeted me, he thanked me for the invitation to the soirée and assured me he'd be present. When I asked him if the invitation was an inducement to see Olympus or you, he didn't hesitate to assure me in no uncertain terms, it was to see you. He also informed me his intentions were serious."

"I'm happy to hear that," I said. "But I'd like to try to support myself—at least for a while. Just to prove I could."

She looked genuinely distressed. "Oh, my dear child, if only you knew how it pains me to hear you speak that way. You don't have to live with me. I'll admit I wanted you to love Olympus as I do. And I wanted your children to inherit it."

"When you loved it that much, you should have had a family of your own to inherit it."

"I had my opportunities, but I devoted myself to seeing that you got the best education imaginable, that you traveled extensively so you could converse on any number of subjects and countries. You were my brother's daughter."

"I appreciate all you did for me," I said. "I only wish there was some way I could repay you."

"There is." My aunt's features were remorseful. She held up a hand as I started to protest. "I know you wish to leave here. I will help you in any way I can, my dear. I'm responsible for you. Be assured I'll not interfere with whatever course you choose. I shall write Jeb MacDowell an invitation immediately. Will you take it to him tomorrow?"

"I'll be pleased." I'd been wondering what excuse I could invent to go to town tomorrow to see Louis Taylor. Now I needn't make one.

She laughed. "You sound as if you would be."

I changed the subject. "Have you eaten, Auntie?"

"No, my dear. Melisse is bringing up a tray. I'm exhausted. I had a busy day."

"In Flagton?" I wondered what could have kept her there until dark.

She nodded. "Some business acquaintances were at the inn. I've learned someone who handled many of my financial dealings has abused my trust."

"I'm sorry to hear it." I really was, as I could well imagine the culprit would pay dearly for it.

I'd have thought myself heartless except that I knew she had done Mama a great wrong by letting the town think the duel had been fought because Armand's father had called her a witch. Because of that I questioned my aunt's loyalty to me. But I took pains not to reveal it.

I had sense enough to know that if I wished to pursue my quest regarding the true story of Mama, I would have to be most discreet—as clever as my aunt, and that would take a great deal of skill. I only hoped I was capable of it.

She told me again that she would write the invitation to Jeb MacDowell and have Melisse leave it on the table downstairs for me to deliver tomorrow—unless, she added, I would prefer Henry to deliver it.

"I think," I said, "it would be nicer if I did. Particularly since his invitation will be tardy in arriving."

"Good thinking, my dear." She touched her cheek to mine and bade me good night.

After she left, I sat in thought for a long time. I remembered my promise to Armand to search for the letters his papa had indiscreetly written to my aunt. In a house of so many rooms, they could be hidden anywhere. But no matter which room they were concealed in, my greatest difficulty would be getting an opportunity to search for them. And how could I manage that, when I'd stated I was leaving Olympus after the soirée? There'd be no chance before. Tomorrow was Friday, and extra help would be arriving to decorate the ballroom and downstairs rooms in the house, others to help in the preparing of food. I didn't know the population of Flagton, but I had an idea there would be over a hundred people present. Knowing my aunt, I was certain it would be a lavish affair with no expense spared. If she had been doing this out of the goodness of her heart, I'd be impressed. But I knew she was doing it for herself, and not for me as she had stated. She was using me as an excuse, and I did not like being used. But I *was* looking forward to seeing Adrienne again, for I felt that one day she and I would be fast friends.

SIX

Mr. Taylor received me graciously, his smile as warm as I remembered it on our first meeting. His morning jacket was a hunter's green and served as a fitting complement to his fair skin and white hair. With soft silk shirt and black flowing tie, he seemed more like a scholar than an attorney. His astute gray eyes studied me carefully while not seeming to.

I apologized for coming in the morning, but stated I felt my meeting him was urgent. He waved aside my apology, saying, "I'm honored to have the daughter of Daphne and Thomas Moniere pay me a visit. You're the image of your mother, you know."

"So I've been told. It's she I've come to talk with you about."

He evidenced momentary surprise, then suggested we relax in the library, where it was cool and looked out on the garden and river beyond. It was a pleasant room.

Two walls were lined with bookcases, neatly stacked with books varying in size and, I was sure, subject matter. A third wall held paintings of landscapes. A black marble fireplace was framed by ceiling-to-floor windows. Large leather chairs added to the warmth of the room.

Mr. Taylor motioned me to one and excused himself, stating he would have a light repast sent in to us.

From where I sat I had a view of the garden, which was a riot of color. I could envision Mr. Taylor sitting here, relaxed and content, surveying its beauty and that of the river beyond.

He returned immediately and our conversation centered on light pleasantries. Shortly, a maid entered the room and spread a cloth on a table set before one of the windows fronting the garden. She laid service for two, placed a low bowl of roses in the center of the table, then set out two plates heaped with a delicious fruit salad. A dish stacked with dainty sandwiches was added, and for a beverage there was a tall pitcher of lemonade. She filled our glasses, then left as quietly as she had entered.

Mr. Taylor led me over to the table and seated me. His manner was courtly, and I felt quite at ease in his presence. I again apologized for coming so early in the day, but he quickly shushed me.

"I'm alone too much. And to have a guest who reminds me of a lady I thought a great deal of in the past has given me a lift, and, I may add," his smile was pensive, "turned back the clock."

"Thank you, Mr. Taylor." I took a few forkfuls of food, complimented him regarding it, and then launched into my reason for being here.

"I hope you'll forgive my frankness, Mr. Taylor, but I've been told you thought a great deal of my mother."

"I loved her, my dear," came his quiet reply.

"My aunt said you did, but that she was faithful to Papa's memory."

"Be assured she was," he said.

"She never gave you the slightest encouragement?" I asked.

"Not beyond allowing me to pay my respects and to discuss our mutual love of poets, particularly the Romantics and their works." His eyes regarded me curiously. "Forgive me if I'm surprised by your question, but even from Daphne's daughter, I consider it rather intrusive."

"I'm sorry, Mr. Taylor, but I had to ask."

"Why?" he prompted. Though he didn't have the appearance of an attorney, he had the inquiring mind of one.

"I heard a story regarding you and Mama yesterday that has given me pause for thought."

"What kind of story?"

"It was ugly, and were Mama alive, I'd ignore it. But her good name is involved. In effect, it was that you were quite a jealous person and not above challenging a gentleman to a duel if you thought she might have a romantic interest in someone else."

He set down his fork and touched his napkin to his lips. His features gave no hint of what he might be thinking. "Whatever are you talking about?"

"It's difficult to put into words. I didn't think it would be, or I'd not have come. But sitting here, facing you . . ." I paused and noted a scar on his upper left cheek. "You did take part in a duel, didn't you?"

His hand raised, and his forefinger lightly traced the scar. "Yes. I was very young. A game of chance was involved. I was cheated and challenged the individual to a duel. His name is unimportant, since he's been deceased for many years."

"You killed him?"

"Goodness, no. He grazed me, and I did him, and our honor was satisfied. But because of it, he had to leave New Orleans. I have an office there, though I have two competent young men who have taken over a great deal of my work. But that is of no interest to you."

"Do you handle all of my aunt's affairs?"

"Not all, but many. And her interests are quite extensive."

"She told me she holds a mortgage on most properties in town."

"And the surrounding countryside."

"And she owns the bank."

"Is that displeasing to you?"

"No."

"Then why did you refer to it?"

"Because of the soirée Saturday night. The townsfolk dislike me. I know they want nothing to do with Olympus, but she's forcing them to come, under threat of losing all they hold dear."

"My loyalty to your aunt as a trusted employee prevents me from making any comment on that. If that's why you came, I'm afraid your visit is doomed to failure."

"My reason for being here concerns my aunt only indirectly," I said.

"I'm an attorney, Miss Julie. As such, I like to get to the heart of the subject as quickly as possible."

His manner was gracious, his tone quiet, but I sensed a growing impatience.

"I'm sorry. It's just that the subject is distasteful and I don't know whether my relating it will antagonize you."

"Let me be the judge of that."

"Was my mother ever your mistress?"

"Good gracious, no! Who dared slander your mother's good name by making such a statement?"

I lowered my eyes against his anger. I couldn't bring myself to speak the name of my aunt.

He said, "Louisa Leloude! She hated your mama and, as I well know, now bears that same hatred toward you."

"I visited her yesterday."

"That took courage."

"Yes. But she received me graciously. From her I learned something that disturbed me greatly and set me thinking."

"Concerning your mother?"

I nodded. "I learned from another party Mama took the blame for the duel which Armand Bergeron's father and mine fought."

"Wasn't that the truth? That the duel was fought because Lester Bergeron called her a witch?"

"No." My reply startled him. He regarded his plate, then pushed it to one side.

"Miss Julie, please don't force me to keep asking questions. What is the true story regarding the duel?"

And so I repeated everything Armand had told me. The color receded from Mr. Taylor's face, then returned as his anger arose. But he remained quiet until I had finished my story.

"I hadn't the slightest suspicion of such a thing," he said.

"Do you believe the story Armand related to me?"

Without answering my question, he asked one of his own. "How did Armand happen to tell you that? The last I knew, he made a public statement to the effect that you had predicted Lizbeth Guthrie's death. Of course, I disbelieved him. I sensed he was antagonistic toward you because of the duel in which he lost his father."

"I lost mine also."

"True. But it was your papa who challenged Lester Bergeron. Now tell me how you happened to be in Armand's company. Because you must have been."

"I was," I admitted and related, in detail, how I'd gone to Mama's suite, found the shepherdess costume, donned it, and gone down to the Apollo fountain. I told him of what almost happened to me there and of Armand's shock to see it was I he'd almost choked to death instead of my aunt, whom he'd believed it to be.

Mr. Taylor appeared genuinely perturbed by what I'd revealed. "What possessed Armand to do such a thing?"

"As you must know, my aunt holds mortgages on his properties. She called them in."

"Why?"

"Because he said I predicted the tragic death of Lizbeth Guthrie—which I did not."

He looked thoughtful. "I didn't know your aunt was Lester Bergeron's mistress. It would be like Daphne to assume the blame for the duel in order to spare Lester's wife. Your mother was a warm, compassionate lady who would cause no other human being on this earth unhappiness. She did have the gift of foresight, though she never revealed it after your Papa's death."

"I can't believe I have it," I said.

He regarded me kindly. "Did it ever evidence itself during your growing years?"

"Never."

"Then the first time was during your illness when your were in the hospital, near death, and hallucinated."

"Yes. Dr. Tanney told me it wasn't unusual for patients to see themselves dead. Though, with me, it was death through strangulation. When Armand was choking me that night, I thought I was blessed or cursed with the gift of foresight. Because I'd seen myself dead through strangulation lying at the foot of the Apollo fountain."

"Then you had a dream regarding your aunt, Mrs. Leloude, and Adrienne. Your aunt informed me of that yesterday."

"Yes."

His eyes were staring into mine, though they seemed not to see me. "I'm wondering if your mother is, in some way, trying to communicate with you. Trying to tell you something."

My eyes widened in sudden awareness. "Of course. Trying, perhaps, to get me to prove her innocent of wrongdoing."

He sighed. "You still haven't told me all of that. Now I'll be quiet until you relate it in detail."

"My aunt wrote Zaffery Leloude a letter. He was away and his wife opened it, believing it might contain an urgency of some kind. The letter stated that you were lovers and you were suspicious of Zaffery and my mother.

My aunt wrote that she feared you might challenge him to a duel, and she reminded him that he had a family and should stop seeing Daphne to avoid a scandal."

"Oh, my God. I swear Daphne was never my mistress. I had the highest respect for her. And I'll also swear she was never Zaffery Leloude's."

"Then why would my aunt write such a letter?"

He pushed his chair back, rose, and strode in silence the length of the room. When he returned, he paused by the table and looked down at me.

"Perhaps your aunt was Zaffery Leloude's mistress. Just as she was Lester Bergeron's."

"Would she do that to Mama?"

He nodded slowly. "I'm beginning to get the picture, and it's ugly. But my hands are tied. She is all-powerful in this town and holds mortgages on most of the properties. Thank God, mine is free and clear. Knowing what I do now, my loyalty to her ceases—unless Louisa is lying. And that I doubt. Did she show you the letter?"

"No."

"I wish she had. I wonder if she still has it."

"I was so astounded by her revelation, I didn't think to ask her. But it isn't all that simple."

"It's very simple," he said, "after what you've told me. I'll have to remain quiet until after the soirée, but then, if Louisa still has that letter and Zaffery will admit his guilt, your aunt will never want the story to come out. With that hold over her, she'll not further harass the people of this town who are in her debt."

"It *isn't* that simple," I repeated.

"What do you mean?"

"Louisa is responsible for Mama's death," I said.

"Oh, no," he disputed. "Daphne fell and struck her head on a marble bench."

"Yes," I replied. "But Louisa was in a rage. She confronted Mama and threatened her. Mama denied it, but fled before Louisa's rage and in her flight lost her footing, fell, and struck her head. The blow was fatal."

"Who told you that?"

"Mrs. Leloude. She's been burdened with it all these years. She and my aunt are the only two who know about it."

He eyed me thoughtfully. "Perhaps you'd better tell me the rest of what Louisa told you."

I did so, and he listened attentively. When I finished, he said, "Please say nothing of this to anyone. However, if we're unable to clear Daphne's name—though be assured I shall do everything possible to reveal the truth—at least we will remove the threat your aunt is now holding over everyone." He picked up the pitcher of lemonade, but I refused more. I'd eaten my salad and nibbled at a sandwich. He refilled his glass and sipped the beverage as he moved about the room, his features reflective.

"I'm sure Yvonne hasn't the faintest suspicion anyone in town knew of her affair with Lester Bergeron. Nor will she want it known, even after all these years. People in this town know me. They were aware of the affection I bore your mother, and even though they called her a witch, they knew she was a lady. What I'm thinking is that your aunt also seduced Zaffery. He spurned her and your aunt deliberately sent that letter, knowing he was away, and Louisa, fearful it might be an emergency of some sort, opened it, as she was meant to. Zaffery could never reveal to his wife it was your aunt because of the hold she had over him in a financial way."

I set my napkin on the table and rose. "Why do you suppose my aunt came back here, knowing the people don't feel kindly toward her?"

"Revenge," Mr. Taylor said. "She waited many years—until you were grown. When you hallucinated during your illness, it gave her the idea. I believe she deliberately told Armand Bergeron about it so that he would believe you were also a witch. She didn't know he had already heard the true story of the duel from his father's second. Unfortunately, he died four months ago. He was a disinterested person and bore an excellent reputation in town."

"Why isn't she frightened by the dream I had of her in the cemetery?"

"Perhaps success has made her reckless. It might even prove her undoing."

"I wouldn't want anything to happen to her, Mr. Taylor. Despite what she did to Mama, I don't feel vindictive."

"Which is to your credit. Nothing will bring your mama back to life. But this can't go on. With each victory she'll become more and more ruthless."

"You know she took Armand's properties from him, but gave them back, so she isn't all bad."

"That could be part of her strategy, you know. I think she's out to humiliate and destroy the town of Flagton."

"But then there would be no one to admire Olympus."

"Olympus will eventually become a museum, particularly since I suppose you'll not remain there."

"I'm leaving immediately after the soirée. My aunt knows."

"And where will you go?"

I smiled. "I should be able to find employment as a governess. I like children, and I'm well-educated. I speak four languages and know the social graces."

"I don't think Bruce Manning will let it progress that far. He loves you."

"You know him?"

He nodded. "I don't know if you would allow it, Julie, and this isn't the proper time to discuss it, but I would like to take the place of your father. I admired him greatly. Both he and your mama were idealists. Their love was for people rather than for possessions. You've done them proud."

"I want Mama's name cleared. Yet how can it be done without hurting Mrs. Leloude?"

"I don't know," Mr. Taylor admitted. "Perhaps we can find a way. But we must exercise extreme caution until after the soirée. Please do nothing to antagonize your aunt."

"I give you my word," I said. "And now I must go."

"I'm glad you came, my dear," he said.

He was facing me, regarding me with benevolence. His hands lightly touched my shoulders, and he bent and kissed my brow.

"Bruce is a lucky young man."

"You're a little premature, Mr. Taylor. He hasn't even proposed."

He smiled. "One doesn't need foresight to predict that. He's already talked with me about you. I told him how well I knew your parents and the high respect I bore them. I even told him I would like the honor of leading you to the altar on your wedding day."

"Should it come to pass, I will be honored to have you do that."

"Thank you."

I left, encompassed by a warm glow, pleased I'd had the presence of mind to come. I headed for the general store to deliver the invitation to Jeb MacDowell.

Jeb was shy, but manly and more than pleased to receive the invitation. He informed me Adrienne was driving into town later in the day. As he spoke, his eyes focused on the open doors, seeking the first glimpse of her. I told him my aunt was looking forward to meeting him. He appeared dubious, but thanked me anyway. I gathered he already knew how people in town felt regarding the invitation, which was really not an invitation at all, but a command to appear or be punished.

On another one of those sudden impulses, I found myself heading for the bank to pay Gene Duvall a visit. I remembered my aunt's imperious voice and his distress the day he left Olympus, and I wondered how he would greet me.

He had an office at the rear of the bank, and he appeared startled when I was led in by a young clerk. He seated me alongside his desk, then resumed his chair.

"You're looking well, Miss Julie," he said.

"So are you, Mr. Duvall. I was passing and thought I'd stop by to pay my respects. I suppose you will be at the soirée."

"Oh, yes. Yes, indeed." His laughter was jovial, yet it seemed forced and obviously was, since there was really nothing to laugh about. "Wouldn't miss it, Miss Julie. When I think back to the magnificent receptions your aunt used to have," he shook his head in remembrance, "I can't wait to attend this one."

"I'm glad," I said. "I guess about everyone in town will be there."

"Just about," he said.

"I hope they're looking forward to it," I said innocently.

"I'm sure they are," was his discreet reply.

We were interrupted by the young man who had ushered me in after I'd given my name. He placed a note on Mr. Duvall's desk and stood there. Mr. Duvall excused himself, glanced at the note, then told the clerk to inform the gentlemen he would see them shortly and please to wait. The clerk replied courteously and left. I had an idea whoever was out there awaiting entrance to the sanctum sanctorum had already been told it was Miss Moniere who was taking up Mr. Duvall's time. Now that I knew my aunt owned the bank, I understood that the name, though not revered, carried grudging respect.

But the note had upset Mr. Duvall. He paled and thrust it into his pocket, and his trembling hands gripped the sides of the desk. I feared he was about to have a seizure of some kind.

"Are you ill, Mr. Duvall?"

"No." He breathed deeply to regain his composure, placed the palms of his hands flat on the desk, and used them as a support to raise himself to his feet. "Please excuse me for a few seconds."

"I'll go, Mr. Duvall." I was already on my feet. "I really had no business coming here."

"Please sit down, Miss Moniere," he urged. "I want to talk with you. I'll be back directly. I have some medication I must take."

He headed for the door behind his desk. I resumed my seat, settled back in my chair, and watched him exit. He closed the door behind him; then I heard a second door close. I wondered if it led to another office, or if he had gone outside for a breath of air. Certainly, the contents of the note had upset him.

Ten minutes later I was still seated and was about to get up when the door opened and two gentlemen entered, followed by the young man who had brought in the note.

The three looked around. One was corpulent and moved with an air of authority; he headed directly for the door behind the desk. He went through it, and I heard him open a second door.

"He must have sneaked out this way," he called back.

The second man regarded me, not certain just what my business was here. The corpulent gentleman returned to the office of Mr. Duvall.

The clerk eyed me and addressed the two men. "As I told you, this young lady is Miss Julie Moniere, Miss Yvonne Moniere's niece."

The corpulent man said, "Did your aunt send you here?"

I ignored his question to ask one of my own. "Just what is going on?"

The corpulent one said, "I'm Sheriff Haymes. This is my deputy, Mr. Deeks."

I acknowledged the introduction, then repeated my question.

"Guess there's no need to keep it a secret," Sheriff Haymes said. "Your aunt has filed charges against Mr. Duvall. She's accused him of misappropriating funds."

My shock was evident. And I now realized the reason

for his hasty flight. I glanced at the bank clerk who had brought in the note, wondering what it had contained.

The Sheriff addressed the clerk. "What did you tell him, Sammy?"

"I just wrote a note that you were out here and wished to talk with him. I told you he was with Miss Moniere. I wouldn't've known who she was, except she came up to my cage when she came in and told me."

"I thought Sammy meant your aunt," Sheriff Haymes said. "What was your business here, Miss?"

"My call was a social one," I said calmly. "I was having a pleasant talk with Mr. Duvall when this young man came in with the note."

"What did Gene Duvall do when he read the note?" The Sheriff asked the questions. His deputy stood nearby taking down notes.

"He excused himself and went out that door." I motioned to the one behind the desk.

"Did he appear nervous?"

"Not unduly."

I kept my manner calm, as if I couldn't imagine what the fuss was all about. In truth, I felt only sympathy for Mr. Duvall. I could imagine his lot hadn't been easy, with my aunt as an employer. I found myself even hoping he might escape the clutches of the law, though it was evident Sheriff Haymes was an astute law officer. While speaking, he picked up the various papers on Mr. Duvall's desk and scanned them. He told his deputy to check the drawers to see if there was any incriminating evidence or a weapon of any kind.

I stood up. "I'm sure you gentlemen will excuse me."

"Not yet, Miss Moniere. When did Gene Duvall leave?"

"As soon as he read the note," I replied blandly.

"You mean you sat here for ten minutes?" Sheriff Haymes eyed me with annoyance.

"Oh, yes. He said he'd return."

"Well, no sense in our staying here. Better get to his

home. If he's not there, we'll have to start a search for him. You may go, Miss Moniere."

My feeling was still one of sympathy for Mr. Duvall. I ignored the stares of the employees as I walked between the two rows of cages, heading for the front door. Sheriff Haymes and his deputy left through the rear.

The young clerk caught up with me at the door and opened it. His features were distraught as if he felt he would be dismissed for Mr. Duvall's getting free. He probably would be.

He said, "I'm sorry you had to go through that. I only hope your aunt won't be angry with us."

"You did nothing wrong," I said, managing a smile in at attempt to reassure him. "My sympathies are with Mr. Duvall."

He was too flabbergasted to make a reply. I bade him a good day and returned to the carriage.

When I arrived home, my aunt was in a highly distraught state. I assumed it was because of Mr. Duvall. I was wrong. Apparently she didn't yet know he'd made his escape. She immediately ordered me to accompany her upstairs. I did so, no longer surprised by her arrogant manner. It was a side she'd kept well hidden from me, but once she'd removed her mask, she made no further pretense of quiet gentility.

I followed her along the wing she occupied and noticed several of the doors were opened wide. Doors she told me had been locked.

She motioned to them. "Have you been in any of these rooms?"

"No, Auntie, I swear."

"Do you know who could have entered them?"

I thought of Armand, but moved my head negatively.

Her eyes flashed indignantly. "They've not only been searched, but ransacked. Who would do such a thing, and why?"

"I can't imagine," I said.

"I remembered the key to the french doors in your suite was missing. Someone must have appropriated it and used it to gain access to the house."

"Is anything missing?"

"Not that I know of, and of course every object is inventoried. But it's the principle of the thing. Who could have committed such destruction, and why?"

"I can't answer your question."

"There'd be no need for Louis Taylor to steal the key, since he has one to the front door. Gene Duvall!" she exclaimed. "I trusted him all these years, and he cheated me. Appropriated considerable sums from the bank, using them to gamble. He also made bad investments in an attempt to recoup. He'll pay. So will the culprit who did this."

She was moving from door to door, with me behind her. She had reason to be angry. Draperies had been torn from their rods, rugs thrown back, bedcovers tossed aside, pictures taken from the walls and thrown on the bed or dropped carelessly on the floor. One had a frame broken—as if it had been stepped on.

"Who?" my aunt exclaimed in growing anguish. "Who? Who?"

Her question was unanswerable so far as I was concerned. It was a relief to have her attention distracted by the sound of the door gong. She moved briskly to the landing. I had an idea who it would be. Sheriff Haymes and his deputy, Mr. Deeks.

They already stood obediently at the foot of the stairs, regarding my aunt. She, in turn, studied them. I knew she was wondering what they were doing here.

"Well?" she asked as she started down the stairs.

"We're sorry to have to report that Mr. Duvall escaped before we could get our hands on him. We'd have got him, except your niece was with him and he told his clerk to have us wait and . . ."

My aunt flashed me a look of anger which she quickly controlled. "You didn't tell me, Julie."

"I haven't had time, Auntie."

She nodded. I expected her to reveal to the sheriff and his deputy what she'd just discovered upstairs. But she made no reference to it, just continued down the stairs. Not knowing what else to do, I followed.

"I suggest you gentlemen instigate an immediate search for him—unless you have knowledge of his whereabouts."

"We already checked his home. He didn't return there."

"He's probably absconded."

"If so, we'll send out descriptions of him."

"See that you do—and immediately. There's no need to waste further time here. Be assured, he'd not dare set foot on the premises."

They appeared relieved to go, and it was understandable. My aunt was still in a high state of agitation. She motioned me into the sitting room.

As I followed, I said, "Why didn't you tell them about the ransacked rooms upstairs?"

"I shall wait until I take inventory. If nothing is stolen, there's no need to complain."

"True," I agreed.

I thought of the letters Lester Bergeron had written. Letters Armand had been unable to find. I wondered if he had created that mess upstairs. I'd be unable to learn until the soirée tomorrow night. I wondered if my aunt would cancel it. I hoped so.

My hopes were quickly dashed when she said, "We'll say not a word of what happened upstairs to anyone. I want everything to appear quite normal tomorrow night. I'll expect you to look your best. Goodness knows you have the gowns to do so."

"Yes, Auntie," I replied.

"As for Gene Duvall," she said scornfully, "he'll pay dearly for doublecrossing me."

I had no doubt of it, but I remained silent. She poured herself a glass of sherry and downed it in two swallows. She refilled her glass and came over to stand before me.

"What were you doing at the bank?"

"It was such a lovely day I hated to come back. I really went in just to kill time."

"Where else did you go?"

"To the general store to deliver the invitation to Jeb MacDowell."

Her smile was bitter. "I don't think Louisa will be very happy at Adrienne's choice. I'm amused."

"He's a fine young gentleman," I replied. "I think Adrienne displayed excellent taste."

"Where else did you go?" she demanded.

"I visited Louis Taylor. You told me he was fond of Mama, and I wanted to know more about her."

"You could have asked me."

"Yes," I admitted, "but I've seen little of you since we came here. Either you've been busy in town, or you've sequestered yourself in your suite."

"I wasn't idle. I had hoped you would take over some of the many duties connected with the running of Olympus, and also my other interests, but you let me down. You've proved a great disappointment."

I could have told her she had done the same to me, but I had no wish to antagonize her further. Mr Taylor had cautioned me to exercise discretion, and I felt his advice was sound.

"I can help you inventory the rooms that have been ransacked," I said. "Or perhaps it would be wiser to have Sheriff Haymes check them. He might find a clue leading to the culprit."

"You will say nothing to anyone about it." Her voice was a command.

"If you wish to keep it such a secret, why did you even tell me?"

"I wondered if you'd had a hand in it."

My complacency left me. "In heaven's name, why would I do such a thing?"

She shrugged impatiently. "I don't know. I'm just terribly upset discovering that Gene violated my trust. How could I have been so mistaken in him? Oh, I'm sure he intended to replace his theft of money, but he made bad investments. Also, he gambled. To think a man could have fooled me! I've prided myself all through the years that I've never been taken in by one of them."

"When did you learn about Mr. Duvall?"

"Yesterday. I told you I had been with business acquaintances at the inn. They were private investigators. One visited here two days ago. He left just as you were returning after being with your doctor."

"Oh, yes."

"I became suspicious of Gene about two months ago while we were still in Europe. I wrote for an accounting of certain securities. His reply was long delayed, and when it finally came, it was evasive. That's why we returned home. We'd have tarried in New Orleans only briefly, except that you became ill." Her smile mocked me. "My concern wasn't for you nearly as much as it was for what Gene Duvall was up to. I'd already hired private detectives to observe him. The information they garnered concerning his shady activities left me no recourse but to have him arrested. If you hadn't been in his office, he'd be behind bars now. You afforded him a means of escape."

"And you're angry with me."

"Yes, I am."

"Do you wish me to leave?" I stood up and faced her, our eyes feuding. I was tired of being berated, and I wondered how I could have been so gullible as to believe her a gracious, warm person who truly loved me.

"No. You owe it to me to remain. You've been rebellious since we arrived at Olympus. I'm beginning to think you hate the place as much as your mother did—and my brother."

"I don't think it's the place I hate. Nor do I believe my parents hated it."

"Then why have you been so difficult?"

"I wasn't aware I had been."

"You are now."

"Perhaps it's because of the manner in which the wealth of this family was accumulated."

"That shouldn't bother you. My grandfather was hanged for his crimes of thievery. He paid his debt to society with his life. I feel not the slightest guilt for all my worldly wealth. I revel in it, and certainly it has done much for you."

I said, "I appreciate all you've done for me."

"I doubt it," she retorted. "I doubt it very much."

"Are you still giving the soirée?"

"Indeed, yes."

"But with Mr. Duvall's arrest?"

"He hasn't been apprehended yet."

"I have no doubt but that he will be. The news came as quite a shock to him."

"Just what happened?"

I told her in a few sentences of how he had reacted when he'd read the note. Her smile was one of triumph. I turned away, wondering how I could endure remaining here until after the soirée. Apparently she read my mind, for she said, "You don't like me any more, do you Julie?"

I stood up. "You aren't the woman I thought you were."

"No matter what you think of me, I advise you to remain here until after the affair tomorrow night. If you don't, I will destroy Flagton and everyone in it. You know I have the power."

"What proof do I have that you won't do it anyway?"

"None," she replied quietly. She refilled her glass and carried it over to stand before me. "You can only hope the evening passes off without incident and with everyone putting their best foot forward. If it does, they may return to their homes and sleep easy."

"May I be excused, Auntie?" I was too repelled by her behavior to remain in her company. Also, I sensed she had been imbibing alcoholic spirits since before my return, for her words were slightly slurred, and as she approached, I saw her weave slightly.

"You may go to your suite." Her tone was insolent.

"Thank you."

I turned and left the room, but looked back as I started to mount the stairs. She had emptied her glass and was filling it for a fourth time. I was sick at heart. I'd never seen her intoxicated before. I'd never even known she overindulged in spirituous liquors.

Melisse brought me a tray on which was a steaming plate containing roast lamb with mint jelly, mashed potatoes, and carrots. Hot rolls, cake, and a steaming pot of coffee completed the meal.

"Do eat, Miss Julie," she urged. "And don't be frightened. Melisse will stay with your aunt. It's not easy for her, knowing how the folks resent her."

It was the first bit of talk Melisse had volunteered, but she quickly placed a forefinger over her lips. I nodded understandingly and said, "Thank you, Melisse. I know my aunt is overwrought. Things haven't gone well for her since we came here. And I haven't helped matters."

"You do what you feel best for yourself. You are a person who must always be honest . . . here," she placed her hand over the area of her heart, "and here." She touched a forefinger to her brow.

I nodded. "I can be no other way. That's why . . ." I didn't finish the sentence.

Melisse patted my shoulder lightly. "Melisse understands. You are lady. The good doctor knows. The town will know. You wait and see."

I smiled my appreciation, but made no answer. The way things were going, I had strong doubts about the town. But thoughts of Bruce lessened my anguish.

Melisse brought a chair over to the table and motioned me into it. Then she left, with a departing nod of encouragement and a plea that I eat my supper. I did, amazed at my appetite. Afterwards, I placed the tray on a table outside my door. Strangely, after I closed it, I turned the key in the lock. I'd never done that before, but should my aunt take it into her head to pay me a visit, I'd not allow her admittance. I wanted no further altercation.

I'd left a lamp burning in the sitting room, but my bedroom was without illumination, and I lay there with my troubled thoughts. Sleep was out of the question, and I longed mightily for Bruce's comforting arms, and the sound of his deep voice reassuring me all would turn out well, for the house seemed to hold an ominous air foreboding evil.

I wondered if my aunt's moment of triumph would be the soirée tomorrow night. Or whether it would happen the following day when she would call in the mortgages on all the properties and thereby destroy the town and its inhabitants. If such an act was in her mind, I wondered if it was in my power to forestall it. I could think of only one way. To agree to remain with her, or if I married Bruce, to make this palazzo our home. It would be a form of blackmail, and I doubted if he would agree to it. He was a compassionate man, yet I couldn't see him knuckling under to a cold, heartless woman.

I stiffened as the sound of a doorknob turning reached my ears, but I quickly relaxed, knowing I'd locked the door leading into the hall. I heard it again, followed by the soft rattling of the knob, as if someone wished to gain my attention. I slipped from bed and went as far as the door leading into the sitting room. I heard my name spoken softly, then repeated. I eyed the door leading into the hall when I heard the knob being turned again, this time impatiently. It didn't move. My glance flicked to the french doors. A light tapping sounded on one of the frames of glass, and my name was spoken softly, but with an air of urgency.

I recognized the voice, and I moved quickly to the door, turned the key, and admitted Adrienne. She had a negligee over her nightdress, but her feet were bare.

"What are you doing here?" I glanced worriedly at the

door leading into the hall as I spoke. "My aunt might hear you."

"Let's go in your bedroom," she whispered. "I had to come and thank you for extending an invitation to Jeb for tomorrow night."

We moved soundlessly but swiftly to the bedroom. I noticed her feet were moist and touched with blades of grass she'd picked up during her nocturnal journey here. I got a towel for her to dry them.

"I'm glad to see you," I said, "but why did you come here?"

She spoke as she applied the towel energetically to loosen the blades of grass. "I had to. Mama told me tonight you'd paid her a visit. She likes you very much. She told me why you came, and also the story of Papa and your mama. I don't believe it, and I said so to Mama."

"Thank you," I said gratefully. "I don't, either."

"I also told Mama she should tell Papa she told me. He'd understand."

"Why do you want him to know?" I lit my bedside candle so we could see one another.

"So he can tell us the truth. Whatever it is."

I thought I knew, but I made her no answer. I couldn't until after the soirée. Mr. Taylor had suggested the wisdom of silence until then, and I was in complete agreement.

I said, "Your mama is fearful your papa might hate her for what she did."

"Especially if your mama was innocent of any wrongdoing.

"If she was innocent, then whom do you suspect?"

"Your aunt."

She mistook my astonishment for disbelief. "Don't be angry, Julie, but your aunt is very beautiful and she never married."

"What has that to do with it?" I was not yet prepared to admit I agreed with her reasoning.

"Everything."

"I still don't understand."

"No."

"Then I'll be frank. I believe your aunt is the type of woman who must be adored by all men. She could never be faithful to any *one*. And to her, each man is a conquest."

"Where did you ever learn that?" I couldn't believe the shy, insecure girl I'd encountered at the inn was the same girl uttering this gem of human behavior.

"I did an awful lot of reading while I was growing, and after I was grown. I learned a lot about people, and then when I observed them, I'd try to see into which category they'd fit. That's what I thought about your aunt even before Mama told me about the letter she sent Papa."

All I said was, "You're far more observant than I. But I wish you hadn't come here tonight. If my aunt ever knew you came here . . ."

"Didn't you tell her about my coming here?"

"Never."

"You're a true friend, Julie. I understand you and Bruce Manning are practically engaged."

I smiled. "Not yet."

"You will be." She spoke with assurance.

"Everyone seems to be better informed than I."

"You can't keep secrets in a small town. Besides, everybody knew his interest in you was more than professional after Lizbeth Guthrie was killed. If anyone even uttered a word about you, he told them off in no uncertain terms. He even told the Guthries, though he was quiet about it there. What happened to her wasn't your fault, and they know it. She was very jealous of Armand. She was furious when he brought you there. That night they quarreled, and afterward, she went for a ride. She should have known better. It was dangerous and she knew it, but I suppose she was so angry."

"I'm sorry it happened."

"I know you are. Certainly it didn't help you. But

people will come around. And it won't be long. You wait and see." She touched her cheek to mine. "I must go now."

I nodded agreement. We were at the door, and she stepped onto the small porch. She waved a brief farewell, then moved briskly to the stairs.

I closed the door, locked it, and sat down in a rocker by the window. There was no sleep in me. I was grateful Adrienne had come, but concerned lest my aunt hear her. But I'd been cautious and had spoken only in whispers.

However, far from cheering me, Adrienne's visit had only made me more aware of my loneliness. It was the palazzo, I knew. So large and so cold.

I thought of the suite my parents had occupied. Without a second thought, I dressed, got my bedside candlestick, unlocked my door, and stepped into the hall. I wondered if those rooms had been desecrated as the others had been. I hoped not. To me, it was the only sanctuary in the house. There, perhaps I could find peace of mind.

I was relieved to find the door unlocked. I closed it behind me and stood there, accustoming my eyes to the gloom. The candlelight scarcely penetrated the darkness, yet I felt not the slightest fear. Tension drained from me within these walls, and I moved with ease over to the table. I touched the flame to the five-armed candelabrum to wipe out the darkness. I lit two single candlesticks on either side of the mantel.

There was a rocker to one side of it, and I sat down and let the gentle motion of the chair further relax me. My eyes were closed, and there was a half smile on my face. I felt the presence of my long-dead parents in this room, and I was soothed by it. I wondered if my aunt had ever come into these rooms. I doubted it, for she couldn't help but feel a trace of guilt at their untimely end.

I also wondered whether Armand Bergeron had entered this suite. I felt he had, but had withdrawn as if it were a hallowed spot. He knew the true reason his papa had fought the duel with mine and so he would feel no vindictiveness toward Mama. His malicious attack on me that night at the Apollo fountain had really been directed at my aunt. The secret hatred for her he'd harbored within him had caused him to lose his reason for a few moments.

I thought of the letters he'd been searching for and wondered if he could have been responsible for the vandalism committed in those rooms. Somehow, I couldn't believe it.

And Louis Taylor. What would be his interest in making a search of the palazzo? Also, having a key, he could have made a leisurely search, disturbing nothing and giving not the slightest evidence he'd made an extensive investigation of the rooms.

Gene Duvall came to mind. I doubted that he even knew of the existence of those letters. I looked at the half-finished child's sweater Mama had been knitting at the time of her death. I picked it up and held it carelessly, so much so that one of the needles slipped free of the stitches and fell back into the basket. The pointed top caught in the wicker bottom and stuck upward at an awkward angle.

I tried to pull it free, but it resisted my efforts. I put down the sweater and used both hands to worry the needle free of the basket. Instead, the whole bottom pulled away, though the sides didn't move. The needle was still in it and I lifted it, expecting to see the table beneath. But there was a second base to the basket. What I'd uncovered was a hidden compartment. In it was a tied bundle of letters.

Love letters of my parents! I picked them up, wanting to open them, yet knowing they weren't meant for my eyes. I'd dispose of them, for they didn't belong here. Not with both my parents deceased. Then I glanced at the name on the envelope. It was addressed to my aunt. I pulled the top one free of the stack and took out the letter.

Dear Yvonne,

Enclosed are your gloves which you left behind

during your last visit to Ann. Your visits mean a great deal to her and your vibrant personality has done much to help her forget the pain which is always with her.

She has asked me to express her appreciation for your thoughtfulness. I wish also to add mine.

Flagton will be forever in your debt. Sad that they have shown such resentment toward Daphne—whose only sin was trying to warn others of impending danger. I hope that, with time, they will come to their senses. Daphne is the epitome of goodness and the love she and Tom bear one another is beautiful to behold.

I pray one day my beloved will be blessed with a return to good health. My faith is great and I believe in God's compassion.

Ann informed me you discussed some books you believe she would enjoy and asked that I stop by for them. I will do so on Saturday when my presence will not be necessary on the plantation.

I must add a final word—you have captivated our son Armand. He is forever asking when the beautiful lady will come again. You have quite spoiled him with gifts.

In grateful friendship, I remain,

Lester Bergeron.

I replaced the letter in its envelope and eased it back into the tied stack. I pulled out another at random and felt growing resentment as I read it.

Dear Yvonne,

It is most indiscreet of me to write after last evening, but I am filled with guilt and remorse. I beg your forgiveness and assure you it will never happen again.

I only hope my despicable behavior will not deter you from continuing to visit Ann. Your visits brighten her day. Since you always come on Tuesdays and Thursdays at two in the afternoon, I will arrange to be absent from the house at that time.

Again, I ask your forgiveness and express my sincere regrets.

The signature was that of Lester Bergeron. I replaced the envelope in its proper place in the stack and pulled the bottom one free. I couldn't help feeling a touch of pity for Mr. Bergeron, despite his wrongdoing. He had fallen under my aunt's spell as I now knew everyone had, including myself. I had always believed her to be a lady of high character.

As I read the final letter, I could sense Mr. Bergeron's agony and knew the utter ruthlessness of my aunt. It read:

Dear Yvonne,

What a fool I was, decrying my helplessness to resist you when all the time you were the seductress. Now you threaten that unless I promise to continue our sinful relationship, you will present Ann my letters, written in the heat of my infatuation for you.

At present, I am trying to get up the courage to inform her of my weakness. Also, you are holding over my head the threat of taking my lands from me, leaving me without even a house to shelter my ailing wife whom I dearly love. I am filled with self-loathing for my infidelity.

I cannot stop you from wreaking what vengeance you will, but I will not see you again. This letter is my final one. Do what you will.

Sincerely,
Lester Bergeron.

I replaced the letter, set the stack back in the secret base of the basket, replaced the sweater and slipped the stitches back onto the needle. I rested the article in the basket in nearly the position it was in when I picked it up.

I could understand why Armand hadn't searched this suite. One could sense the love and happiness that flourished in this sanctuary and would withdraw. As for me, I felt a sense of peace just sitting here. I rested my head against the wicker back and rocked slowly, my eyes closed.

Now I knew why my aunt had been so upset with the disorder of the other rooms. She knew someone had been searching for something. What she didn't know was that it was Armand Bergeron. If he could have found the letters, he would indeed, have a hold over her. A hold that would let everyone in her debt sleep more easily if she feared the contents of Mr. Bergeron's correspondence to her should become known. Even many years after his death.

I also believed I knew why Mr. Leloude's manner had been one of defeat. He had remained quiet all these years, letting Mama take the blame which was really Yvonne's. He, too, had been unfaithful, and his conscience smote him, yet he could do nothing about it lest he lose his lands and leave his family penniless. Lester Bergeron had been ready to do that, but he didn't know the extent of my aunt's vindictiveness. She had practically ordered him executed because he disdained her. In doing so, she had also signed her own brother's death warrant.

I wondered if she had suffered pangs of remorse because of it. Was that why she had raised me? Enrolled me in the most expensive schools, taken me on vacations that took me to the four corners of the earth? Made my life a sort of fairytale existence? I'd never known fear or want. I'd been kept away from Flagton and this palazzo which, for my parents, had sealed their doom. This room gave strong evidence they would have been happier in a humble cottage, for their needs and desires were simple. Apparently, despite my background of luxury, I'd inherited their sense of values. No doubt the good sisters where I'd been educated had helped to formulate my character, or had developed what was already inbred in me.

"What are you doing here?" I was so immersed in my thoughts I jumped at the sound of my aunt's voice.

I'd not even heard her enter, but she stood inside the door, holding a candlestick, though there was small need for it in this room. I'd taken no precautions against the light leaking beneath the door, and I'd lit several candles. She looked haggard, possibly the result of overindulgence in the wine. But its effect had worn off, for her voice was firm and as cultured as always.

"I couldn't sleep," I said.

"Nor could I." She set down the candlestick and sat in the rocker facing me. "I'm sorry I behaved so rudely. I was upset when I discovered the condition of the rooms. I was going to open them for tomorrow night and allow the guests to go on a tour of the house. It's been many years since anyone set foot in here."

I doubted anyone had any desire to, though I sensibly made no reference to it. "When do you suppose it was done?"

"It had to have been done before our return," she said.

"But I thought you sent the servants on ahead to get the palazzo in readiness."

"My goodness, child, it would take an army to do that. I gave the butler a message to be delivered to Louis, listing the rooms I wished cleaned. He oversaw their work, and they did well."

"Yes, they did."

She started to rock, but quickly stopped and placed a hand to her head, as if the motion did her little good. She seemed to take no notice of the sewing basket on the stool alongside my chair, yet I sensed her concern. I wished I had concealed the letters on my person, but perhaps they were safer here. Since nothing had been disturbed in this room, she might believe it was the safest place for the letters. I wondered why she hadn't destroyed them, once Armand's papa had been killed. Perhaps womanly vanity.

"Julie, are you angry with me? Am I the reason you couldn't sleep?"

"My feelings *are* of concern."

She frowned in puzzlement. "For whom?"

"Both of us."

"I don't understand." A consummate actress, she looked the picture of girlish innocence.

"This affair tomorrow night you've forced on the people of Flagton."

"Is that what worries you?" Her smile was one of relief.

"Yes. Has it ever occurred to you that we might be in danger?"

"From what?" She looked amused.

"From whom, Auntie, not what. Have you forgotten that dream I had?"

"Of my pleading with you to come help me?"

"And my seeing the cemetery, along with the sculptured figures of my parents. I'd never seen them before."

"I still say you undoubtedly saw drawings sent me by the sculptor for my approval."

"Perhaps." I made my voice doubtful, hopeful of instilling fear in her which might put an end to her scheming.

"I have no doubt of it." She spoke with assurance. "If you're trying to persuade me to cancel the affair tomorrow night, you're doomed to failure. In me, you have a worthy adversary. So has the town."

"I'm sure they know it now," I said.

"They've known it all along. Perhaps," she mused, "they thought I might mellow with age, but my determination only grew stronger through the years."

"Determination for what?" I asked.

"To make them crawl and beg for mercy, but they'll get none." Her eyes glittered with callousness.

"And what will you do to me?" I asked.

"Nothing," she said. "You have no part in my plans.

You did have—I wanted you to carry on. To follow in my footsteps."

"You mean you wanted me to learn to hate these people as you do?"

"That's what I mean."

"But why?"

Her eyes took on a faraway look and her smile grew reminiscent. "My grandfather was hanged in this town."

"Did he deserve it?"

"That's not important."

"It is."

"To you, yes. Very well, I'll tell you. Perhaps he deserved it. He killed an employee. But he had money. He offered a king's ransom if his life would be spared. Anywhere else it would have been. He was turned down. I was just a little girl at the time, but I worshipped him. Before he was taken to prison, he told me that if they hurt him, I must punish them. I must never forget what they did to him and one day, when I was grown up, I must make the whole town pay for what it did to him."

"But the people who live here now had nothing to do with his death," I exclaimed.

"Their ancestors did, and so they are also guilty. I kept my word to Grandpa, and I shall continue to do so."

"You won't live forever, Auntie," I said.

Her mocking laughter filled the room. "Are you threatening me? Will I die violently as my brother did—or like Lizbeth Guthrie?"

"God forbid!" I exclaimed. "Don't you have even a vestige of forgiveness in your heart?"

"Not a vestige," she said airily.

"How can you hate innocent people?"

"They're as guilty as their ancestors."

"They're guilty of no crime. They've done no wrong, nor did their ancestors who abided by the law."

"It's a cruel law."

"I won't deny that," I said. "But it was the law. They could do nothing other than abide by it."

"And so shall I," she said, rising. "I want what is due me and I shall, in the near future, own all of Flagton."

"Then you're determined to wreck these people," I said.

"Destroy them, make paupers of them." She picked up the candlestick and continued speaking as she walked to the door. "A pity you have your doctor. I would do the same to you. Well, I must get some sleep. The house will be a beehive of activity tomorrow. You must not leave it. I will need your help."

"For what?" I asked, knowing she had imported many servants from New Orleans, along with the members of two orchestras. They were to arrive at dawn.

She paused at the door and turned to regard me. "At the present I can't think of anything. But I felt it was a more courteous way of telling you you were not to leave the premises. I'm sorry, Julie, but I don't trust you. Since I learned Gene Duvall violated my trust, I feel you, too, bear watching."

"What about Louis Taylor?"

"He can be trusted. He sees only good in people. Or perhaps I should say, he is incorruptible."

She had moved out of the doorway, and her voice trailed off as she spoke. I knew what she meant. Though he had served her loyally in his profession, her beauty and wiles were wasted on him.

My first instinct was to go to him, tell him of my aunt's plan, and enlist his help in warning the people of Flagton to remain away from the soirée, for it would do them no good to come. The evening was to be her final act of revenge before calling in the mortgages on their properties.

Then caution prevailed. Perhaps it would be wiser to wait in the hope I might arouse a trace of compassion in her. My common sense told me that would be the more judicious course to take, and I felt Louis Taylor would agree.

With that decision made, I got up, blew out the candles,

and left the suite reluctantly. I didn't touch the letters. I felt they would be safer there. I believed my aunt was of of the same opinion.

SEVEN

The house was a bustle of activity all day. Floral experts from New Orleans came to decorate the house with bouquets from the extensive gardens on the grounds. Tantalizing aromas drifted from the enormous kitchen built directly behind the house. Certainly the guests would be given a banquet to remember, for every dish known to an Orleanian was being prepared. Seafoods of all kinds from bouillabaisse to dishes containing shrimp, oysters, and crabs. Meat dishes of beef, veal, pork, and ham. Also sweets of every description, and beverages for the individual's preference.

The servants bustled about the place, supervised by Martin and Melisse when necessary. She paused once to inquire as to my health.

"No worries, Miss Julie?" she asked kindly.

"None, Melisse."

Her eyes looked doubtful. "Try not to be frightened."

"I have small reason to be, with all the servants bustling around."

"And soon you will be hearing music coming from the ballroom. The musicians wish a little time to practice and to discuss what each orchestra will play."

I knew it would take more than music to lift my spirits. "How is my aunt?"

"Cheerful today."

And she was. This was her triumph, and nothing must go wrong to mar it. I had to stifle the feeling of pity I felt when I regarded her moving about with an air of competence, her eyes glittering with excitement. I saw her only once through the day to speak to, and then briefly. There was no mention made of our meeting last night in the suite occupied by my parents. It was as if it had never occurred. I wanted mightily to go there and see if the letters were still intact, but she seemed to be everywhere and to do so would certainly have aroused her suspicion.

"It's going to be a lovely party, Julie."

I agreed, complimenting her on her appearance. For that, I was rewarded with a captivating smile. She did look feminine and beautiful. A large rose was in the waistband of her voile dress, another in her hair. I could understand how she had enchained the opposite sex. She knew how to enhance her comeliness, and certainly she was gifted in the art of allure.

She rested a hand lightly on my arm. "Please don't think too harshly of me, *ma petite*. And please believe I want everyone who comes to enjoy themselves."

I wondered how they could, but I gave her the answer she wanted to hear. "If they don't, it won't be because you spared the slightest expense."

She was pleased by my reply. "It's worth it. And I'll say this—to reassure you. If it turns out to be a pleasant evening, I may surprise you."

Her meaning was obvious, but I wasn't convinced. "I don't understand."

"Yes, you do. You want me to be more lenient with these people. To forget what they did to my grandfather."

"The people who will come did nothing to him—or to you."

"So you said. And I'll grant it's given me pause for thought. It was the way your parents felt. Perhaps they were right and I have been wrong all these years. Tonight will tell."

My smile was hopeful. "I'm glad you feel that way."

"Believe me, my dear niece, I do."

With that she was off, calling to a servant who was carrying a large mirror and headed in the wrong direction. I wished I could believe her. If I'd not seen those letters last night, I might have. But too much had transpired. She had lied to me. She had let Mama take the blame for Lester Bergeron's death and that of her brother, when she had been the cause of it. She had maligned Mama when she sent that letter to Zaffery Leloude, knowing he was away and it would be opened by his wife.

I wished all day that Bruce might pass this way on his visits to the sick and be able to spare the time to pay a brief visit. But I was doomed to disappointment.

However, Sheriff Haymes called to report Gene Duvall had thus far eluded them and he feared he had succeeded in escaping. The sheriff assured my aunt he had sent telegrams to nearby cities with a description of Gene and a detailed report of why he was wanted. He also stated the search would continue in these parts. He offered to place some guards on the estate if she was fearful he might return. She scoffed at the idea, saying he'd probably stashed a sum of money in some other city and would head for wherever it was. For the first time, I asked if her loss was great. She replied it was well over fifty thousand dollars in cash, plus several thousand more in negotiable securities.

As much as there was to be done, my aunt would not allow me to be a part of it. I wondered whether, in her quiet way she was punishing me. She knew time hung heavy on my hands. I wandered from room to room, observing the servants setting up extra chairs and tables, for the refreshments would be served informally at many small tables in various rooms. That would give her an opportunity to move about freely among her guests. In that way, they could not avoid her. The advantage was, as always, hers. But I sensed the good breeding of the people would carry them through a difficult evening.

The strains of the music filled the house, large though it was. My aunt, Louis Taylor, and I received her guests in the large reception hall. As they entered, they were announced by Martin. Her memory I felt to be amazing, and I marveled at how she was able to converse with such ease with them. It was as if she'd been corresponding with them during the past sixteen years when she'd resided in Europe and had been kept informed of even minor incidents in their lives.

Whether a lady had an aptitude for sewing, or playing a musical instrument, or was one who gave liberally of her time to the activities of the church, my aunt knew and brought it into the conversation with ease. Some evidenced their astonishment with a slight raise of eyebrows, or a momentary lapse of speech from which they quickly recovered. It was apparent their surprise was as great as mine, but my aunt pretended not to notice. Even Louis Taylor gave her a side glance when she asked a gentleman if the thief who had stolen a valuable heirloom from his home had ever been apprehended.

When the gentleman replied affirmatively, my aunt informed him she would like to discuss with him the purchase of the object. At his reply that he had been informed it was worth a king's ransom, my aunt stated that she had it. All told so graciously and humbly, as if she held no power over him in the form of a heavy mortgage.

The gentleman couldn't contain his surprise. I suspected he would be glad to sell, as with that he could pay his debt on the property and be a free man. Yet I wondered if she was sincere about making the purchase. I still felt she was playing a game. If so, she was a magnificent actress.

When there was a momentary lull in the arrival of the guests, Louis addressed my aunt. "You seem genuinely glad to see these people again, Yvonne."

"I am," she said, favoring him with a smile. "Perhaps it's because of Gene Duvall. A sad thing. I wonder if he made life difficult for them during my years of absence."

"If he did, wouldn't it be at your order?" His words were spoken so gently she could not take offense.

Yet she seemed not inclined to, for she raised a chiding forefinger. "Now, Louis, are you making me out a Simon Legree?"

"You're much too beautiful to qualify for that. And you know it."

His manner was both respectful and courteous, yet he left no doubt he knew her reputation as regarded the people of Flagton. She knew it, too, but she also knew Louis. He worked for her and was completely loyal to her. What she didn't know was that he now had detrimental information about her—something he had not known until I told him. I wondered how she would have reacted, had she known. I had no further time to dwell on it, for Martin announced the arrival of Mr. and Mrs. Zaffery Leloude, their daughter Adrienne, and Mr. Jeb MacDowell. They, like the other guests, were received graciously.

I noticed Mr. Leloude's manner was now relaxed. The haggard look in his eyes had been replaced by one of warmth as he regarded his wife. I knew then her talk with him had wiped out the years of heartache for both. She knew the truth—that my aunt had deliberately sent that note, knowing Louisa would open it because her husband was away. I knew, too, she had confessed to her husband that she believed she had caused Mama's death.

For the first time, doubt assailed me, and I wondered

if Mama's death had been accidental. Yet who would murder her?

A cold shiver passed through me as the answer came. I glanced sideways at my aunt, engaged in idle chitchat with Louisa. She was referring to the church work Louisa had been so active in. Louisa, though surprised at my aunt's knowledge, answered graciously.

The Leloudes and Jeb moved on. The servants offered them libations from trays filled with glasses. Some were spirituous, and some were not. Adrienne waved to me and her lips mouthed something I didn't comprehend, but gathered it was to say she would see me later. I nodded, and she smiled in satisfaction.

Through all of this, I managed to hide my unhappiness that Bruce had still not made an appearance. I told myself that being a doctor, he could have been delayed by a patient who needed care. Yet I wondered why he hadn't even sent a message. Nor had Armand Bergeron come. Was he defying my aunt's edict? I could think of no other word to use in reference to the invitations that had been issued.

A lady scarcely five feet in height and dressed in pale lilac from her head to her satin slippers entered. Even her silver hair was topped by a bonnet covered with sprays of silk violets. She exchanged a few words with Martin, who seemed a little puzzled, but a firm nod of her head ended further argument.

He turned and called out the name as she'd given it to him. "Missy Ettie Brown."

She must have been in her eighties, yet her skin was unwrinkled and her blue eyes held a merry twinkle. She eyed my aunt with high interest, her mittened hand already extended in greeting.

"So you've come home, Yvonne." Her voice was high-pitched, but had a musical tone. "Didn't think you'd ever have the nerve."

"Good to see you, Missy Ettie." My aunt laughed good-naturedly and smothered Missy Ettie in an embrace that caused her bonnet to slip its moorings.

"Humph. You're mighty loving. But I ain't softening. Didn't come 'cause I was afraid of you. Just came to see how you'd aged. You haven't. Not a wrinkle in that beautiful vain face."

"Thank you, Missy Ettie."

"You're welcome." She looked around and spotted a waiter with a tray of glasses. "What's in them?" she asked of Louis.

"Champagne," Louis volunteered.

"That's what I like." She turned back to me. "So you're Julie."

"Yes, Missy Ettie."

"Bend down so I can give you a kiss."

I obeyed, and she gave my cheek a birdlike peck. "You look like your mama. Always loved to catch a glimpse of her. A real beauty she was. A pity about her and your papa. Such a waste."

"Thank you for having kind memories of them," I said.

"Never did believe the stories they told about her being a witch. Now I hear they've tagged you with the label."

"I'm afraid I'll have to disappoint them," I said.

"You do that, honey." She gave a firm nod of her head. "I'm going to get me a glass of that champagne. Guess I'm the last one here. Got a good crowd, Yvonne. Not that anyone would dare stay away."

My aunt ignored the jibe. "Everyone seems to be enjoying themselves."

"If they're not," came the caustic reply, "they better give a good imitation of it."

"You're unfair, Missy Ettie," my aunt said.

"No, I ain't," came the quick retort. "Come on, Louis. I want a dance in the ballroom before I sip champagne. Used to dance there years ago. Best dance floor for miles around."

Louis excused himself and guided Missy Ettie to the ballroom. The string orchestra was playing a Viennese waltz. I was glad, thinking it would be more fitting for her. Having met her, I knew if a gavotte were being played, she'd dance to it, and I was sure she could.

My aunt said, "Please excuse me, Julie. It's time to move among my guests. I notice some are already seated at the tables placed around."

"May I go upstairs, Auntie? I'm really tired from standing."

"By all means, my dear. But don't remain too long. I want the folks to get acquainted with you."

I assured her I wouldn't and moved to the stairs, going directly to my suite. It wasn't fatigue that made me wish to come up here, but rather Bruce's absence. I missed him, and though the atmosphere in the house was cheerful enough, it served only to make me more aware of how much I loved him.

The very thought of him warmed me, and I was grateful, for certainly the shock of learning my aunt was not the woman I believed her to be had been great.

I moved about restlessly, from time to time going to the window, hoping for a glimpse of a doctor's wagon approaching Olympus. Dusk was fast changing into darkness, but I could see, here and there strolling about the grounds, several people observing the plantings and formal gardens.

I was about to turn away when I caught a glimpse of my aunt, moving swiftly along the path of the topiary garden. The sculptured shrubbery was tall and close together in those parts, but the way was faintly lit with Japanese lantern. Her chiffon gown billowed around her as she moved with seeming purpose along the path. She paused abruptly and looked about her, as if to make certain she wasn't observed. She slipped a piece of paper from the bodice of her gown and held it close to a string of Japanese lanterns to read it. She concealed the note again and after a cautious look about to see if she was observed, she moved swiftly along the path where the high bushes concealed her as she made her way to the stairway leading to the Apollo fountain.

Once I realized where she was headed, I broke out in prickles of apprehension. I remembered the dream I'd had of her, standing before the sculptured figures of my parents in the cemetery. Now my dream was about to come true. She was in danger! I knew it. I had to get to her.

Could it be that Louisa Leloude had been playing a game with me and her husband? Or was it Armand Bergeron? He'd not presented himself, and I wondered if that could be the reason. Was it he who had sent a note to my aunt, asking that she meet him at the Apollo fountain? Or Zaffrey Leloude? Was he enraged at the trick my aunt had played? A trick that had caused Louisa to pursue my mother causing her to suffer a fatal fall? Or so Louisa believed. Would I ever know?

I had to get down there to prevent another murder. I headed for the french doors to pursue her when a light knock sounded on my sitting room door. I'd have ignored it, but the door opened and Adrienne slipped through, shutting the door behind her.

"I had to come and tell you that everything is fine between Mama and Papa. They talked with one another. I want to thank you, Julie, for all you did."

"I really did nothing," I said quickly. "But you look radiant."

She beamed. "Jeb and I are going to be married. Isn't that wonderful?"

"Wonderful. I'm so happy for you."

I embraced her and urged her to the door. She was bewildered by my behavior, but I had to get rid of her.

"Won't you come down and talk with Mama and Papa?"

"Are they both downstairs?"

"Of course. They're feasting on jambalaya in the east sitting room."

"I'll be down directly. I want to get a fresh handkerchief."

"Do hurry," she said.

I almost pushed her through the door. She was startled, but I had no time to think about it, much less apologize. I could reach the fountain much faster by using the stairway outside my sitting room than by going through the house proper.

I ran to the doors, unlocked and opened one, and practically flew down the stairway. Without pausing, I headed for the path between the topiaries that led to the stairways. I know I startled several people as I ran past them. It was a hot night and moonless, the darkness relieved only by the dim glow of the Japanese lanterns. There were many of these, but they stopped some distance from the twin stairways, and with good reason.

My aunt had stated she didn't want anyone going down them lest they take a fall. It was a sensible decision, for the steps were made of rough stone and a fall could result in a severe injury. I came upon it suddenly, made aware of it only by the sound of the water splashing into the descending fountains. I moved cautiously now, for I had no wish to fall. I called my aunt's name as I descended, as loudly as I could but I doubted that she could hear it above the splashing water.

My eyes strained to pierce the darkness so I might see the area at the bottom, but it was hopeless. I was two-thirds of the way down when I realized my foolishness in coming without a light of any kind, but it was too late to return. I was already winded from the run, and I was tense with concern for my aunt. If it was true, as Adrienne had stated, that Zaffery Leloude was inside the house, only Armand came to mind. Was his hatred of my aunt so great he would resort to murder?

I finally reached the bottom and spoke her name. I repeated it over and over, again raising my voice to be heard above the splashing of the water in the Apollo fountain. I could see no one, but the darkness was intense. I placed my hand on the marble lip of the fountain and started to move slowly around it. I'd reached the halfway mark when my foot, advancing slowly, touched something soft.

I froze. I didn't have to stoop and touch it to know what it was. I sensed it was a human form. And it was that of my aunt. It had to be. I made myself bend down, and hands moved outward in an exploring manner. I touched soft, filmy fabric. Chiffon. I dropped it and got down on my knees. If I hadn't, I'd have fallen, for I was trembling with the horror of my discovery.

I spoke my aunt's name again, but I knew she'd not answer. I could make out her form and though the outlines of her face were indistinct, I reached out again and touched her hair, remembering a tiara there. Since it was made of diamonds, she'd always secured it carefully in her hair whenever she wore it.

The tiara was there! I made myself touch her skin. It was still warm. My fingers traced her face, pausing before her slightly parted lips. I felt no breath. I bent down closer to speak her name and placed my other hand beneath her neck to raise her. But her neck wasn't bare. I cried aloud as I felt the silken cord which was around it. I tried to loosen it, my fingers frantically seeking the knot. There was none. It came free in my hands. It had been held tightly only until breath left her body.

"Get up!" the words were a hissing whisper.

I opeyed and started to turn. Something was pressed hard against my back.

"Don't move!" Again, the command was whispered, but so harshly I dared not disobey.

From a distance, I heard my name called. The voice was faint and almost drowned out by the fountains. It was Bruce! He had come and he was seeking me.

"This is a gun in your back. If you call out, you'll be dead. Walk over to the conifers."

I obeyed. A few steps brought me to where they encircled the area around Apollo's fountain.

"Get behind them."

This time I paused. If I went into the forested area,

I might never come out. I decided to gamble on his shooting me. I had to let Bruce know.

"I wouldn't call out if I were you, Miss Julie!" This time he spoke aloud.

"Mr. Duvall," I exclaimed.

"Yes."

"You killed my aunt."

"I did. And I'll kill again if I have to."

"Why would you kill me?"

"My job isn't completed."

"Why did you kill my aunt?"

"Because she turned me in to the authorities."

"She had a right to. You stole from her."

"Yes," he admitted. "But she knew I'd been doing it for years."

"She countenanced such theft?" I was astounded.

His laughter was soft but bitter. "She had no choice."

"What do you mean?"

"She killed your mother."

"Indirectly." Apparently he knew about Zaffery Leloude and my aunt.

"No. Poor Louisa thought all these years she did it." He laughed. "Yvonne didn't bargain on Louisa's confronting your mother with the letter Yvonne had written. But Louisa did, and her rage was such she lost her reason and pursued your mother. Yvonne picked up a small marble statue and struck your mother with such force that she killed her. Knowing the grounds, Yvonne retreated behind shrubbery and pretended to happen on the scene of your mother's fallen body and Louisa in hysterics because of what she believed to be an accident. Yvonne told Louisa your mother must have fallen."

"May I turn around?" I asked.

"No."

"How do you know all this?" I asked Mr. Duvall.

"I happened to be a witness to the murder."

"Of my mother?"

"Yes."

"So you blackmailed my aunt all these years."

"I did. I forced your aunt to write a letter in which she admitted the murder. I kept it all these years. However, I foolishly left it in the bank. She returned unexpectedly, and yet she seemed so friendly when she visited me that day in the bank, I was caught completely off guard. Of course, I should have known better. Since she was once my mistress, I knew what a relentless person she was. She had the keys to the bank, but she was too smart to search for the letter. I wasn't as smart as I thought. I'd placed the letter in her file thinking she'd never suspect it was there. But she hired private detectives to search for the letter. She furnished them keys to the bank. They found it. Without that, I had no hold on her. Who would believe me? Particularly since she already had a case against me for theft of funds from the bank."

"And so you killed her."

"Strangled her with the cord taken from the draperies of the suite you occupied. I'd just entered it and appropriated the cord when you had a nightmare and I had to beat a hasty exit."

"Had you come to murder us?"

"Only if I was intercepted."

"Did you come back?"

"I did. The following night, but she must have heard me, for she was not in her bed. I entered her suite with the determination to strangle her. But again, I had to retreat, fearful she might be lying in wait with a gun. I knew she'd not hesitate to murder me, particularly since she had nothing more to fear from me. Once again, I departed via your suite, still with the cord. But I used it finally."

"Did you send her a note tonight?"

"Yes. Once darkness fell, it was easy to stroll the grounds with so many about. I handed the envelope to a servant and asked that he deliver it immediately. He did." Mr. Duvall chuckled softly. "He was carrying about a tray of drinks. I took one, compliments of your aunt."

"Wouldn't she have recognized your handwriting?"

"Yes, but I printed the note and signed it with Armand Bergeron's name."

"How contemptible."

"No more so than your aunt. I wrote that I was smitten by her charms and pleaded with her to meet me at Apollo's fountain. She could never resist such flattery. Though still beautiful, she's no longer young, and to have a gentleman both handsome and suave as Armand was write her a note begging for a rendezvous would be too much for Yvonne to resist."

I started to turn, but the gun was jabbed harder into my back.

"Take care, Miss Julie," he commented.

"Was it you who ransacked those rooms?"

"Yes."

"What were you searching for?"

"The letters Lester Bergeron wrote to your aunt. I guess she must have destroyed them."

"Why did you want them?"

"To heighten my hold on her. In a weak moment, she told me about them. She found it quite amusing. I didn't. Lester's sudden end was more than his ill wife could bear. She followed him in death a month later. If I could have got my hands on those letters, she'd have been at the mercy of the town. She was merciless. She used your mother twice to save her name."

"Would you have given Armand those letters so that the town could have a hold on her?"

"I was thinking only of myself. I'm as complete a rotter as your aunt. She brought Flagton to its knees. Her crowning humiliation was tonight, forcing them to come and pay obeisance to her when they despise her, yet dare not reveal it. Nor did they dare not come. But their gesture won't help them."

"How do you know?"

"She ordered me to see each and every one of them and inform them if they did not attend the soirée, the mortgages on their properties would be called in. I did so. I had to, even though she told me she was going to foreclose on them anyway."

"Did you tell the people that?"

"No. At the time I didn't know she'd hired private detectives to find the letter she'd written confessing to the murder of your mother."

"When did you find out?"

He seemed to want to talk about it, and I was striving desperately for time.

"Your aunt sent a message for me to come at once. I did so, and it was then she told me of the soirée and ordered me to see that her debtors—that was how she referred to them—accepted the invitations she was sending. Her manner toward me had completely changed, and I was puzzled by it."

"What do you mean—changed?"

"Before—years before, and in all the letters she wrote me—she was sweet and docile and made me believe her manner toward me was one of complete trust. But that afternoon she was rude and arrogant. Knowing her as I had in the past, I realized there was a reason for it. When I returned to the bank I went directly to her file and discovered the confession missing. I knew then she'd have her revenge on me, and after the bank closed, I checked the books. I could tell they'd been examined, and scratches on the wooden exterior of my desk indicated the drawer I'd always kept locked had been tampered with. When I opened it, the ledger accounting for the moneys I'd appropriated and securities I'd sold was missing."

"So that's why you came here that night to murder her."

"My intent was to threaten. She was vain and loved life. However, I believed if I got the cord around her neck, she'd weaken and surrender the confession and the ledger and give me further written assurance she'd do nothing to injure my reputation. I didn't want my wife and son hurt."

There was not need to remind him that if he'd always

thought of his wife and son, he'd not be in this situation. He knew it as well as I.

"Why didn't you plead with her?"

"I had nothing to bargain with," he said bitterly. "Besides, your aunt intended to wreak her revenge on everyone in Flagton. My turn had come. With the possession of the letter, her triumph was complete"

"So that's why you murdered her."

"Yes. She destroyed me, but I apparently have one last vestige of decency left in me. That evening at my home I wrote a confession telling everything I knew. It was a final desperate attempt to force her to let me alone. But I never had a chance to threaten her with exposure. It would have done no good. She knew I'd never reveal my relationship of years ago with her. I wouldn't want my wife hurt any more than she will be. The knowledge that I've been a thief and betrayed the trust your aunt placed in me will be enough for my beloved wife to bear."

Still stalling for time, I said, "The people of Flagton must hate you as they do my aunt."

He disputed that. "They know I had to do her bidding. Everyone here did, except a few like Louis Taylor, or your doctor." He jabbed the gun harder into my back. "Don't call out to him, Miss Julie."

"Killing me will do you no good."

"Killing your aunt will do Flagton good, will it not, Miss Julie?"

"What do you mean?"

"You know what I mean. You seem like a decent sort. There is no will. You inherit everything. Have you inherited her desire for vengeance? Have you, Miss Julie? I must know."

He paused, and all of a sudden I realized I was holding the cord he'd used to strangle my aunt. I wondered if he would use it on me. Or would I be murdered by gunshot? I judged it to be the latter. I let the cord fall to the ground and braced myself for the bullet to crash into my body.

Instead, he continued his revelation. "I failed to get

the letters, but she'll never threaten the people here again."

"Julie!" My name was shouted again, much closer this time, and there was an urgency in Bruce's voice. I was certain he was now at the foot of the Apollo fountain. I'd remain silent no longer. If I was going to be shot, at least Gene Duvall would be close enough to be captured. I called out Bruce's name.

At that instant a shot rang out. I expected to fall, but I didn't. Instead, the crash of a falling body came from behind me.

I screamed and ran in the direction of the clearing, reaching it just as Bruce's arms extended for me. I went into them and started to sob hysterically. He comforted me, gathered me up in his arms, and brought me into the clearing skirting the fountain as he headed for the stairs.

"Gene Duvall is in there." I pointed to the area from which I'd come. "He shot himself."

Bruce said. "I'll take Julie to the house and send some men down."

"I'll stay with the bodies." It was Armand's voice that replied.

"Oh, Bruce, Bruce," I sobbed, "why didn't you come?"

"Forgive me, my darling. Armand and I were closeted at the inn with the private detectives. We convinced them it would be wise for them to talk of their dealings with your aunt. When they told us about the letter she had written, confessing to the murder of your mother, we came here at once, fearing you might be in danger. Now rest. We'll talk later. There's nothing more to fear. Sheriff Haymes has the letter."

I said, "No one in Flagton has anything more to fear."

"No one," Bruce repeated. "Your aunt overplayed her hand. What happened to her is terrible, but what she did to others, and especially to your mother, was shocking."

"My aunt is dead, isn't she?"

"Yes."

"She was strangled with the gold cord missing from my suite."

I couldn't say any more. They'd find the cord where I'd dropped it. Exhaustion claimed me. I was trembling with the shock of my discovery and what I'd been through.

Bruce brought me to my room and gave me a sedative. The guests lost no time leaving. I was glad I didn't have to see them. I could well imagine their shock when they learned what had happened. Later would come their relief that they would never again have to fear the wrath of my aunt.

My aunt was laid to rest in the cemetery behind the palazzo, but at the opposite end from where my parents lay. Mr. Duvall's body was brought back to Flagton, where he was buried. Despite his wrongdoing, his funeral was well-attended. He left a letter confessing all and begging forgiveness of his widow and grown son.

I told Sheriff Haymes everything Gene Duvall had related to me. I'd already related it to Bruce, telling him of the location of the letters Lester Bergeron had written to my aunt. After Bruce checked to see if they were still concealed in the basket, we decided to let them remain there for Armand to collect. I hadn't informed Gene Duvall the letters were at Olympus all the time. It would only have added to his despair. I figured he had not invaded my parents' suite because of a feeling it would have been sacrilegious to do so.

The day following the murder and suicide, Armand paid me a visit. I informed him then of the location of the letters, suggesting he go and retrieve them. In answer to my question, he stated he'd not made a search of the suite, commenting that first of all, he didn't believe they'd have been there. Secondly, the appearance of the rooms revealed the love my parents had borne each other, and he couldn't bring himself to touch anything in it. My aunt had picked the best place in the palazzo to conceal them. But it revealed how completely lacking in feeling she was for anyone and how she would go to any length to protect herself.

Armand destroyed the letters after making public their existence and the true reason for the duel. He insisted on that, saying that even though Mama had been long dead, it was only just that her name be cleared.

My aunt had not made a will, but since I was her only heir, I was the sole beneficiary. I discussed with Bruce what I wished to do with Olympus, and he was in thorough agreement. My plan was to present the grounds and palazzo to the State. It was, in fact, a museum. As for the mortgages, when I learned of the exorbitant rates of interest my aunt had charged the townspeople through the years, I returned the mortgages to the people along with a letter stating that their period of indebtedness was ended and the realty was now theirs.

The State accepted Olympus without hesitancy, especially when I turned over securities that were to be placed in trust to be used for the upkeep of the building and grounds. Even my parents' suite has been left intact. It's a part of the story of Olympus and lends further interest. Several fantasies have grown up surrounding those two rooms, but I do nothing to discourage the tales. Bruce and I know the true story of a great love two people bore one another. I am the result of their love, and I like to feel that I behaved as they would have wished me to and as I know they would have, had they lived.

I've never since hallucinated or had dreams of a frightening nature. I suppose Dr. Tanney was correct—that people near death do hallucinate. Yet I can't help thinking that Mama, in some way, came back and put that picture in my mind. Whether to put me on guard against danger, or to warn that my aunt was not all she seemed, I don't know. But when I visit the cemetery and stand before the graves of my parents, I feel a great serenity.

Bruce and I were married immediately following my aunt's burial. Louis Taylor gave me away, Adrienne was my bridesmaid, and Jeb was the best man. It was a lovely wedding, and the town turned out for it as evidence of their good-will.

The wedding reception was held at Bruce's home—which I now share with him. Adrienne and Jeb's marriage followed shortly after, and we have become fast friends.

I have been accepted by the people of Flagton, and there is no more talk of my being a witch. Nor of Mama's having been one. That's all in the past. Some citizens even came to me and admitted they'd been guilty of castigating Mama. Their confession was followed by a sincere apology, which I always accepted.

The private detectives related their part in the recovery of the letter Gene Duvall had forced my aunt to write. They also presented correspondence between them and my aunt. All of it was published in the newspaper, as was Gene Duvall's confession. The town knew, finally, that Mama was an innocent victim of my aunt's chicanery. And I realized her reason for bringing me back was my hallucination. She hoped to frighten the town into believing I had my mother's gift—that I was a sensitive. She intended to use me as a future threat to their peace of mind. Once we arrived, she lost no time telling of it.

Louisa and Zaffery Leloude also revealed their part and the role they had played. Though Louisa decried the fact that she believed the contents of my aunt's letter to her husband, she's a changed person now that she knows she had no part in Mama's tragic and brutal end.

No trace was ever found of the letter my aunt wrote, admitting her guilt in murdering Mama, and we believed she destroyed it the moment it came into her possession. However, the detectives had read it, and it bore out what Gene Duvall had told me.

And so Olympus still stands, as does the Apollo fountain. Bruce and I will return to it once a year, but only to visit the suite occupied by my parents. I now know the joy they once shared and the happiness those rooms gave evidence of, for ours equals it.